THE OTHER SIDE
OF SILENCE

Sylvie Nickels

Published in 2012 by Oriole Press (through FeedARead.com
Publishing – Arts Council funded)

First Edition

A CIP catalogue record for this title is available from the British
Library.

By the same author
The Young Traveller in Finland Phoenix House, 1962
The Young Traveller in Yugoslavia Phoenix House, 1967
Travellers' Guide to Yugoslavia Cape, 1969
Travellers' Guide to Finland Cape, revised 1977
Welcome to Yugoslavia Collins, 1984
Welcome to Scandinavia Collins, revised 1987
The Big Muddy – *a canoe journey*
       down the Mississippi Oriole Press 1992

Fiction
Another Kind of Loving Antony Rowe, 2005
Beyond the Broken Gate Oriole Press, 2007
Long Shadows, Oriole Press, 2010
Village 21, *an anthology of short stories,* Oriole Press, 2011

Educational aids
Assassination at Sarajevo Jackdaw Publications 1966
Caxton and the Early Printers Jackdaw Publications 1968
Scott and the Antarctic Jackdaw Publications 1971
The Vikings Jackdaw Publications 1976

In memory of Annikki
&
in friendship for Matti and Ritva

Oxfordshire, early summer 2010

1

It was Aristotle's fault that Pippa opened her email that evening. She had returned home late from the History Society, dog tired and longing for bed, grateful for once that Jude was away so that she would have it to herself. Briefly she wondered how he was getting on in Las Vegas before her attention was claimed by Aristotle, weaving round her legs, insistent that he wanted to go out.

Pippa, muttering resignedly, opened the back door, switched on the kettle for a mug of herbal tea, stood watching it as she drummed her fingers on the kitchen table. As she poured out tea, her attention was caught by the blinking screen-saving message on the laptop by the telephone. *'Night 'night'* it said. Hardly original. That had been Jude's idea.

Might as well check the email.

Unusually there was only one message. As always, she remained cautious about opening any message from an unknown source, and she was on the point of trashing it. It was the subject matter which intrigued her. 'Next of Kin' it read, followed by three question marks.

Dear Sir or Madam, she read. *We may be related. I live in a place called Kittilä in northern Finland. I hope you don't mind me contacting you especially as I believe the family cupboard holds a skeleton. I saw a translation of a book by someone called Joseph Eastman. I had an uncle called Jooseppi, which is Finnish for Joseph.* It was signed Liisu Itäinen.

Crouched over the screen, Pippa re-read the message. The 'Sir or Madam' would be due to the fact that she often abbreviated her full name, Philippa, to Phil. Phil Eastman was how she advertised her yoga classes on line. She knew, however, that she did have a very strong connection indeed with Finland. Her grandfather had come from there, an escaping Russian soldier stranded on some frozen Finnish lake shore during that unforgiving Winter War. But why

5

should this woman (presumably) associate Joseph Eastman with her uncle Jooseppi?

And a skeleton in the cupboard? How intriguing. What would Father have made of that, supposing there were any connection? And then a memory intruded: a telephone call from the police soon after Father's death. Something about a cold case. Or perhaps this email was a scam. There were so many about. Someone had got her email address from a website she'd visited and decided to make contact for some nefarious purpose. Though she couldn't think what or why. Or may be this was a genuine enquiry. Could it simply be a coincidence that this Liisu's uncle had the same name as her own father?

She had never been that interested in family history, perhaps not surprisingly given her long non-relationship with Father. It was one of the reasons she had joined the local History Society partly to see if she could latch into the current mania for genealogy, and partly because she was aware of an underlying feeling that somehow she had missed out with Father. She had become sufficiently intrigued to join a website called Genealogy.com and become its zillionth member.

She was about to re-read the email when Aristotle announced his presence by that characteristic sound that was half *miaoul*, half purr. When Jude was there he delighted in standing at the kitchen door loudly calling "Totty, Totty, Totty."

"Your cat has a very strange name," a neighbour ventured once.

"It's my bloke's sense of humour that's strange," Pippa said cheerfully.

"Why not call him Frankie short for Frankenstein," Jude suggested. "God knows his creations were ugly enough." Aristotle had curled his lip; the dislike was mutual.

Jude had not yet learned to distinguish the aspects of Pippa's life that were truly important to her. It was hardly surprising even though they had met soon after her arrival in Western Australia nearly 20 years ago. It began as a whirlwind affair of sharing mutual enjoyment of Australia's Great Outdoors, good food, concerts, the occasional rave, not to mention sex. Indeed sex had been a revelation to Pippa whose experience of it, constricted by living under her father's jurisdiction was practically nil. In Australia she had let her hair down in every sense.

6

2

Life with Jude epitomised everything she had missed out on back home. It was Fun. They had therefore felt no need to exchange much information about their earlier lives. Jude knew she had come to Australia to escape an authoritarian parent; she knew he was the son of a couple of Ten Pound Poms. They had rented an apartment on the outskirts of Perth and settled down in mutual acceptance of each other's life style. In due course they had moved to Queensland's Sunshine Coast where Jude established a successful travel agency and became a part-time surfing instructor; and Pippa a yoga teacher with a penchant for meditation. For quite long periods they were apart – on several occasions Jude had gone for longish periods to set up an office in New Zealand or elsewhere in Australia, and he went for extended stays with his mother back in W.A. until she died some years later. Pippa had joined friends on several cruises, a form of travel Jude could not abide. Each had their own group of friends who occasionally mingled at beach parties.

So, no, Jude had no idea of Aristotle's place in her life. And, as far as she could remember, Father had simply ignored him.

Watching him as he went straight to his saucer of water, Pippa found herself thinking of the man who had dominated so much of her life and, for the most part, seemed so daunting. The trouble was Father had always seemed old; and his permanent frown of concentration gave him a sombreness which added further to his years. A memory came out of nowhere. She was about ten years old, and had answered the telephone because Father never did and Mum was in the garden. A young male voice had asked if this was the house of Professor Joseph Eastman and if he could speak to him. His name was Karl and when she had queried it he had explained it was German for Charles.

Pippa had left him holding on and gone to find her mother, Frances, in the garden. "Your father's out," Mum had said. "No he's not," Pippa protested. "Yes, he is. Don't argue," Mum had said. Since she had always been told how wrong it was to lie, Pippa assumed Father had gone out without her knowing, only to discover he was still in his office. Perhaps that's why the memory remained so clear.

7

And then there was the time when she was twelve, perhaps thirteen. Her brother Robin, two years her senior, was at boarding school. She had just outgrown the tomboy stage and was beginning to grow her hair. Father had ruffled it as he passed her chair at breakfast – he was invariably the last at table – and muttered something.

'Yes, it does suit her, doesn't it?' Mother had said, so it was clearly a mutter of approval. She had not remembered him ever commenting on her appearance before.

Pippa knew Father had been born in Finland, which looked a long way north on the map. There had been a war, and Father and Grandmother Annikki escaped to another country when Father was a baby. Mother did not know what happened to Grandfather Josef and said it would be better not to ask as it upset Father. There was also mention of Grandfather Josef's sister and for a while Pippa was intrigued at the idea of having a Russian great-aunt and perhaps even a clutch of Russian cousins. But Mother said the sister was much younger than Josef and Father really did not want to talk about her.

And at that stage in her life, the last thing Pippa wanted was to upset Father. 'A desperate old fossil' was Robin's summing up of their parent. But for some reason it was a time when briefly she had desperately wanted to please Father. Now, so many years later, she could no longer remember why, but she distinctly remembered a time when her regard for him almost amounted to hero-worship. Perhaps because he really had been very clever.

Something was rubbing against her leg. Pippa looked down at Aristotle who was clearly aware of Jude's absence and thought it was time to go to bed.

"OK," Pippa said.

On the way up she took two books – an atlas and a dictionary - from the shelves of her father's study, almost unchanged since his death. Checking the atlas, she saw that Kittilä looked very small and was a measurable step above the Arctic Circle. Then she checked the name Itäinen in the Finnish-English dictionary. It meant 'east or from the east', Eastman perhaps? As Jooseppi was Finnish for Joseph.

"Curiouser and curiouser," she told Aristotle.

But he was already curled up on the bed, and the email could wait until tomorrow.

Dreamscape

That night she dreamed of Father. It was quite different from the dreams she'd had following his death three months earlier. Those had simply continued the nightmares of each day as he declined deeper into dementia that destroyed the only thing she found admirable about him: a brain fine-tuned by decades of reading, thought and argument.

Professor Joseph Eastman. He had been among the top in his field of comparative culture; probably at the top of his chosen area, the cultural interrelationship between the string of small nations forming what he called the European Fault Line, destined to be pawns in the power games of stronger neighbours.

The new dream was of long ago, of that time when she had briefly come close to worshipping her father, wanting desperately to please him. In the dream she remembered him as he had been: tall, angular, slightly stooped as though permanently approaching a low door.

An exciting idea had come to her one day when she heard Father playing some music by Sibelius. She had suddenly been struck by the fact that the music sounded just like the Finnish landscapes looked. She had seen many pictures and films of Finland, and had been enchanted by the huge skyscapes with their rolling clouds moving over dark forests and sparkling lakes. It looked so big and silent and she longed to go there. And this music sometimes swirled like a storm, and then became quiet like a still evening. She had remembered asking her mother if they could go to Finland for a holiday, but she had been adamant that they could not. It would make her father unhappy she said, though she did not explain why.

Pippa had thought a lot about the landscapes that looked like the sound of the music, and then she'd found a book that Father had been studying. At first she thought it was a fairy story because there were illustrations of strange beings, and birds that could speak. In particular there was a swan, very elegant and sad-looking. But why on earth would Father be reading a fairy story? In the end she asked him about it and he said the picture was of the Swan of Tuonela and there was a piece of music about it, which he played for her. Then it had all clicked into place: the landscapes, and the story, and the music.

9

Father had told her about the book which had a very complicated story, with characters with long unpronounceable names who did brave things. In the way that dreams have of telescoping whole sequences of events, she'd gone into Father's study when he was out, holding her breath at her own temerity until she thought she would burst with fright. She'd found the book and then went through all the tapes he had by his record player, and found several whose names echoed some of the names in the book. When both her parents were out, she'd played the music and found once again that the pictures it created in her head matched the stories. While listening to the music she'd scribbled some notes, and now she began to put them in order, matching the music to the stories, and then to pictures she drew of the landscapes. She soon filled exercise books with neat tiny writing and drawings. Drawing was one of her favourite things. Even Father said she was good at it.

In her dream, she clearly saw the drawings and tidy notes which she had eventually shown to her father. He'd studied them while she watched every flicker of his expression. At last he'd looked up at her with eyes that smiled and made him look gentler than she had ever seen him. "These are interesting observations, Philippa," he'd said. "Tell me how you came to make them." And she'd thought she would burst with pride.

She had answered all his questions as best she could, while he listened, nodding approvingly from time to time. At one point Mother had called them for supper, but he had responded impatiently, "Not now, my dear. Philippa and I are engaged in important discussions."

In the dream, Pippa had felt so emboldened by this unique sense of rapport with her parent that she asked, "You know when you left Finland during that war, Father? What happened to Granddad Josef?" Then she added very boldly, "And did he have any brothers or sisters?"

It was as though a light had been switched off behind his eyes. He said in that sharp dry tone that was his most familiar form of address, "Terrible things happen in wars, Philippa. It is better to avoid staring into the past and to work for a better future."

The dream-Pippa, reflecting her adult self, had wanted to argue, *but how can you work for the future if you don't learn from the past.* But Father had returned his attention to her research and,

10

terrified of losing again that warm feeling of approval, she had quelled her curiosity.

He had spoken to her for a long time, longer than she ever remembered him speaking to her before. She couldn't remember it all, but the gist was that he was really proud of the way she had extrapolated her ideas; but he issued a strong warning of the dangers of being side-tracked by the imagination. It was very important that she should not create conclusions simply to match her expectations.

When he had stopped talking, there was quite a long silence. Then Father had leaned towards her conspiratorially. "Before we go in for supper," he said, "I want to show you something. But you must not tell anyone. It's a big secret just between the two of us."

Wide-eyed, Pippa had murmured under her breath 'hope to die', which was the most solemn oath you could give when someone told you a secret. Father had led the way out of his study, down the hall and to a door that Pippa had never noticed before. She began to say "But I've never seen …." in a hoarse whisper, and he had hushed her, finger pressed to closely tight lips. The door opened into a tiny room, a narrow slit of space between door and window, with a big cupboard filling one wall. Father had brought out a key, put into the lock, turned it slowly. As he pulled the door open, he looked at her again, and said so quietly that she only just heard him: "Remember …. big secret. Not even Mother must know." His grip on her shoulder was firm, almost painful.

She had peered round the cupboard's opening door and became aware of a figure crouching inside. It wore dark clothes and heavy boots. She started back, alarmed, but Father's grip strengthened so that she had to suppress an 'ouch'. "It's all right Philippa. There's nothing to be afraid of any more." Then she saw that the figure was very still, and when she put her hand out to touch it, she felt how cold it was. She crouched down so that she could see it better, and saw its head was at a very peculiar angle, as though the neck were broken.

She had looked up at Father. "It's dead," she said, half question, half statement.

And he had smiled at her so affectionately and said, "Yes, I told you Philippa, there's nothing to be afraid of any more." But as he closed the cupboard door, he added something very peculiar. It sounded like "…. wrong boots…."

11

1

In Western Australia, Pippa leaned on the rail of the ferry that linked South Perth with the main part of the city across the Swan River. It was June, 1990. Whatever else she thought of her present circumstances, it had to be said that this was as fine a city view as you could get. The city's forefathers had had good sense. Apart from the small central cluster of high-rise buildings, they had decreed that the city should spread horizontally rather than vertically. And goodness knows, it wasn't as if there were any lack of space. The sprawling green parks that bordered the river were evidence of that

She just wished she like it more. When Bunty, one of her closer mates at college had said, "Well, if you want to get away from your Dad for a bit, why not go to Oz?", it had seemed a great idea. The older she got, the more impossible Father became. It wasn't that he said a great deal, but the house seemed to vibrate with his disapproval: of what she wore, of where she went, of the time she came home, of whom she came home with. One of Father's grunts or mutters could convey a wealth of negative feeling towards whatever was happening at the time. From time to time he allowed himself a comment such as, "I once had high hopes for you Philippa," leaving the ensuing silence to tell her how far she had failed to live up to them.

"I don't understand how or why you put up with it," said Bunty, among others. She was one of the few of Pippa's friends who had been to the house. She was also one of the few who could ignore Father's negative comments or vibes. Bunty had added "God help you if you bring any boyfriends home."

That was something Pippa learned to avoid.. Not that she had many boyfriends, though she did lose her virginity uncomfortably and unpleasurably in the back of a car. For a short while she regretted that such a momentous event should be so immemorable. "Don't worry," Bunty said when she reported it. "It does get better." All the same, she suspected that the austere reputation of her home life had gone before her. The more likeable young men who ventured to take her home after some concert or dance were usually greeted by a front door opening to reveal her father's forbidding presence and a comment such as "Ah there you are Philippa," followed by the closing of the door again in the face of the hapless young man.

"He's impossible," she told her mother regularly.

But Frances had taken to computing like a duck to water and was preoccupied with classes and projects that took up most of her time. "You must decide what you want for your life," was the only advice she gave.

So in due course Pippa had contacted Bunty's friends in Western Australia, who said they would find her a place and a job, "no probs". Initially the house shuddered with Father's disapproval, until he apparently decided to ignore her and her plans. When she left, he pecked her on the forehead and said he hoped she would not regret her decision.

She had arrived in Perth a couple of weeks ago. Bunty's friends, Rowena and partner Jack, met her at the airport and took her home to a sprawling bungalow where they had prepared for her a small but comfortable bed-sitter where she could stay until she got herself sorted. They had arranged an interview for her at one of the hotels in town whose manager they happened to know. He agreed everyone would just love her Pommie accent and gave her a job as a receptionist. On her days off she explored the city.

Now, as they approached the landing stage and the lush vegetation of the riverside parks and gardens, she reminded herself of how lucky she had been to fall on her feet so quickly. *If only,* she thought, *she could like the place more. What was it that made that so difficult?*

She found a seat near the ferry landing and thought about it. The answer was quite simple. Every Aussie she met exuded self confidence. Each one seemed to know where they were going, how they were going to get there, and what they would do when they did. Whereas she never had, except that she wanted to escape Father's dark shadow. And now she had she was still none the wiser.

2

She was aware of someone lowering themselves on to the seat beside her. "It may never happen," a pleasant male voice said.

"Pardon?"

"Your expression is like a forecast for the proverbial wet week."

"Are you Aussies always so unspeakably rude?" Pippa flared. "Even to total strangers."

"'unspeakably rude'," he mimicked. "I guessed you were a Pom. I'm Jude Jamieson by the way. And you...?"

In spite of herself, Pippa responded, "Pippa Eastman."

"Well, at least we're no longer total strangers. Pippa, that's a nice name." She turned to meet the amused look from a pair of very blue eyes, a rugged outdoor face topped by a thatch of straw-coloured hair. He went on, "I'll call you Pip - you know, the sort you get when someone gives you a sour look."

"I don't recall asking you to sit here," Pippa.said.

There were a few moments of silence between them, interrupted by city noises - a chattering group of students passing, a child yelling, traffic and the slosh of water as the ferry took off again across the water.

He said, "No, you didn't. But you looked sad and you have an interesting face." He waved an arm to take in the surrounding scene. "You look ... well, you look so different from all these people who know exactly what they're doing and exactly why they're doing it." *Good Lord, he might have been reading her mind.* "Anyway, Pip, just tell me what you do when you're not sitting looking miserable, and then I'll leave you alone."

His grin was wholehearted and infectious. Pippa returned a small smile. "I left England because things were miserable and came here only to find I'm miserable here."

"Some people take their misery wherever they go, but I don't think you're one of them. If you have half an hour to spare, I'll take you to a place where you get the best ice cream in the Antipodes."

It was particularly good ice cream, and afterwards they strolled through the centre of the city while Jude pointed out the small 19th century buildings crouching among the high-rise, among them the Cathedral, a number of other churches, the Town Hall and a couple of theatres. He told her he'd just been visiting his mother who lived in South Perth, and had noticed Pippa standing by the rail on the ferry crossing.

"Of course you won't realise that I'm a Pom, too. Both mother and I are. We're Ten Pound Poms, if you're not too young to know what they are."

No, she wasn't too young, and had read about the post-war offer of the Australian Government to increase its population by giving austerity-ridden Brits a new life in exchange for a tenner.

"And she likes it here?" Pippa asked.

"Loves it. She's a hairdresser over in South Perth, and lives near Perth Zoo, where she can hear all kinds of growls and roars and pretend she lives in the jungle. Mind you, her partner Greg is an artist and hairy enough to qualify for jungle status."

Pippa laughed, found she was enjoying the company of this relaxed man. She registered that his mother had a partner, so presumably Jude's Dad had died or gone off.

"Perhaps you'd come with me one day to meet her for tea, still prepared impeccably in true English tradition. Or if that sounds a bit daunting, how about us doing an art show? There's a new exhibition of Aboriginal Art at the Art Museum. You look like an art exhibition person."

Pippa liked the sound of that. Art had been one of her better subjects at school and even Father had been quite complimentary about some of her water colours. It would be a nice change to visit something with a companion. They arranged to meet on her next free day at the ferry station, exchanged phone numbers, then Jude saw her on to the bus that would take her back to her new home.

15

That evening Rowena issued an invitation to a neighbourhood barbecue party at a local park for the day of her rendez-vous with Jude. When she explained she already had a date, and the circumstances, Rowena said, "Well, just be careful who you get picked up by. You've no Dad to look out for you here." So Father's reputation had preceded her to Australia.

Her unexpected encounter with Jude had undoubtedly boosted her morale. Pippa found she was much keener to try participating in whatever was available. Rowena went to a weekly yoga class and Pippa joined her to find she had a flair and mobility that quite surprised her. "You're a natch," the teacher told her. "You should take this up." So she enrolled for a regular class. She also joined Rowena's group of dog walking friends. Not that Rowena had a dog, but the twice weekly arrangement featured a walk in the cool of early morning through Perth's parks on both sides of the Swan River, linked by a bridge at either end.

3

"Hey," Jude greeted her, a few days later. "You look different."

"Less interesting?"

"Prettier as well as interesting. What's been happening to you?" So Pippa gave him a rundown of recent days and he said a little sadly, "Hm, I don't think Pip suits you any more. Let's stick to Pippa."

As they strolled up Barrack Street, he asked, "Do you know anything about Aborigine art?" Actually, she did. Keen to learn as much as she could about her new home, she had read up as much as she could before she left the UK. Aborigine art had sounded one of the more interesting aspects of a country in which most things were otherwise part of a brave new world..

"A bit," she said. "It sounds interesting, all that stuff about Dream Time."

Jude shrugged. "I'm not sure I go in for that myself. Down to earth, that's me. I mean how can you really take seriously the idea that trees and even rocks have a spirit?"

"You can make anything sound ridiculous if you oversimplify it. What do you think an Aboriginal might make of our Black Holes and parallel universes?"

"Yeah, but at least we can examine these scientifically. OK so give me your take on Dream Time."

It was a bit like being back at school, Pippa thought. "I can't say I have a take on it exactly, yet. I've done a bit of reading. But I can accept the idea of a great nothingness out of which the ancestral spirits emerged (and, no, I don't know how). Then these spirits travelled through the darkness creating song lines through which they named and brought into being everything that has become part of our landscapes. In due course, the humans came - about 40,000 years ago I believe - and became guardians of the land until a lot of other humans arrived and started messing it up." Pippa grinned. "That's probably over-succinct. Perhaps the art show will flesh it out a bit."

"OK. I'll try and keep an open mind."

As they crossed the railways the cluster of buildings housing museums and art galleries came into view. They spent nearly three hours at the exhibition, taking in a break for a visit to the shop followed by coffee and cream cake. Pippa looked at Jude over her steaming mug. "So?"

Jude swallowed a mouthful of cream cake. "I'm impressed. Not that I'm any the wiser about ancestral spirits and that stuff. But I like the style - especially the way the pictures are created out of a barrage of dots, broken up by symbols." He flipped through some cards he had brought and produced one in various tones of sand. "Look - there's the camp fire with the smoke rising, and kangaroos tracks all around."

Pippa smiled at his enthusiasm. "Not forgetting the invasion of possums a bit further away. But the dot paintings are comparatively recent compared with rock art which goes back over 40,000 years. Some of them show animals and birds that died out yonks ago."

"Yeah, I noticed there's a great emphasis on flora and fauna and geological features."

"Which brings us back to the spirits which exist in the landscape. You can understand why some of these people take a great

17

objection when someone wants to build an airport or factory on the land of their ancestral spirits."

"Not sure I can go that far. Feel like some more cake?"

Pippa laughed. "I had noticed your predilection for gooey things. Go on then. But how do you manage to stay so slim?"

"I'm glad you noticed that too," Jude said over his shoulder as he went off for more cake.

It was a fun afternoon, and there were more fun occasions to follow as they went out for meals, a couple of theatre visits, a barbecue with Jude's friends. So it was not a great surprise when he invited her back to his small apartment.

"My experience of sex hasn't been great," Pippa said.

"Who said anything about sex? Though come to think of it, I might give you a different take on that, too."

And he did.

A few weeks later, Jude found a bigger apartment and they moved in together. They fell into an easy-going routine. Pippa's work at the hotel meant that she periodically worked unsocial hours. Jude's at the travel agency quite often took him away from Perth: to conferences in other parts of the Continent and sometimes on a reconnaissance trip abroad. The resultant semi- independence suited them both. Jude was a tolerable cook and they shared the chores. The sex got better. Father would have been horrified, Pippa thought, and the idea quite cheered her.

After six months. Pippa's yoga teacher suggested she should seriously consider doing a teacher training course, so she did. It was quite intensive on top of her work at the hotel, requiring a thorough working knowledge of physiology, but Pippa loved it and the prospect it brought of eventually running her own classes. Yoga people were special, she felt at ease with them and their lack of need to chatter. Jude thought they were a bit odd, but in a nice way.

And then, after three years, just as Pippa was coming to the end of her training course, Jude came home one day and said he had been asked to open a branch of the agency on Queensland's Sunshine Coast. What did she think? They crossed the Continent on an exploratory visit. The rather hedonistic life style that went with it was not quite

Pippa's choice, but there was some magnificent wild mountain country on the Queensland-News South Wales border. They moved over there in 1994.

It took a bit of getting used to. The Sunshine Coast was built for the main purpose of servicing pleasure. After a few months Pippa announced she was rather bored with it and they moved into an apartment in Brisbane. In due course, Jude protested at living in a city and they found a cottage just over into New South Wales, near a small town called Murwillumbah. It was near the lower slopes of Mount Warning and its cloak of rain forests. Wallabies occasionally wandered into their garden and they learned to be wary of the less welcome presence of leeches. Pippa put an advertisement in the Murwillumbah paper for her yoga classes with pleasing results. Jude's branch of the travel agency was soon flourishing and in his spare time he gave surfing classes.

Sometimes Pippa wondered if she and Jude were really suited to each other. He had a way of skating across the surface of life, of sitting on the fence when it came to the major issues, that sometimes grated. Then he would be away for an extended period, expanding a new branch here, or replacing a sick manager there; and she really missed him. Once or twice she had a brief affair in his absence, but it never felt right. She suspected he did the same. They never discussed it, but their coming together always seemed to be mutually joyful.

Then letters from Robin began to refer to their mother's ailing health and hint that Father was getting just a bit odd. In 1998.Pippa booked a flight for her first visit home.

Oxfordshire, summer 2008

1

"Philippa! Philippa!" Joseph Eastman called as loudly as his quavering voice would allow.

Downstairs in the kitchen Pippa pulled off the rubber gloves she was using to clear the sink and called back "Coming, Father."

He was as she had left him, his thin face a similar discoloured white as the bank of pillows against which he was propped. She must get into Banbury and buy some new ones.

"Philippa, who is that fellow I saw this morning? And what's he doing here?"

"That was Jude, Father. He is a friend of mine from Australia. Arrived a week ago."

"How long is he staying?"

"I don't know. Father. But he has come a long way. So it will be for a while."

"I don't like him in the house. He disturbs my work."

It was some years since Joseph Eastman had worked, and they had had this conversation three, perhaps four times that day. Not to mention the day before, and the day before that. In fact, Jude had kept out of Father's way virtually since he arrived, but time meant nothing any more to Joseph Eastman, and today or a month or more ago merged into one,

"Don't worry, Father. I'll keep him out of the way."

Jude marvelled at her patience with this man who had once filled her with awe, at times even fear. It was impossible to explain how this querulous old man was no longer that person. She had come to regard him as a sick, somewhat tiresome child.

2

It was ten years earlier in a different century, indeed millennium, that she had last come here. Her parents had recently moved out of Oxford to the outskirts of Daerley Green, 20 miles to the north. Her mother was ill – wouldn't 45 years living with that curmudgeon make even a saint ill, as her brother Robin put it? And then quite suddenly she collapsed. Pippa had already booked her flight home and now managed to advance her departure by a few days. Just enough to be able to spend some hours of several days with her mother in that gem of a hospice where she ended her days.

"He's getting very forgetful," Mother had told her several times. "It's worrying."

"You leave us to worry about that, Robin and I."

Much of the time, her mother had slept, but occasionally Pippa would look up to see her looking at her with an intensity that was almost tangible, and then she would start telling her something that was clearly of great significance to her. On these occasions she spoke quite fluently, and on one of them she said, "You probably don't remember that your father had a Russian cousin. A much younger one - she tried to get in touch with him."

"What happened?" Pippa asked.

Mother was tiring now. "Nothing," she said, with a struggle. "He'd never met her and he was adamant that he had left all that part of his life behind him. Perhaps one day you might contact her. I think her name is Margarit." She sighed. "And anyway, who would be able to figure out the workings of your father's mind?"

Who indeed? Pippa's bafflement must have shown in her expression, for her mother suddenly said, "Don't be sad, darling. I've had a great life."

"Have you, Mum? Really?"

"How can you doubt it. Your father and I were ideally suited." Seeing her serene smile, Pippa knew there was no way she could question this remarkable statement and that she had better accept it even if she did not understand it.

On another occasion she said, "I should have gone with him that time he returned to Finland. Something happened that changed him."

And towards the end, "There has been some man - two men trying to contact your father. One is called Hans, the other Karl. Your father will not speak to them or say why they make him angry."

A skeleton in the cupboard? Pippa wondered. But it was hardly something she could ask her dying mother. She knew that Father had returned to Finland while she was still a baby, but of course she didn't know what he had been like before.

A couple of times her father had turned up at the hospice, and sat silent, with a lost helpless look. It was disturbing because she had never seen that look on his face before. Later she learned it was part of his deteriorating condition.

The new house on the edge of Daerley Green was a five-bedroom so-called executive home, a term popular term in the latter part of the 20th century. Her parents had already put their stamp on it. Two of the bedrooms overlooking the fields at the back had been converted into a study with attached shower room and toilet. The study held a single bed in case Joseph was in the mood to work into the night.

Her mother had converted a third bedroom into a study for herself equipped with the technology to convert her considerable collection of photographs into digital images and print them in the form of postcards and greeting cards. The photographs were taken all over the world during her frequent journeys with Joseph. She had also created a website from which she ran a small mail order business. Pippa had been astonished by her mother's skill and enterprise and understood better how she had survived and flourished through these difficult years. Some of the photographs had been blown up and decorated the upstairs and ground floor halls. A living room opened into a dining room connected with a large kitchen. There was a small library-cum-study with floor-to-ceiling bookshelves and some of the treasures from Joseph Eastman's travels. They had also acquired a young cat called Aristotle, rather a monster of a ginger cat which, early on in her visit, had an ugly encounter with some creature of the night and bore the scars in the form of a big bump on his right cheek. Pippa had tended to his wounds and been rewarded by ever deeper affection. The cat appeared to have a curious relationship with Father, as they spent a lot of time in each other's company, but did not appear to communicate.

In addition to the house and the cat there was a rather ancient VW campervan parked up along the side of the house. Mother had written to tell her about it and how they used it to travel round the country when his father was on a lecture tour in order to economise on hotels. Economy was another of his new phobias. Pippa cleaned it out, brightened it up and used it as her office while she was there, running her laptop off the car battery through the cigarette lighter. It also provided an escape from the increasing demands of her father.

A few days after Pippa's arrival, as if everything were now in order and she could let go, Mother died. Father did not do God, so there was a simple but moving Humanist service at the crematorium. Pippa, who was not yet entirely sure whether or not she did God, slipped into Daerley Green church for quiet headspace several times.

Father had made it clear he did not want her to stay and that he could manage quite well, thank you. In fact, once the funeral was over, he did seem much more his old self: more brusque and gruff. At times downright unpleasant. In particular she remembered a phone call from someone called Karl who had asked to speak to Professor Joseph Eastman. Father had become red with anger, refusing to take the call, so that she had been obliged to make some excuse to the caller. A distant memory had surfaced - a boy asking for her father many years earlier and her mother's insistence that he was out.

She went to see his doctor who agreed that her father was showing signs of mental decline though he had refused any tests that might help in making a diagnosis. Well, that followed. However, the doctor also said that the changes might be very slow and it was much too early for her to be thinking of completely re-organising her own life. Then a miracle happened. Robin announced that he was shortly moving to the Oxford branch of his firm and he would keep an eye on father.

Still not entirely convinced that it was the best thing to do, Pippa returned to Australia. It was soon after that she and Jude had moved into the cottage near Murwillumbah and for some time life became extremely busy establishing a new home, a new office for Jude and new classes for her yoga. News from Robin was reassuring. Father had even started writing a little.

All the same, Robin's email went on, *his domestic skills have never been great so I've arranged for a home help and a gardener. The home help is called Klaudia and is Polish. I hoped she was not expecting to improve her English with our silent papa, so it was a bit of a surprise to find them giggling over something Father had said in Russian and which was apparently quite rude in Polish. In fact, all round there is a welcome softening of his nature.*

Perhaps that was part of his condition, too, though Philippa. But the news was generally encouraging and Jude told her not to look for trouble where there wasn't any. She contented herself with sending a message to Klaudia via Robin, asking her to email her if any problem arose and Robin were not available.

Weeks and months turned into years. Jude went off for several months to open a branch in New Zealand. Pippa went on a cruise with some yoga friends round Indonesia, and sent her father postcards. There were even occasional letters from him, talking about the book he was working on. True he kept mentioning that a strange woman had taken over the house and was ordering him about. Pippa wrote to explain that the strange woman was a home help Robin had asked to keep the house tidy, but it did not stop Father from repeating his comment. Gradually Pippa realised that since he forgot she had already answered it, it was likely that he had also forgotten he had already mentioned it. From time to time there was a worrying report from Robin, but he had spoken to Father's doctor and these alternating periods of deterioration and remission were apparently normal.

And then came the email from the neighbours. Joseph had been found wandering aimlessly round the monthly market. He had been quite aggressive when someone tried to take him home. This had happened half a dozen times. Soon after, an email came from Klaudia: *Mr Eastman forget I come and he lock me out. Next time OK. Next time forget again. Is difficult. But now I have key.* Pippa called Robin. He said, yes things were falling apart a bit. He was going to move in for a while where Father liked it or not.

24

It was a huge relief.

In the meantime, Father's letter became strange. *Your brother has come to live here for reasons I do not understand. It disturbs my work.* Pippa correctly assumed that, in truth, there was no serious work to be disturbed.

And then most inconveniently, Robin fell in love. She was called Marion and there was 'no one like her in the world'. She had come to work in the Oxford office and they had clicked straight away. She was two years younger, not beautiful, but striking and clever. And on and on. Pippa was delighted for them both, but sensed there was about to be an upheaval in her own life. There was no way you could expect even the most understanding woman to take on Father.

"Don't worry, Rob," she said. "I'll come back and sort something out."

The need for this had become increasingly apparent from her father's letters over recent weeks. Robin's presence in the house seemingly made no difference to the progression of whatever Father had. Dementia or Alzheimers she called it in her head. Every letter rambled on continuously about her mother: how she had gone out somewhere and failed to come back. When she had told Jude she planned to go home he'd said, "Why now, you've never bothered about the old fart before?"

"He's ill, Jude, that's why. I can't expect Robin to take full responsibility. Anyway I shan't be long."

3

She had gone in the New Year of 2008, leaving Perth in temperatures in their upper 30sC and arriving at London Airport in a downpour of rain and sleet. Robin met her at the airport, having moved in with Marion a couple of days earlier. Aristotle had given her an ecstatic welcome. Father had expressed neither surprise nor pleasure at seeing her, immediately informing her that her mother had gone out and not come back. Pippa had made them both a cup of tea and sat with him at the breakfast bar in the kitchen.

"Father, don't you remember Mother died a long time ago. We had a nice service at the crematorium."

He had looked at her, frowning, for a while then his face lit with comprehension. "That's right, how could I forget?"

But he went on forgetting with only gradually diminishing frequency for several weeks.

They developed a kind of flexible routine. Klaudia came three times a week now and did most of the cooking, preparing extra portions for the freezer. Pippa started a yoga class in the next village and began to develop a series of private lessons which she did in other people's homes on the days Klaudia was there and on evenings when Robin could Father-sit.. This was flexible enough to adapt to her father's needs. Robin had power of attorney and kept them solvent. To begin with Father had spent a lot of time in what he called his studio, adapted from the garden shed. Gradually this decreased and he took to reading, initially in the downstairs study, then in bed. When Pippa took a look at the writing he had left on his desk, it proved to be a series of jottings of unconnected ideas that made no sense. Aristotle mooched round the house, spending quite a lot of time in Father's room, sometimes curled up at the bottom of the bed. He and Father seemed to ignore each other as they always had, while creating a curious impression of companionship..

And then there had been that odd phone call. "My name is Karl Schmidt. Could I speak to Professor Joseph Eastman please?" A pleasant voice in accented English. A distant memory returned again. "Karl as in Charles in English?" she asked. There had been a pause, then a laugh. "Exactly so. May I speak to the Professor?" Then the other memory of her mother "A man called Karl has tried to contact your father. It makes him very angry."

"I'm sorry, I'm afraid he is really quite ill."

A grunt of commiseration. "I am sorry to hear. Perhaps I will call in a week or two in the hope he is better." He rang off before Pippa had time to say there probably would not be much improvement.

On another day she opened the front door to find Jude on the doorstep. "You said you wouldn't be long," he accused.

"You might have emailed."

"Yeah, and you would have found some way of dissuading me." As if anyone could dissuade Jude from anything on which he had made up his mind.

Pippa introduced Jude to Father and Aristotle both of whom clearly disliked him on sight. It was not practicable to conceal a large Australian in the house, so she installed him in the campervan. Father had most of his meals in his room, so Pippa and Jude had theirs in the kitchen, trying to remember to keep their voices down. It was all a bit of a farce, but it worked. When she asked Jude what he did with himself all day, he said airily that he had been walking or in the library or in the pub. He certainly knew far more about the local countryside than she did. She suspected he was also drinking a bit too much.

And then in the middle of one night, Pippa awoke to find her father stumbling about the landing clasping his chest. She called for an ambulance and he was admitted to hospital with a pulmonary embolism. He died two days later while she held his limp hand.

As he had always made it clear that he was an agnostic, Pippa arranged for a Humanist Funeral at the crematorium. A Humanist celebrant had come to the house and spent an evening discussing Father's life, the kind of music he might want, some possible readings. Throughout the discussion, Aristotle sat on Pippa's lap, contributing the occasional *miaoul*.

Pippa had put a notice in a University publication and a couple of the broadsheets and was astonished to find the chapel almost full. A few strangers came to take her hand after the service, murmur condolences; some commented on his considerable contribution to a lesser known branch of history. Jude stayed in the background, but she was glad to have him there. Aristotle spent most of the day on Father's bed.

A few days after the funeral there was a strange telephone call. The girl's voice sounded very young and she asked to speak to Professor Eastman with some urgency. When Pippa explained that her father had only recently died, the girl sounded unexpectedly distressed.

"That is sad news," she said. "I wished very much to speak to Herr Professor."

Herr Professor? So she was probably German. Perhaps she was a student? But no, she sounded far too young.

27

"Is there anything I can do to help?" Pippa asked, not able to imagine what it might be.

"No, no." The girl began several sentences, stumbled, then paused. At last she said, "My name is Greta Schmidt. My grandfather knew very well Herr Professor. But now it is too late." The line went dead. Schmidt? Wasn't it a Karl Schmidt who had rung on an earlier occasion?

And then came an even stranger call: a police inspector who wanted to speak to Professor Joseph Eastman. Pippa initially told them he was not at home, without enlarging on it. Yes, she agreed she was his daughter.

"Could you tell me when he might be returning home?"

"He won't be returning home," Pippa said. "He's dead." And to her own surprise she burst into tears.

An embarrassed police inspector apologised profusely for disturbing her at such a time, and then tentatively asked whether she had any idea where he might have been in 1970.

"All over the place," Pippa said tartly, pulling herself together. "He was an internationally known historian and lectured all over the world for heaven's sake. What's all this about?"

The inspector murmured it was to do with a case that had been brought to their attention, but in view of the Professor's demise she would not be bothered any more. Pippa found herself asking what case he was referring to.

"It was a very long time ago," he said. "In Finland. I suspect this is the point when it becomes a cold case, in every sense of the word."

Airborne, 2010

"Breakfast, Jude. Wake up!"

Thirty thousand feet above the Atlantic, Jude Jamieson opened an eye in response to the gentle dig from his neighbour. He glanced at his watch. Five a.m., an outrageous time for breakfast. Five a.m., UK time, 10 p.m. in Las Vegas where the gaming halls would be humming right now. And in two, three hours he would see Pippa. Perhaps a bit more, as she was always late. He smiled, visualising her face, rather triangular with its pointed chin and broad cheekbones under the thatch of bouncy dark hair from which she now tinted out the odd grey streak. Not beautiful, but special.

"Penny for them," said his companion, as the tray bearing his plastic breakfast was placed on his fold-out table. Josie was petite and blonde, quite different from Pippa, prettier but without that special quality that had kept Jude uncharacteristically faithful for a long time now. Well, he reminded himself, at forty-two it was time to stop butterflying even with as charming a blossom as Josie who had made it clear she was attracted to him.

"Actually I was thinking of Pippa."

"Your woman?"

Jude smiled. "She wouldn't admit to that. She's her own woman."

Josie unwrapped a brioche. "What did you say she did?"

"I'm not sure I did say. She's a yoga teacher. And paints bit."

"Eats nut cutlets, drinks herbal tea?" Josie, he had noticed, went in for stereotypes.

"Yes to the herbal tea, but I haven't seen any nut cutlets yet. And she has an appalling cat called Aristotle."

"She does sound – er, a bit special." Josie bit into her brioche, then turned to one of her colleagues seated just across the aisle.

Jude unwrapped his own brioche. There were two slices of shiny ham and squares of cheese wrapped in plastic, a carton of yoghurt, a tiny pot of marmalade, a small plastic glass of orange juice and an empty cup. He thought back over the past few days in which they had all over-eaten and under-slept: a promotional trip for a group of mainly travel agents specialising in US holidays, plus a couple of other travel writers like himself. The travel writers had been old buddies and seemed pretty well joined at the hip, as well as unimpressed by his own commission from *Whizz,* a rather new London-based monthly for the well-heeled international set. As a result he had spent most of the time with the agents The itinerary had combined a stretch of California coast near San Francisco, a day in Yosemite National Park, and a visit to Las Vegas. Yosemite had suited him best and, given the choice, he would have spent the whole time exploring those amazing forests of giant redwoods and sequoias under the ice-sharp mountain peaks. For many of his much younger companions it was their first trip so far afield and they made the most of the lavish entertainment. Watching them, it made him feel quite old as well as a bit homesick for the wilder parts of his homeland.

"You're an Aussie," one of their hosts had said as they sipped iced drinks overlooking a beach near Santa Barbara. "This must remind you of home."

"Home's emptier," Jude had replied. But then home was emptier than anywhere else he had been so far; certainly emptier than Pippa's bit of Middle England where the villages were separated by just a few miles of Oxfordshire's rolling farmlands.

Pippa's village of Daerley Green, twenty miles north of Oxford, had picture postcard qualities, though the house she lived in with her father was on an estate on the edge of it, and indistinguishable from a myriad other estates up and down the country. Pippa had flown home when her mother was dying and had returned, concerned about her father's mental condition. Years later, she had gone back again to look after him. She had not asked Jude to come, but Oz had seemed emptier than ever without her. Jude's partner Craig did most of the day to day running of the agency and assured Jude he was more a hindrance than a help. So he just went.

He and Joseph had taken an immediate dislike to each other. OK let's be honest about this, Jude thought, each of them felt they were the more entitled to Pippa's attention. He was not proud of it. As Pippa pointed out, her father, now with advanced dementia, was not in a position to make rational judgments while he, Jude, was. The truth was that, after their carefree life in Western Oz, it was a hell of a shock to find every day and every decision circumscribed by the needs of an old man of whose fine brain all trace had gone. There was also a weird ginger cat called Aristotle with a big bump on his face. Jude called it Totty and it clearly disliked him as much as Pippa's father.

"You're a bit of a selfish bastard, aren't you?" Pippa said, early on.

"I don't remember you having a lot to say in your father's favour back home," Jude pointed out.

"No, well he was difficult. But now he's sick. That makes things different."

For a while life had been no fun at all. Pippa had started giving yoga lessons, fitting her hours in with those when her home help or her brother Robin was available. Fortunately Robin was OK, but mostly preoccupied with a new love in his life. When Pippa was not teaching, she was tending to her father. Jude would have helped more, but Joseph Eastman could not stand the sight of him.

So Jude went for long walks and came to learn the subtleties of this countryside, so much greener and more gentle than what he was used to. With Pippa's agreement, he had the campervan checked out and began to explore further afield. He came to be enchanted by the warm stone-built villages and their churches that not only looked but smelled of great age. He found the reputedly reserved Poms were in fact delighted to talk to a stranger who admired their homes and he enjoyed a 'proper cup of tea' in several of them. He temporarily lost himself in a network of narrow lanes, meeting only the occasional tractor. He began to wonder why, all those years ago, his parents had decided to leave this land, leading to the next question of where, amongst these island confines, he might find trace of his own father. Then he wondered why he did not start looking, and acknowledged the underlying fear of what he might discover.

He also became a regular at the local, The Trumpet. Everyone there said what a fine brain Joseph Eastman had, though they also agreed that he had always been a difficult man. Jude went to the library and spent some hours reading his books. Despite their subjects, they were surprisingly easy to read. They were all about rather obscure times in European history. Not only obscure times, but obscure places: small countries that kept changing shape and name in a ragged line between what Jude thought of as Western Europe and the

31

great bulk of what had been the Soviet Union and its sphere of influence.

Something was nudging him again. Josie said, "Are you going to drink that cold coffee, or do you want some fresh?"

He jerked himself back into the present of breakfast up in the sky, and handed his cup back for an exchange.

"You were miles away," Josie said. "So tell me, are you descended from one of the criminals who were deported to Australia, whenever?"

He smiled and shook his head. "Sorry to disappoint you, but I'm only second generation, and descended from one of the Ten Pound Poms."

"What on earth was a Ten Pound Pom?"

So Jude embarked on a brief history lesson of how, following the Second World War, Australia wanted to encourage more Brits to come to this young and developing country, and had offered the opportunity for a new life in return for payment of £10. And many people, especially the young, had been glad to leave the austerity of post-war Britain and take up the challenge.

By the time he had finished, Josie was losing interest. Soon after the breakfast trays were collected, the captain announced that they would shortly begin their descent, and Josie went off to the loo. Looking out of the window, Jude saw the sprawling green of Britain far below, and realised how much he had missed it in the arid setting of Nevada. He went on watching as thin lines turned into railways and roads and moving dots into motorway traffic. He was aware of Josie slipping back into her seat.

"So you must still have quite a few relatives over here," she said.

"Some," he agreed. But he didn't tell her, any more than he had yet told Pippa, that finding one in particular, had been another big motive for coming here.

Reunion 2010

Pippa was catapulted into wakefulness by the shrill of her alarm reminding her that she was to meet Jude at Birmingham Airport that morning. Aristotle was washing himself at the bottom of her bed. From that angle, showing his left side, he still looked very handsome. She lay still watching the neatness of his movements as he fanned out his claws, his tongue meticulously probing between them.

And then, despite the promise of a warm August day, she shivered. The dream had left a disturbing hangover. Its causes were obvious enough. Father had been and would long continue to be a preoccupation of her subconscious, and that absurd email referring to skeletons in cupboards had tipped it into the realms of the surreal. Anyway this hadn't been a skeleton, but fully clothed even down to its heavy boots. The whole thing was macabrely absurd. And what about that weird comment Father had made right at the end, even if she couldn't remember exactly what it was.

She suddenly felt very happy that she would be seeing Jude soon. Things had not always been very harmonious since his arrival from Australia, but now she needed his presence and his reassurance. All the same she would not tell him about the dream. She could just imagine him throwing back his handsome head in a bellow of laughter. As for the email, in due course she would decide whether or not to reply.

She tended, as Jude was pleased to point out, to leave things until the last moment. In fact, she thought she had set off in good time, but there was a hold up on the M40 and she arrived a good half hour after he would have emerged from Customs. No probs, as Jude would say. In case of hold ups on either side, the waiting one would go to the ground floor café. He was there at a table by the window, a beer before him, leafing through a magazine. Pippa stood watching him for a moment, enjoying this first sight of him.. He really was very good looking; chiselled, fit-looking too in the way that Aussies who did a lot of sport managed to look, as though fitness was intrinsic to their genome. Young-looking too: much younger than his forty-something years.

He must have sensed her watching, for he suddenly looked up and gave that smile that enchanted her the first time she saw it. "Hi Pips!" An arm signalled her across.

"So you didn't allow enough time," he continued now as she approached, and he hooked a chair for her with a foot.

"There was a hold up on the M40."

"Yeah, yeah." He leaned forward and kissed her. "Miss me?"

"Surprisingly. Aristotle didn't of course."

"Tell me something new."

Pippa came over and took the seat opposite him, "Well," she began, and before she could stop herself continued, "I've discovered I have a skeleton in the cupboard."

Blue eyes widened in surprise, then amusement. "Now, I know it's time I came home."

"Just a silly joke. Some woman in Finland thinks we may be related," Pippa said quickly, but she had noted and warmed to his reference 'came home'. "I'll tell you later. Now, tell me about Vegas,"

"Busy and expensive; a bit depressing watching all those people chasing the pot of gold at the end of the rainbow. A lot of kids too. Not allowed to gamble of course, but presumably beginning to assume that this is what you're expected to do when you grow up. But Yosemite, that was something else. You could get drunk on the air, and I've become a dedicated tree hugger."

"And now I know it's time *you* came home." But Pippa found she liked the idea of Jude hugging trees. "Anyway, how about we do just that: go home?"

On the way he told her more about the trip, focussing almost entirely on Yosemite. Then he broke off to ask, "Tell me more about this skeleton in the cupboard."

"Not much to tell. The email came from someone called Liisu, lives way north, beyond the Arctic Circle and thought we might be related."

"Why would she think that?"

34

"Maybe because of her surname, Itäinen, which means person from the East: Eastman for example. And she had an uncle called Jooseppi, which is Finnish for Joseph."

"Well, that's a pretty tenuous assumption."

Pippa paused while she followed the exit at Junction 10, negotiated a couple of roundabouts and headed into the lanes of north Oxfordshire. Finally she said, "I have a feeling about it. And she mentioned a skeleton in the cupboard."

"Hm. It's a bit hard to imagine Joseph with a secret life."

"On the contrary. There's a load of stuff from Father's past that is a closed book as far as I'm concerned. What happened to my Russian granddad. for example? Why my grandmother dragged father over to Sweden when he was still a babe-in-arms. Maybe this Liisu could fill in some of those gaps. Anyway tell me some more. What about the Californian coast? And San Francisco?"

So for the rest of the journey Jude filled her in with their visits to the city and local resorts. As soon as they reached home, he humped his luggage up to their room, then flopped on to the bed and said, "I'm bushed, Pips. Do you mind?" And was asleep almost like the flicking of a switch.

It was not what Pippa had envisaged for the day. She spent the next few hours re-thinking a new course of yoga she was planning for a retirement club, popping in to check up on Jude from time to time. In the event he took her by surprise as she was standing in the kitchen chopping up onions, peppers and courgettes for a *ratatouille*. Hands were clasped round her waist, her head pulled back against him as he leaned to kiss the crook of her neck. She felt the familiar promptings of desire, deepening as he raised his hands to cup her breasts.

"You'd better stop that right now if you want any supper tonight."

Jude stood back. "I could forego supper, but I guess we'll make better love on a full stomach. Anyway, I have some questions." He took a serrated knife from a drawer and joined her in her vegetable chopping,

"So fire away."

"While we were in California, I got talking to a guy whose dad spent a lot of time in Oz. He said I reminded him of his father. Outdoor type, you know. In his case a keen horseman. I was a bit surprised that he went on at such length, then it turned out that his dad had died only a few days before. Cancer. He said it was terrible to see him change from someone so fit to a bag of bones." Jude paused. Pippa went on chopping, waiting. Then he went on in a rush, "It made me think of your Dad, and how I had never really known him. Not as a person. But I had got to know him in a different way through his books. I read quite a lot of them, you know."

"No, I didn't know."

"In the library, filling in time when you were so busy and preoccupied. They were really surprising, easy to read and full of stuff I didn't know. About different countries in Europe. Yeah, of course we've got a lot of those people in Australia – Poles, Czechs, Slovaks, Serbs. But I'd never really stopped to think about the places they came from. I got to think that I wish I'd know him better, made more effort."

Pippa stopped chopping. "He was impossible to get to know, however much effort you'd have made. Especially by the time you met him."

As if she had not spoken, Jude went on, "And the same applied to my Dad. I never really made an effort."

Pippa tipped the chopped vegetables from the cutting board into a casserole dish, put it in the pre-heated oven, took Jude by the hand and led him into the living room.

"This is weird," she said. "You've never spoken about your childhood before, let alone your Dad. Well, I knew your Mum had that rather dishy partner when she died - Greg, wasn't it? But I suppose I just assumed your father just went away."

"There's not much I want to remember about my childhood, least of all my Dad." Jude sat in one of the armchairs, arms resting on his knees, looking up at her. "He was a drunken sod - and, yes, he did just go away. But may be I should have tried to find out why."

Australia 1965-1974/Oxfordshire, summer 2010

1

The truth was that Jude had very little recollection of his early childhood, especially of the transit camp, and those he did have probably were distilled from the colourful descriptions of his mother, Anne. Predominant was a blurred impression of intense heat.

"They were actually hosing the huts to cool 'em down." He could still reproduce in his head his mother's voice shrill with indignation at finding herself in such a place. The misery was made even worse because it contrasted with the idyllic journey in the cruise ship *Canberra* and because she was pregnant with him. She and Dad had never known such luxury, and they made the most of it. Morning sickness had curtailed some of Mum's activities, but Dad had made up for it. Once arrived at their destination, the pregnancy must have been dire in such conditions and so far from home, but it contributed to a very close friendship with Dorrie who shared the Nissen hut with them. The thinness of the partition wall allowed for little privacy so Dorrie was left in no doubt as to the depths of Mum's misery or the deteriorating state of her marriage.

Dad had worked on and off. The idea was that they should save to move out of the transit camp to an apartment of their own. He got jobs on construction sites, down at the docks at Fremantle, but he became more and more unreliable and they never lasted long.

Later his mother said Dad had always been something of a drinker, but never like he was on board ship on the journey over. And once they were installed in the hostel, it got worse. He found the conditions degrading, the Aussies unfriendly, and said the whole thing had been a terrible con trick.

"But it was the same for everyone," as Mum had said. "It was as if there were a devil in him just waiting for an excuse to burst out." She'd even thought for a while they should pack it in and go home. But she had been about and seen enough to know that Australia could offer a really good life, especially for the tiny human who was showing increasing signs of wanting to get out there and join in.

Her son was born in a hurry. Dorrie had rushed her to emergency on a spring day in 1965. Dad was out drinking as usual and in due course came to drool over the scrap of red squawling humanity in his mother's arms. They christened him James and called him Jimmy. He had always hated it and changed it to Jude when he went to University.

Of his father, Mum rarely spoke and never without bitterness, so presumably such memories as he had were his own. And they were confusing. Blurred and confusing. They were invariably of a huge figure that was either maudlin or aggressive. If he thought hard about it, he could smell the sweat that always accompanied his father's embraces. That and the pervading whiff of alcohol, though he wouldn't have been able to distinguish it as such at the time. Though he hadn't particularly enjoyed Dad's affectionate attentions, at least they were not frightening. In jolly times, as he got a bit older his father had taken him to the beach or fishing or ice cream parlours where he had stuffed him almost sick with gaudy confections. Dad himself was accompanied by a seemingly inexhaustible supply of cans of liquid whose smell Jude continued to associate with his father long after he stopped seeing him.

In contrast the dark moods were forever associated with his mother shouting and weeping, and then Jude would scuttle away to hide in a cupboard or under a bed. Sometimes there was the sound of blows and his mother's face would be red and swollen. And then one day she told him, "Your father has gone away. He won't be back for a while." Only he never did come back. It was ages before Jude found the courage to ask where he was, and that was on the eve of their departure from Adelaide to Perth in Western Australia. "How will Dad find us?" Jude asked. "He'll find us if he wants to," his mother replied. And because he never saw him again, Jude assumed it was because Dad had chosen not to.

There were other memories. One in particular was of toddling through the city streets clutching his mother's hand. There were a lot of other people and he had been terrified of losing her. Much later she had explained that all the people in the transit camps were marching in protest because the rents had been put up. Dad had raged about it for days, but was too drunk to come on the march.

It was soon after that he had gone, and Jude spent a lot of time with Auntie Dorrie while his mother went to school. He liked being

38

with Aunt Dorrie, not least because she had a niece called Beverley who was always coming round. Jude had had a crush on her and, in true Australian tradition, had truncated her name to Bev the Beaut. She certainly was a 'beaut' with her thick chestnut hair in the pageboy cut of the time. Not that she took much notice of him, as she had a string of hunky boyfriends. In between, she sometimes took him and Aunti Dorrie up into the hills for a picnic and taught him the rudiments of bird recognition among the colourful parakeets and rosellas. He was more interested in her than in the birds, but came to take a fancy to the magpie-lark, bold as a street urchin, with its long cocked-up tail. Anyway Bev was twelve years his senior and had just finished teacher training at Uni. Then she got a post in Fremantle and he didn't see much of her after that.

Mother did really well. He'd though it terribly funny that she should be going back to school, but apparently she was learning to be a hairdresser. Her hair had always been very pretty. Soon after she had finished learning, she got a job, quite locally, in a hairdresser's shop, or salon as they called it. At about the same time he had started school. He had really enjoyed being with so many of his peers. He wasn't very good academically but even at that age he showed signs of being good at sport and won awards for the school which also won him popularity.

He was really fed up when Mum decided to move to Perth. The salon she worked for was part of a group and they were opening a new one in South Perth, offering her the opportunity to manage it. It meant good money and an apartment over the premises. She said she couldn't wait to see the back of Adelaide, her only regret being that she would miss Dorrie who had been such a pillar of support over the years. She also said the weather would not be so extreme. They had both loved it there. Mum had become a different person, happy and relaxed and in due course acquired a partner called Greg. Jude had done well at school, gone to Uni and got a good degree in business studies. He had a vague memory that Aunt Dorrie and Bev the Beaut had paid them a visit, but by then he had a acquired a taste for females nearer his own age. After that he got work experience in a travel agency before setting up a small one of his own. And then one day, returning from a visit to his mother in South Perth, he saw Pippa on the ferry across the Swan River.

2

Jude spilled all these memories out to her a couple of days after his return from America.

"I can't believe you've never told me any of this before. I knew your Mum died a few years after we went to Queensland, but I assumed your father had gone off long before."

"Well, he had, and it's not the sort of thing that crops up when you're having fun. And that's what we were about, wasn't it, having fun?"

"You make us sound very superficial."

"Well, we were, weren't we – in a way both escaping from pasts we weren't keen to remember? I don't recall you talking about your father, except in negative terms, until you suddenly started to worry he was losing his marbles. I mean, what brought that on?"

Pippa was silent, thinking about it. "I suppose because the one thing I had always admired was his mind. Mother had always dinned into me how clever he was, what a hard time he'd had, and how nothing must be allowed to disturb him. And then suddenly the one special thing about him started to disintegrate. I started to read his books again –well, maybe read them properly for the first time, and I found in them a compassion I never found in him. And I couldn't bear the thought of him ending up in some old people's home with no one to visit him."

She looked at him in that direct way she had, which could be quite unnerving. "I didn't really expect you would come."

"Nor did I. I was thinking about that on the flight back the other day. The fact is that Australia didn't feel right without you. And, after a while, I got to thinking just possibly I might try and find some trace of Dad – or at least his family. I know they came from Somerset."

"So in a way we're both looking for lost Dads?"

"You could put it like that."

"I'll help you find yours if you'll help me find mine. Well, I know where mine is, of course. His ashes are scattered round the local wood, and his name is on a plaque in the local Crem. The man I want to find is the one my mother fell in love with."

"It sounds as though the first source to tap might have signed that email you got the other day. Have you answered it?"

"No. And I'm not really sure why."

"I can tell you that. You've never been good at committing yourself."

"Since when were you into psychobabble?"

"Heaven forbid. But I've know you long enough to know your strengths and some of your ever-so-small weaknesses. What's more I think we have them in common. I'm not a great committer either."

After dinner, they went to bed and made love. And then they made love again. Eventually Jude said, "What about that email?"

"What email?"

"The one to Finland."

Pippa grunted and rolled over towards him again.

After breakfast next morning, they composed an email together. *Liisu Itäinen – Yes, there could be a connection as my father was born in Finland, and his name is Joseph (Finnish Jooseppi?). Was Joseph. He died a few weeks ago. I didn't know he had brothers or sisters. What kind of skeleton did you have in mind? Your English is very good. – Greetings, Pippa Eastman*

The reply came within an hour. *Hello Cousin – I am an English teacher at a school here and spent a year in England. Uncle Jooseppi did not have brothers and sisters ,but a cousin; and his mother Annikki, your grandmother had a brother Matti, my father. So you have a great- uncle Matti. We moved north to Lappi (Lapland) after the big war. Uncle Jooseppi came here in 1970, when I was eleven. I thought he was very handsome. After he left, a dead man was found. That is the skeleton.*

"So you are a murderer's daughter," Jude said cheerfully.

"Shut up, Jude." Pippa was doing some calculations in her head. "So this Liisu is about 10 years older than me. And it's true,

41

Father did go to Finland in 1970. I was only a few months old so can't remember. But for a while when he got back, Mother said he was in a rare good mood. "

"Perhaps he should have murdered a few more people."

"Shut up, Jude," Pippa said again as she started another email. *Hello Cousin – this is amazing to find I have a new family. Please tell me all you can remember about my father. I have been living in Australia most of my life.*

This time the answer took a little longer to come. *I will try and describe to you. Remember I was very young. At first I was a bit frightened, he seemed angry, stern. Then he went away and came back happy. He read me stories in English and told me how pretty baby you were.*

Father had never read to her in her life. How pretty baby she was? Were they talking about the same man?

She read on: *He sent me cards for my birthday for a few years. Then nothing. I'm very sorry he died.*

"I wonder where I went wrong," Pippa said. "Why he didn't read stories to me. Or send me birthday cards." She looked thoughtful. "Come to think of it, Mother did say that he changed a lot after a visit to Finland when I was baby."

"Mine didn't either," Jude said "Read stories, send birthday cards, I mean. May be being very clever is as self-absorbing as being drunk. Except I don't remember Dad taking notice of any other kids." He suddenly took in her expression. "Hey, you're upset."

Pippa sniffed, blew her nose. "Not really. It's nice to think someone has good memories of him."

"We could go visit this Liisu."

"We ought to go back to Oz. At least you ought. I need to stay and sort things out, at least sell the house, make sure I haven't any more hidden relatives."

"Oz can manage with me a while longer. Craig's doing a good job. He actually enjoys running the show. And, apart from the 'dosh' Ma left, I'm doing all right with Whizz. In fact, I guess they might quite like a piece or two on the frozen north." He nodded at the email. "Does Liisu have anything else to say?"

42

Pippa looked at it again. "Yes, she does. Why not come for a visit, she asks?"

"Well, there you are then."

"Let's fix up the old camper van and go by road," Pippa said. "But I need to finish going through Father's papers first."

1

They decided to travel to Finland in early September. Pippa remembered her father saying that the autumn colours in northern Finland were quite spectacular. They even had a special expression for it: *ruska-aika,* or russet time.

A further exchange of emails with Liisu confirmed that this would be a good time for her, too. *The mosquitoes will be finished by then* she added.

"What about the animal?" Jude asked.

"If you mean Aristotle, the neighbours adore him. He can get in and out and as long as he's fed and in his own surroundings, he'll be fine."

After a couple of evenings poring over road maps of Europe they decided to cross to the Hook of Holland, drive into Germany to pick up the autobahn network to Denmark. Then the mini crossing to Sweden and so to Stockholm for the ferry over to Finland. They would use camp sites for overnight stops. The campervan had a small fridge and a very small shower/loo, Pippa began planning any other equipment they would need en route, and started on a list of provisions.

"I hear they do have shops in mainland Europe," Jude said.

"Ha-ha. We don't want to waste too much time shopping."

In between the planning, Jude continued his researches on his family. Then, returning from Oxford one day, he said, "I think I'll go down for a few days to Weymouth before we go. Check parish records."

"Do you want me to come?"

"I'll probably concentrate better on my own. But I'll expect you to have tackled that garden shed by the time I'm back."

He'd been on about it for weeks, referring to it as 'that garden shed' knowing very well that to Pippa it was 'Father's studio'. The solicitor had gone through it rather thoroughly soon after Father's death. Most of his relevant papers had been in the downstairs bureau and the solicitor reported the studio contained only papers connected with the Professor's work. There were, he added, some books that appeared to be old diaries written in a foreign alphabet.

For some reason Pippa kept finding reasons to postpone a thorough check of the studio. There were still strong memories of sneaking looks through the window to see Father dozing over a book or staring into space with unseeing eyes.

"What will you do if you find some great work in progress?" Jude asked.

"It's highly unlikely," Pippa had replied. And perhaps that's what she was afraid of: finding the anticipated treasure store turned out to be an empty shell.

And if so, did it matter?

She found it did matter. The childish memory of that brief period of hero worship, muddled in with echoes of her recent dream, proved to have more reality than that of the stern parent who had blighted her growing years. If they had a father like that, they'd run away, friends said in various ways. She'd hated and resented their pity, and she solved the problem quite simply by ceasing to invite them home. Finally, she had solved it definitively by moving to Australia.

She headed for the studio as soon as Jude had gone, inserting the key in the lock of the studio door and thrusting it open with unnecessary vigour. A shaft of sunlight and waft of wind followed her in. She sat at Father's desk watching the minute motes of dust dance and drift. The door swung almost closed behind her. In the dimness, the ray of sun and dancing dust motes disappeared, and what remained was thick silence. Pippa found she had been holding her breath as she listened to it, and let it out slowly. Then she looked at the surface of the desk. The solicitor had left it impeccably tidy: a small pile of wirebound notebooks, a tray of pencils neatly aligned, a small box covered with material that looked Asiatic, a clock that had stopped at 7.30. P.m. or a.m.? Did it matter? There was also a pile of journals from the history society of which he had been a member and to which he had often contributed. They were dated from a few months before his death. She wondered whether he had even looked at them.

So what now? She opened the box. It was almost full of stamps: foreign stamps tidily cut out from envelopes containing correspondence which he maintained with fellow academics all over the world. Had once maintained. She studied their postmarks, ranging over a period of some years. She remembered her mother mentioning that he collected them to give to a local hospice, and felt her throat contracting. It was not the sort of thing she would imagine him doing and felt a wave of sorrow that she had known him so little. Well, at least she could put that right, take them to the hospice. She would do it today. Or tomorrow. When she had probed further into the dusty silence.

She pulled the pile of notebooks towards her. The top one was full of scrawls that were illegible, except for the occasional word. 'Fear' was one that appeared regularly. Pippa sat looking at it quietly. Had he been afraid? Of what? And why? She thought of that dream in which he had taken her to a cupboard she had never seen before and, as he opened it, she had seen the cold, crouching figure, and her father had said she need never more be afraid.

"Don't be absurd," she said, and the silence shivered with her words.

She looked at the notebooks lower in the pile. The writing became easier to decipher, and she guessed they were written at an earlier period in his failing mental state. The word fear continued to appear, alongside 'power' which had been crossed through with 'corruption' and finally 'not power but fear corrupts'. That famous quotation: *power corrupts, absolute power corrupts absolutely.* Who had said that? She'd looked it up. Whoever it was, Father was disputing it; challenging it with the thought that not power but fear was the greater corrupter.

She sat quietly in the silence thinking this idea through. Why did people want power? Throughout history famous leaders had sought to conquer others and gain more power, That was true, but it was not power for the sake of power; it was power in order to get more land, more wealth, more everything, consumed by fear that if they did not have more they would lose what they had. But what about Mahatma Gandhi and Martin Luther King who had sought to create change without violence. And got murdered for their pains, Pippa reminded herself.

As she delved further into the notebooks, the earlier ones, Father's writing became quite clear. The bottommost notebook was almost continuously decipherable. On the first page he had written the quotation, attributing it to a 19th century British historian called Lord Acton : *Power corrupts, absolute power corrupts absolutely.* He had followed this with a series of ever-bolder question marks. On the next page he had listed the names of several countries: Finland, Estonia, Poland, Czech Republic, Slovakia, Slovenia, Croatia, Serbia, Bulgaria, Romania. After a moment she recognised them as the components of what he had often referred to as the European fault-line, interlinked smaller countries whose history had always been dominated by the demands of neighbouring big powers. She had recently finished re-reading his last book, published some time ago just as his mind began to play tricks on him. It had expounded his theories that challenged earlier ones that these countries had merely been the prey of such giants as the Habsburg Empire, the Ottomans, the Soviet Union, the West. Instead he suggested, quoting examples, that often they had been weakened from within by historic fears that threatened the integrity of their culture and beliefs. And nowhere had shown this more graphically than what was now known as the former Yugoslavia.

Pippa had been impressed by his arguments and the way he had backed them all with historical examples of the interaction between different ethnic groups. In the case of the former Yugoslavia, the suspicion between Croats and Serbs had been historic, divided as they had been for centuries between the Habsburg and Ottoman empires. It had been compounded in the Second World War when the Croats became allied with the Germans and condoned the slaughter of countless thousands of Serbs in horrendous concentration camps. Pippa found herself regretting that she had not taken an earlier interest in her father's writing, assuming them all to be very clever and probably difficult to understand because that was how she had come to think of him as a person. Of course many of his books had been published while she was in Australia, but she remembered with a twinge of guilt that he had sent her a copy of one which came out soon after her departure. She could not remember commenting on it and he had not sent any more. Her mind wandered back to those days and her feelings of anger towards him because she regarded it as his fault that she had turned her back on her home country. Was there not just the possibility that she could have made more effort to find the sensitivities that she was now beginning to learn lay behind his austerity?

She jumped as the door of the studio suddenly swung wider, briefly allowing the return of a shaft of sunlight. As it closed again, something furry wound round her legs. "Oh Totty," Pippa said, reverting to Jude's name for Aristotle. "I don't suppose you've ever been in here before."

"*Miaowl*," said Aristotle, and as if to prove her wrong set about a purposeful survey of the studio pausing in a corner to crouch over something. When she went to investigate, Pippa saw that he was drinking from a bowl that father had put down to catch drips which occurred when the rain came from a certain direction. When Aristotle had finished, she picked him up and carried him back to the desk. After a moment, he lifted himself on to it and began a systematic exploration, nudging at the notebooks with his nose, patting the aligned pens with a tentative paw. Pippa watched him affectionately, glad of his company, as he ventured across the desk on to the window sill, insinuating himself round a very dead potted geranium, sniffing it as he went past. She felt a twinge of guilt that she had not watered it, or at least transferred it to a more hospitable place. Her father had liked growing things. Gardening had been the only hobby she remembered him enjoying.

"While you're in investigative mood," Pippa told Aristotle, "could you find some old diaries said to be written in some strange alphabet?"

The cat wove once more round the dead geranium, crossed back over the desk and jumped down on to the floor. In the dim light she saw him move into the back of the studio, behind a set of filing cabinets, then disappear from view.

"Aristotle?"

There was a short silence followed by some scrunching noises, another silence, then the sharp clatter of something falling, followed by a feline squawk of surprise. Pippa got up to investigate. Aristotle

48

was crouching behind the filing cabinets, mouth open in a silent hiss of disapproval at an upturned bowl of bulldog clips now scattered on the floor. Pippa gathered them back into the bowl, stroked the animal's head, but he remained in a tense position.

She followed the direction of his gaze and saw what she had not seen before. Set into the wall behind the cabinets was the door of a cupboard. Pippa frowned. If she had not seen it before, why did the cupboard look so familiar?

And then she knew. It looked just like the cupboard Father had taken her to in that dream, when he wanted to share his great secret with her. The cupboard door which had opened to reveal the cold, dead figure of a man that had given Father such satisfaction.

Pippa grabbed Aristotle and headed for the door. It was only when it was closed and locked behind her and she began to feel the warmth of sun between her shoulders that she stopped shaking inside.

2

In the kitchen her mobile was ringing.

"Hi Jude." She had been running and it came out in a gasp.

"Hi Pips. You OK?"

"Fine. How's the research?"

"I'm finding a load of stuff. Probably a married uncle and a spinster aunt."

"That's terrific. Have you made contact with them?" She couldn't stop her voice shaking. "Do you want me join you?"

"Absolutely, but not quite yet. Are you really OK? You sound crook."

"No, really. Just a bit of a shock. Aristotle and I have been in Father's Studio, and we found a secret cupboard."

"What's in it?"

"I didn't stop to find out." Pippa's brain went into overdrive. "Just came in to make a cup of tea before investigating further."

"Right, well let me know what you find. And I'll be back in about three days." He was about to finish, then added, "Love you."

Making a cup of tea seemed a good idea. She put the kettle on, got a mug from the shelf, flicked a teabag into it and thought about her conversation with Jude. She was really pleased he was making some progress, but a lot could depend on the outcome. Aristotle sat on the windowsill watching her, then began cleaning his paws in that meticulous way that always fascinated her, each claw extended so he could really get his tongue between them. When the tea had mashed sufficiently, she went to the door.

"Come on Aristotle," she said, "let's go and find out what's in that cupboard," and he jumped down to follow her, until he saw she was heading down the garden, when he turned tail and returned to the kitchen. Emboldened by her break and talk to Jude, Pippa did not pause. After the bright evening light, it seemed dimmer than ever in the studio, until she remembered the two lamps, one over the desk, the other in the ceiling from which the light spread over the whole room. Whatever ghosts she had imagined had gone. She went to the cupboard and opened it. Not a body in sight. Stacked neatly on a series of shelves were piles of A4 lined notebooks and some worn exercise books. Picking out one of the latter, she saw its cover bore a few printed words in Finnish. One of the words, *paperi,* clearly meant paper. These were probably what the solicitor had described as diaries.

She took a couple more from the pile, leafed through them. Initially bewildered, she looked at the undecipherable script in dismay before grasping that it was in the Cyrillic alphabet and therefore must be in Russian. Then she noticed the neat familiar hand of her Father in the margin. 'Check month' said one, 'Where?" queried another.

On closer examination, she found on the cover of each book there was a reference number and a date. She turned to the other pile of A5 notebooks and saw that these were similarly numbered and dated. Putting two documents with corresponding numbers together it was soon clear that one was a translation of the other. Father had been translating someone's diaries. Of course they would be his father's diaries, her grandfather's, the man who had disappeared at some time in World War II leaving no trace. She found the first of his translations and looked at the first page. *Karelia, Fourth Camp, December 3. If*

Hell is an inferno, dear God how I shall welcome it. It could be any day now.

Pippa read on. *The numbness is almost constant, but this is not the problem. It is when the numbness goes, and the feeling returns like red hot ashes applied to every finger and every toe. Perhaps Hell would not be so nice after all. I have seen men crying like babies with the pain of it, men who mostly come from the countryside and must be familiar with such conditions. I am a city boy, pampered by parent and servants, and wonder how I could ever have taken it so for granted.*

Pippa put her father's translation back on the desk. She could almost feel the cold as she shared the appalling conditions suffered by the grandfather she would never meet. It was a relief to have her thoughts interrupted by the jingle of her mobile. Jude.

"Hi, again," she said.

"I was worried about you. You sounded … well, not like you."

"It's OK. It was just that Aristotle had just found a cupboard, no skeleton in it this time. Or at least I don't think so.

"Hm. Either there is or there isn't."

Pippa explained the sequence of events. "Looks as though I've stumbled upon Grandpapa's diary. Written in Russian. You know, wrong alphabet."

"I thought he was Finnish."

"No, he took Finnish nationality, but he started off as a Russian soldier. I did tell you, or I thought I did. Father has translated it .. the diary. I've just started reading it. Riveting stuff."

"Doesn't sound as though you've done much clearing out."

"I will, I will. I expected I'll get bored with this diary soon."

3

But as she returned to her studies, Pippa knew that was unlikely. She completely lost track of time as she followed her father's neat flowing writing that captured the sheer hell of that struggle between Russian and Finn set among forests and swamp landscapes trapped in the deep freeze of that unrelenting winter of 1939-40. As dusk deepened, she was not aware of automatically turning on the light as she continued to read how, metre by metre, one army group advanced against the other, only to be pushed back or regroup and advance again through another section of petrified forest or sodden swamp. It was a repetition of accounts of exhaustion she had read of other suffering armies on the Somme or at Pachendale.

Grandfather did not say whether or not he, too, wept with the pain of frostbite. Pippa suspected that, despite the pampering parents and servants, he had been brought up in the stiff upper lip tradition that perhaps only the Victorians would recognise. And probably the Finns, too.

At one point she paused in her reading to wonder how he could have written so much in such excruciating circumstances. And then he told her himself. He wrote it in his head to stop the gut-wrenching fear that dogged every step, and then repeated it to himself until he was word perfect for the next time he could put pen to paper. And these times came, if only when they were too exhausted to move, and fell asleep where they lay. He had also invented a kind of shorthand so that he could get it down more quickly. He must have transcribed them later and eventually Father had put them into English. She smiled as she recognised that the translation was in his own spare, formal style and wondered what style Grandfather Josef himself had. Probably under those circumstances, style was the last thing on his mind.

Almost as hard to read were the detached descriptions of death which was as much part of the landscape as the trees and the swamps. Here a soldier lay, his stomach spilling out on the snow; there another lay on his back, eyes closed, teeth bared at the sky. Without second thought, her grandfather had searched each for a crumb of food as well as helping himself to ammunition. She stopped in the middle of critical thought, scolding herself, who'd had a lifetime free of conflict for making judgments on a man whose every step might be his last.

Something warm and soft heaved on to her lap.

"So I'm forgiven, am I?" Pippa fingers threaded through Aristotle's fur as he shuffled into a more comfortable position. She was suddenly aware of a huge tiredness and longed for bed. But they hadn't eaten. She glanced at her watch. Good God, nearly ten o'clock. "I see," she told Aristotle. "It's not affection, it's a reminder that it's long past supper time." She eased the cat off her lap, switched the lights off and returned to the kitchen, led by an anticipatory Aristotle.

After she had opened a tin for him and heated something in the microwave for herself, they both ate briskly and headed for the stairs, Aristotle reached the bed first and was curled up fast asleep by the time she joined him. She slept badly, dreams merging with the reality of the diaries to wake her regularly with sharp jabs of fear. Around 3 a.m., Aristotle moved on to her chest, purring prodigiously and then at last Pippa slept.

She awoke with a hangover indicative of lack of sleep rather than over-indulgence. Aristotle scuttled down the stairs ahead of her. It was surprising how well he scuttled given his age. She let him out and watched him trot down the garden in the direction of his favourite place to relieve himself. An injection of caffeine improved her state of wakefulness and she drank it, leafing through her father's translation of the diaries. She also found a document that did not fit into the normal pattern: a letter addressed to her grandmother Annikki. On the back of it, the sender's address was written in Cyrillic. She checked the postmark, the smudgy date decipherable as 1948. Inside were two pages of undecipherable scrawl in the unfamiliar alphabet.

She returned her attention to the diaries. This time she traced the chronology back to the beginning. From *Karelia, Fourth Camp* it progressed to *Karelia, Camp 37.* Clearly the camps were not of the kind she would recognise. The date of the last entry she had read was in early March, 1940. There were only two more, then a gap before the next long entry headed *Suolampi, May 12, 1940.*

He wrote *Some weeks have been taken from my life. Now I do not know whether it is about to end or to begin again. I do not know how many days I have been here, but every day is the same as the last. I sleep, I try to remember, I sleep, a woman brings me food and I eat, she brings me water and soap and I wash. At first she washed me, but now I can do it myself though it makes me very tired. I am in a small barn, which is like where the cow wintered on my grandparents' dacha outside St Petersburg. I try and remember what the house was like, and our flat in the city, and my mother and sister. They are like snapshots. The woman who feeds me is called Annikki, and she is teaching me Finnish. I can say* hello, thank you, more please, soap, water. *She is very kind and brought her young brother Matti to see me.*

In a subsequent entry he wrote *Annikki has explained what happened. She has a few words of Russian and good gestures. One morning she went for a walk and found me on the lake shore. I was covered with snow and one foot frozen into the lake ice. When she found I was alive, she brushed the snow off me and fetched her father. He did not want to help a 'pig Ruski', but he loves her so he did. They have a doctor friend who removed two toes. Now I am a little better, I notice Annikki is quite young, and even rather pretty. She is also gentle, unlike her father who is the farmer and swears at me. Though I can't understand him, I know he is swearing. Annikki gets upset and sends him away. Perhaps my destiny lies with her. Her brother, Matti is only a school boy. He comes to look at me sometimes as though I am a specimen in a museum, but seems all right. There is another boy, much older, called Kalle, who works on another farm. He came once with Matti and once alone. I do not trust him. I asked Annikki about him, and she said he came here a few years ago as a younger boy. His mother was Finnish and his father German. His name was Karl and he changed it to Kalle. Now I know why I do not trust him. He reminds me of those films they showed us at home about that madman Hitler, and all the soldiers marching like machines. Kalle has cold eyes and moves like a machine.*

He wrote a lot more about Annikki, how she began to spend more and more time with him, and it was soon clear that he was talking about the woman who became Pippa's grandmother. He also described how he gradually became stronger, doing exercises in the barn, and then outside. During this time he became good friends with Annikki's brother Matti. It was Matti who helped him a lot with his Finnish, though Josef said he had to be careful. Matti delighted in teaching him bad words, and then roared with laughter when he used them.

It was about this time that Annikki's father also began to take more favourable notice of him, suggesting to him roughly one day that he might look at the tractor that was not performing well. Josef was good with engines and improved the tractor, so after that he was given an increasing number of jobs round the farm and, in due course, was allowed to asleep in the main building.

Later, Josef referred to a village girl called Kirsti, gentle and pretty and *much too good for the oaf Kalle who dances attendance on her.* He wrote that Kirsti had been adopted by a local farming family, having been sent here by her own family who lived in Karelia on the borders of Russia. From a series of diary entries it became obvious that Kalle and Josef loathed each other. *Even if he did not make it clear that he hated all Russians, I would not trust him.* Joseph wrote. *I know he has had a bad time because his Finnish mother died when he was very young and his German father perished of wounds on the Russian front, but who hasn't suffered tragedy in this accursed war? I fear for Kirsti if she marries him. Annikki is concerned too.*

Then he stopped talking about Kalle and Kirsti and concentrated more and more on Annikki. Three months later she was pregnant with Pippa's father.

Selected extracts from correspondence between Kalle in Suojärvi and Hans in Germany , and from Kalle's diaries, 1938-43 (written in German and translated into English)

September 20th, 1938

Dear Karl – It was a great surprise to learn that you are now living in Finland. By chance I met one of our school friends who told me that after your mother died you went to live with her relatives there because your father was doing important work for our great Fatherland. I remember now that when we last met a couple of years ago, you were going to Finland on holiday. I didn't know your mother had died and I am very sorry.

Do you remember the great times we used to have at summer camp when they taught us to be fit and strong so that we too could work for the Fatherland? I am happy to say that I have now joined the army and have had the great privilege of taking part in the liberation of the German minority of Czechslovakia. It was an amazing experience.

Please tell me your news, Yours, Hans.

September 30th, 1938

Dear Hans - It was wonderful to hear from you, and of course I remember those fantastic times at summer camp. I always admired you because you were so good at everything, and I am not surprised that you are now able to work for the Fatherland. I am full of envy. I know you are a little older than me, and therefore qualify for more opportunities. I am most envious of all that you could be part of our great army liberating the German people in Czechoslovakia. And since our brothers in Austria have joined with us, no one can stop us now. Especially if those stupid English mind their own business.

Yes, I wish I could come home. But because of Mother's death and Father is in the army, my relations here will not let me go back. It is very boring here. I work on my uncle's farm. The most interesting person here is the daughter on another farm. She is called Kirsti, and older than me, but very shy. The people on the farm have adopted her as her own family live in Karelia near the border with Russia and if there is a war, as everyone expects, this could be a dangerous place. I think Kirsti is a virgin and I plan to change that. Have you any suggestions? I remember you told me about that girl in summer camp three years ago, but then you always had more confidence than I do.

Why don't you come here when you have leave? After all, we are good friends with the Finns against those awful Russians. Yours, Karl (they call me Kalle here, but with you I'll keep to my good German name)

October 30th, 1938

Dear Karl - Yes, I felt truly honoured to be there. Such a welcome we got. Any of us could have had any woman we wanted. But the rush of excitement of being part of our great history was more than any woman could give. You could get quite drunk from the roar of the crowds. Don't worry about the English. Their Mr. Chamberlain has made an agreement with our Führer and will not interfere.

If you want a woman, you should come here. But if you want your Kirsti, then you must use some skill. It is not a question of confidence, but of sensitivity. You say she is shy. That girl you mentioned at the summer camp was not shy, but our German girls have a very special and strong character. My dear friend, if you want my advice and your Kirsti is so shy, then you must make her feel sorry for you. Pretend you are sick or that you have hurt your foot or your hand. Better your foot, because you will need your hands. Then she will want to be a mother to you and come close to look after you. I don't think you need further advice from me after that. Yours – Hans.

November 15th, 1938

Dear Hans - I was so envious when I read your letter. I immediately told my aunt and uncle that I wanted to go back to Germany, but they said there is no one to look after me. I do not need looking after, but I need somewhere to stay. Could I stay with your family in Hamburg?

They say here that not all the English are happy with the agreement signed by Mr. Chamberlain. But it should not be a problem. They are a small country and their Empire is far away.

I followed your advice with Kirsti. I bathed my face in hot water and told her I felt sick. She felt my forehead and began to look worried. Then she touched my cheek and that was very nice, so I put my head on her shoulder and she stroked my hair. That was so exciting, but as I was supposed to be sick, I could not do much more. However, she has agreed to come to a dance in the nearby town next week, and then I can hold her close.

People here are getting worried about the Russians. They hate them as much as we do, so perhaps I can do something here. By the way, the newspapers talk about some *progrom* against the Jews, destroying their houses and synagogues. I know there has been a lot of propaganda against the Jews, but that seems drastic. Do you know anything more? - Yours, Karl

November 30, 1938

Dear Karl - I have some leave and have come home to Hamburg, but I must say I feel restless. The civilians do not really understand what momentous things are happening, though of course they are pleased at our success. Girls quite often give me flowers. Though I say it myself, I do look rather fine in my uniform.

I am sorry to say that my family cannot invite you to Hamburg. For some reason they are afraid of staying in the city and are moving to stay with cousins on Luneberg Heath. It is rather primitive there, and anyway I don't think they will have space by the time Mother, Father and my two younger sisters go there. As you say, there is no need to worry about the English. I don't think they will be so stupid as to make war, and even if they do, who will help them? Not the Americans for sure.

About the Jews I am not quite sure. At school I had a Jewish friend and he was a good chap as well as clever, but they said we should not be friends and anyway he soon went away. The Führer says they have done very bad things to our country and he must know. I don't want to harm them but on the whole I think it is best to avoid them. Perhaps we both need to re-read *Mein Kampf.*

Well done, with Kirsti. I look forward to hear how the dance went. If she is shy you had better not rush things. You have plenty of time. - Yours Hans.

December 10th, 1938

Dear Karl - You are right about Kirsti. We kissed after the dance, and it was marvellous, but when I put my hand on her breasts, she pushed me away, though I am sure she liked it. There is another big dance at New Year. At least I speak Finnish quite well now, and that makes things easier. I don't think I told you about Kirsti's friend Annikki whose father owns another farm. I found her alone once in the barn and tried to kiss her, and she slapped my face very hard. She has spirit that one. But Kirsti is prettier, and anyway I like a challenge.

It's disappointing about Hamburg, but you're right, I don't want to go to Luneburg Heath. We had a summer camp there once, and I thought it was a boring place. I think you're right too about the English. They are not very warlike. Perhaps they use their umbrellas as weapons!! Your information about the Jews is puzzling. I remember there was a lot of propaganda when I was at junior school. Yes, I'd better re-read *Mein Kampf*, too. Perhaps it will not seem so difficult now.

I had a long letter from Father. He has been stationed in Prague and says the Czech people are very rude, except for his Czech mistress. He says the winter there is terrible, but it could not be worse than here - so cold. I long to be older so that I can come back to Germany, and perhaps bring Kirsti with me. – Yours, Karl.

April 4th, 1939

Dear Karl - Sorry for the long silence. We have been doing so many manoeuvres that I am constantly exhausted. It is only because I got some chest infection that I can at last have some rest in hospital. So much has been going on that I am convinced there will be a big new campaign soon. It could be against the Poles. According to the authorities, the Slavs are about as bad as the Jews. There could be a problem about this as someone I know listens to the English radio and says they will be very angry if we invade Poland. But clearly the Führer knows what he is doing.

Have you had sex with Kirsti yet? I was interested in your father's mistress in Prague. I have one in Mitstadt, the town near our camp. She is older than me and has taught me a lot, even when I am too tired to do much. It is better to go with older women, though by the sound of it your Kirsti is not very experienced.

I am now a Captain! So you will have to treat me with respect when we meet. I wonder when that will be, old friend? Perhaps if the Finns have a war with the Russians, we will come and help them, then we can fight together. Wouldn't that be wonderful! - Yours, Hans.

May 6th, 1938

Dear Hans - No, I haven't had sex with Kirsti. I think I am in love with her and I am afraid of losing her. But we have talked a lot, and we have a special understanding because we are in a similar situation. She is away from her own family and I am away from mine. I think she is afraid of this sex. But we have kissed and caressed, and I like it very much. But it would be impossible if I had not found someone in the town near here who is not afraid of sex. As you say, older women are the best.

Congratulations on being Captain. And now it is even possible that I can be a Captain one day. There is a big conscription here in case of war, and I shall be eighteen very soon so can join up. Because I am not a Finnish national, I think I will have non-combat duties to begin with. I begin training in Lapland next week and look forward to it very much. Yes, it would be wonderful if we could fight together against the Russians. - Yours, Karl.

June 1st, 1939

Dear Karl - So my good friend is now a soldier. I am anxious to learn if you share my enthusiasm. And I am happy you agree with me about older women. I am sure you will win your Kirsti before long. Please write soon. Yours, Hans.

June 30th, 1939

Dear Hans - I'm afraid I don't share your enthusiasm as I hate the army. No, not the army, but Lapland. Hardly anything lives here, except mosquitoes and blackfly and they live here in their *millions*, mostly on my blood. The Finns laugh at me because I make a lot of fuss, but when every millimetre of you is itching it is not funny. Perhaps the Finns have special blood. The best thing is to follow the reindeer. They go up on to the fells where there is always some wind and less mosquitoes. The other unpleasant thing is that there is no night. The sun shines *all the time*, so it is difficult to sleep. I can't wait to go south again, and for the days to become cold.

But like a good German I will overcome these problems and become a good soldier like you. Yours, Karl.

July 2nd, 1939

Dear Karl - I write to you with a heavy heart and bad news. Two days ago, my son Hans was badly wounded during a military exercise. He fell from a wall and fractured his skull. He has been unconscious for some days and it is uncertain that he will recover. As you can imagine, his mother and I are in deepest anxiety, except that we shall always be proud of him, as I know our Führer is.

I found your last letter in his rucksack, and your address in his notebook. I know you will make a good soldier - Yours in sorrow, Hans Müller, senior.

July 20th, 1939

Dear Hans, - I found your father's letter when I returned to camp, and I , too, am in deepest shock. I am writing to you because it is the only way I know to share my shock, even though you may not be able to read this. We have shared so much in recent months, and now I want to continue to do so in the hope that one day I may have your reply.

I hope one day you learn what a fine soldier I shall become, though perhaps you are watching over me from some unknown place? I would like to think that. In the end I became accustomed to the mosquitoes. Perhaps they poisoned my blood so much that I poisoned them back when they took it. Life is better now we are in the south again, not least because I have my mistress and I can talk to her about you. I do not know if women have the same friendships, but she seems to understand and is very gentle with me. Strangely, because I had not seen Kirsti for so long and did not write to her from Lapland, I found her waiting for me outside the barracks. Perhaps it is true that absence makes the heart grow fonder? I told her about your accident and her eyes filled with tears. Then she kissed me on the mouth and said that when I come back to Suojärvi we must spend time together, so I am hopeful. Yours, Karl

August 15th, 1939 -

Dear Karl - Good news. Hans regained consciousness about two weeks ago. He has a fractured skull and he will be convalescing for a long time. Please continue to write. I read him your last letter and he smiled, especially when I came to the bit about Kirsti. I think she is a fortunate girl to have such a fine admirer. If she proves too instransigent, perhaps you should keep your love for some deserving German girl. - Yours, Hans Müller senior.

September 10th, 1939

Dear Hans - What wonderful news from your father.

So we are at war with those stupid, interfering English. They will soon learn the error of their ways. It is astonishing that they should want to fight us when we are so alike. We are both Aryan peoples, yet they go to war because we want to improve the conditions of the inferior Poles.

You remember you said we should re-read *Mein Kampf?* Well, I did and now I understand much better. In this great work the Führer explains very clearly his aims not only for the Aryan peoples, but also for those who are inferior. He shows how all achievements in the main fields of human activity were almost exclusively Aryan. It follows therefore that the purity of our race must be maintained at all cost. All inferior races will also benefit if the Aryan remains absolute master and spreads his learning through the subjugation of lower peoples. It is difficult to understand how anyone can argue with this, especially the British who are also Aryan.

But I do not need to tell you this, dear Hans. - Yours, Karl.

September 20th, 1939

Dear Karl - How it warmed my heart to see your writing and read your words. I was very proud of your message and of course agree with everything you said. I am still weak and cannot write long. But write to me, and tell me how it is now with Kirsti. Have you achieved your greatest wish? Yours, Hans.

October 10th, 1939

Dear Hans - And how it warmed *my* heart to see your writing. I understand that you must still be weak after such an ordeal.

As for Kirsti, yes, we have had sex at last. It was unbelievable, though I don't think she enjoyed it so much. I think I was too quick, but I will try hard to make it better for her.

My other big news is that I am going on manoeuvres with my regiment - to Lapland of all places, but there cannot be mosquitoes there at this time. I will write and tell you about it. - Yours, Karl.

November 5th, 1939

Dear Hans - How I wish you had been with me in Lapland. In autumn the colours are amazing - every possible shade of yellow, orange, red. In Finland there is a special word for it: *ruska-aika*, meaning russet time. I even wished I could be a painter to try and capture such a wonderful sight. But of course there are more important things to do. Yours, Karl.

November 20th, 1939

Dear Karl - I have never known you to be so lyrical! But you are right, there are more important things. There are rumours of a very big campaign beginning soon. And I am so happy because now I am strong enough to be able to be part of it. We may meet somewhere in this great struggle. What a reunion that will be. - Yours, Hans.

December 2nd, 1939

Dear Hans - I am very confused.. Finland has been at war for three days. On November 30th the Russians attacked the country and now there is general mobilisation. What is confusing is that our Führer has signed an agreement with the Russians in order that they (the Russians) can include Finland in their sphere influence. I am sure the Führer has made the right decision but I do not understand his reasons.

I am really enjoying the army now. I have to say that it is not very well organised - I am sure the German army is better disciplined - but there is good friendship among the men. Many of them are quite rough country folk, but tough as well and that I admire.

We have been doing winter manoeuvres. I have never in my life been so cold and several men got frostbite. As we are all suffering in the same way, it is no use complaining. Now I remember those warm days in Lapland and think I could even welcome the mosquitoes. No one thinks the war will last for long. The Russian army is a million times bigger than the Finnish one, at least that is how it feels. They are everywhere. - Yours, Karl.

March 20th 1940 -

Dear Hans - Thank God the war is over. The Finnish people have had to give a lot of land to the Russians, but they still have their independence. Unfortunately part of that land is where Kirsti's family live in Karelia. I don't think I mentioned she has a brother, Pentti, in the Finnish army. He came to assure her he will take care of her. But I can do that. Very soon I can go back to Suojärvi and comfort her. You will be glad to know that the sex with her has become very good. Now *she* is wanting to try new things. I can't wait!

But I am worried about *you*, my friend. I have not had news for some time. Yours, Karl.

April 15th, 1940 -

Dear Hans - Still no news from you, but I must share with you a very strange story. One of the men from another farm came to tell us that there is a newcomer to the farm which belongs to Annikki's family. Apparently, about the time the war ended, A. was walking in the woods and heard a cry. She found a Russian soldier wounded, lying on the lake shore, with one leg frozen into the ice of the lake. She got help to cut him out and brought him back to the farm where he is now living in a barn while she looks after him. A *Russian* soldi er! Her father is angry. I have told Kirsti she must not go anywhere near, but she is soft hearted and must see him. She said he is very sick and they have taken away two of his toes. I hope he dies.

In the end I went to see him, too, in order to find out how a pig Russian soldier looks when he is beaten. Annikki was with him, helping him to eat. I have never seen her so gentle. The pig Russian looked at me and saw the hatred in my eyes. He tried to say something in Finnish, but I did not understand and left. What would you do, Hans, in these circumstances? Yours, Karl.

April 30th, 1940

Dear Karl - Yes, I am sorry for my silence, but I had a relapse from my head injury.

As far as your pig Russian is concerned, he is the enemy and you must find a way to eliminate him. I am very happy for you that things are so good with Kirsti. I am also happy for you that your war is over, but ours is not. I am still weak, so cannot write much. Think of me, dear friend. Yours, Hans.

June 1st, 1940

Dear Hans, I think of you every day and wish for your recovery. The pig Russian is called Josef and is getting quite strong. Sometimes I see him driving the tractor, or doing exercises in the yard to strengthen his muscles. I have been once or twice to see him, but Annikki or her brother Matti is always there. I will think about what you said about getting rid of him.

Everyone thinks there will be another war with Russia and that this time Finland will ask Germany for help. What will happen to this Josef then? In the meantime the Baltic States of Estonia, Latvia and Lithuania have been occupied by the Russians, which is very worrying for the Finns. They think that now that have had some success, the Russians will want to try again to claim Finland. Yours, Karl.

July 30th, 1940

Dear Karl, - I have been at the front for some time, so your letter has only just caught up with me. But the news gets better all the time. Don't worry about the Russians. If they attack Finland again, I think Germany will help them. Everywhere else the news is good. Now the Italians have joined us. France is ours. Norway is ours. There is no stopping us. And we dispatched the British in their tens of thousands from the beaches of Dunkirk. Aren't you proud? The Führer has made some rousing speeches and seems indestructible.

But you must eliminate this Russian. Yours, Hans

August 15th, 1940

Dear Hans, It is not so easy to eliminate the Russian. He is all the time with Annikki or other people around the farm. And the worst thing is that I think she is pregnant by him.

Yes, I am very proud. And what about the news of our brave Luftwaffe and the destruction they are making of the British air force. But then the terrible news that that R.A.F. bombed Berlin. Our Führer will surely take his revenge and teach them a lesson. Yours, Karl.

Diary entry for the same day - Though I admire Hans enormously, it is very irritating that he constantly writes that I must eliminate the pig Russian. Of course he is not here and doesn't know how difficult it is, especially now he has become quite popular with the Finnish workers because he likes to drink with them. For the moment I cannot see a way.

October 10th 1940

Dear Hans, I have not heard from you recently, but I must tell you that Annikki is now heavy with child and it must be the Russian's. They are always together. She has no shame, looks very happy and does not try to hide it. Josef is now doing more work on the farm and even lives in the farmhouse. I see that he is very friendly with Annikki's brother, who is only a schoolboy, but growing fast.

We read that our brave Luftwaffe are bombing British cities every night.

Please send me a few lines. Yours, Karl.

December 1st 1940

Dear Karl, My silence is partly due to a course I have been following on new techniques called Radar, and partly because my mistress is now my wife and we have a little boy, Heinrich. I am so happy and proud.

The course was very difficult but I managed it. There are many rumours, but of course I must not speak of them. It is sad that this Annikki has no shame. It may be more difficult to eliminate the Russian, but you must do it. Yours, Hans.

December 15th, 1940

Dear Hans - My warmest congratulations on your marriage, your baby and succeeding in your difficult course. I do not see my mistress so much now that Kirsti and I have sex. She (my mistress) wrote me an angry note. Women can be very difficult. I really want a son too, but not like Annikki and the pig Russian. I think her time will come soon.

I shall wait until we are married. Kirsti says that Annikki is very worried because, when the baby is born, Josef wants her to take it to neutral Sweden, and she wants to stay here. Perhaps he can guess that his days are numbered. Yours, Karl.

January 20th, 1941

Dear Hans – A quick message to tell you that the Russian pig's child is born. He is called Jooseppi, the Finnish equivalent of Josef. It makes me sick to hear him squawling and how much attention he gets.

It is many weeks since I heard from you. Yours, Karl.

Diary entry for February 15th – It is now so long since I heard from Hans that I fear something must be wrong. Perhaps the rumours he spoke of have become realities. But what are they?

I so want to tell him my Big News. Annikki's pregnancy has had a big effect on my Kirsti. Now she want to have a baby, too, and that is what I want. But I want us to marry first, so she has agreed. It will happen next month. I have the feeling that Annikki is not very happy about this, but that's too bad.

April 1st, 1941

Dear Hans - Very often I wonder where you are. You remember I said that Josef wanted Annikki and the baby to go to Sweden? Well, they have gone. Her father and brother are moping, and so is my Kirsti. But Josef is like a lost soul. Serve him right. I hear that our Luftwaffe are bombing London every night. Serve them right.

But much more important than any of this is that Kirsti and I were married two weeks ago. Her father has given us one of the farm workers' cottages and she is a wonderful homemaker. The place is so cosy and nice.

How often I wish I could play an active part in this war like you. The days seem very long, each one like the last. Yours, Karl.

April 15th, 1941

Dear Karl - What wonderful news about your and Kristi. Now I hope to hear soon that you have a fine son.

More training is the reason for my silence. Something big will happen soon, but I cannot discuss it, only to say that when you hear of it you will certainly want to eliminate your Josef. So Annikki and the baby have gone. We will catch up with them eventually, and the pig Russian father.

Our success continue. More bombings of the enemies' cities, though I must say some of ours are suffering, too. You probably read that our forces are now in North Africa, and I wondered about this, but now I understand for we have invaded Greece and Yugoslavia. Some of the people of Yugoslavia have welcomed us. Yours, Hans.

June 23rd 1941

Dear Hans - The most amazing news ever. Our army has invaded Russia! Now I understand that our great Führer had special plans when he made a pact with those Russians earlier, giving them a sense of false security. How I long to be part of that huge event. Now it is sure that if Russia invades Finland, we will fight together. Yours, Karl.

September 3rd 1941

Dear Hans - So, Finland is at war with Russia again, but now we Germans are helping them. We have also occupied the Baltic States. Already we have won back those parts of Karelia lost in the Winter War. I was acting as courier for some weeks. It was very exciting and conditions much easier than in the Winter War. I was surprised to find some Finnish Jews fighting with us. I wonder what our Führer would think of that.

It is wonderful to come home to Kirsti. How is your family? Yours, Karl.

June 14th 1942

Dear Hans - I am glad to learn from your letters that things are quieter now on the military front.

Kirsti still talks about how she misses Annikki and little Jooseppi.. When she has given me a son she will have no need to think of them. I am also displeased because Kirsti has become friendly with the pig Russian. She says she feels sorry for him because he is alone. I find it strange that Josef lives here like a Finn, as if everyone has forgotten he is one of the enemy. Our armies have advanced far into Russia. I think my father is there.

Sometimes I dream of our times together at the summer camps and how we vowed we would always stay comrades. And it is so. Yours, Karl.

Entry from Karl's diary, June 25th, 1942 - I have been angry with Kirsti because on several occasions I heard she has visited Josef. Last night when we had sex, I was quite rough with her but afterwards I was very gentle, and it worked. I think she will be more amenable now she knows who is the master.

November 30th 1942

Dear Hans Again, it is a long time since I had news of you. The news from the Russian front is terrible. Our brave Germany army and allies who have been holding the city of Stalingrad in a state of siege for many months are now suffering terribly as the winter conditions become ever worse and their supplies are cut off. There is even greater hatred of the Russians. Apparently Annikki is being looked after in Sweden by some kind of religious organisation. Kirsti is still unhappy to lose her friend and Josef wanders round the farm like a lost soul and Kirsti is quite sorry for him.. If my wife would have a baby she would have more important things to think about. She is not always willing to have sex and then I have to persuade her. Sometimes I go and see my old mistress to cheer myself up. Yours, Karl.

March 3rd 1943

Dear Karl, Yes, we are getting terrible news about the suffering of our brave solders retreating from Stalingrad. With the awful conditions and lack of supplies many are dying. I have met some who have managed to get back to Germany and they say the Russians are unbelievably barbaric.

This makes me think, Karl, that you must do something about this Russian who is living so comfortably in Finland while our poor soldiers suffer. It should be easier now that Annikki and the child gave gone. Do the Germany military know that you have a pig Russian in your midst? I do not understand why you do nothing about these circumstances.

Don't worry about Kirsti. It is a fact that women sometimes need persuading and I think you can do that very well. Yours, Hans

March 15th 1943

Dear Hans, You sound angry and I understand this. We, too, hear terrible news of how our German soldiers have suffered on their retreat. I have been thinking more and more about your suggestion.. It is not right that Josef should be living in comfort while our brave men are dying. I am not at all happy about how much time Kirsti spends with him. Yours, Karl.

Diary entry by Karl, March 10th, 1943 - Hans' idea is brilliant. Why didn't I think of that. I have made some enquiries and found the address of a German military commander which is not far from here. I will suggest to them that they check Josef's details.

April 20th 1943

Dear Karl - I hope to hear that you have done something soon. - Hans.

May 20th 1943   Dear Hans - I sent a message to the German military, telling them they might like to check Josef's origins. A few days later he had gone. No one could give details, but Annikki's father said there had been a telephone call asking Josef to report to the nearest military office, and they had not seen him since. I don't think A's father was very worried, because he had never liked her relationship with Josef. But of course it will be difficult for him to explain to her.

I hope you will agree that this is very satisfactory. Yours, Karl.

Diary entry by Karl, May 25th, 1943 -   Everyone is talking about the disappearance of the pig Russian. Kirsti is constantly crying and when I shouted at her, she ran away to her uncle's house. He sent her back, and then I was very nice to her and everything was all right. Hans is right that sometimes you need to persuade women.

June 1st, 1943

Dear Karl - Well done my friend, Yours, Hans.

1

"After that," Pippa told Jude on his return from Dorset, almost before he had time to unload the car, "everything began to fall into place."

"Doesn't sound as though much clearing out got done," he commented.

"Ah, but it did, it did. Once I'd got that far in unravelling the threads, I put all the diaries away and went to look at Dad's Studio with a fresh eye. I emptied several drawers full of old magazines, and am now gradually sifting through filing cabinets full of correspondence and notes. Some of it is obviously recycling material; some will need a closer sort through in case it relates to publishing queries. Anyway you can probably help with that."

Pippa put the kettle on for coffee. "In the meantime," she went on, "I downloaded yards of stuff from Wikipedia on the Finnish Winter War which helped put Grandad's and Father's story in context. Though of course there are still a million unanswered questions. You can probably help me with those, too."

Jude sat at the kitchen table, looked at her. "I've one or two things to sort out too."

"What? Oh God, I haven't asked you about your researches. I am self-centred beast."

"Just a bit."

"Sorry, sorry." Pippa went over and hugged his head. "I'll pour the coffee out, and then it's your turn and I shan't say a word."

While she made the coffee. Aristotle jumped down from his perch on the kitchen windowsill and ambled over to nudge at Jude's leg. He bent down and tickled the top of his head. "Hello, Totty. Missed me?"

"He probably did. Wasn't a bit keen on the Studio and I'll swear he could see things that weren't there."

"You'll have to learn to curb that imagination of yours."

"Well he was just as spooked by finding that cupboard as I was." Pippa poured out two mugs of coffee, added milk, one sugar for Jude and put it before him. "There," she said. "Your turn now. Off you go."

Jude took a sip of coffee and fished into his jacket pocket and pulled out a worn-looking notebook. "It's all in here and needs sorting out. But to summarise, as I mentioned on the phone, I tracked down a married uncle and a spinster aunt. The married uncle John is a widower and is being looked after by spinster aunt Beatrice, called Bee for short."

"That follows," Pippa said. "I mean spinster aunt looking after widower brother."

"I thought you weren't going to interrupt."

Pippa put a hand over her mouth. "Not another squeak, promise."

"The house they live in is outside Weymouth. It belonged to Margaret, John's late wife, who was also Bee's sister. Still with me?"

Pippa nodded. Jude continued, "Interestingly, when Dad turned up on the doorstep, Uncle John had absolutely no time for him. Regarded him rather as I did as a no-good drunk, but Bee had another take on him." Pippa nodded again, her eyes expressing interest and encouragement. Jude went on, "She found out where he was staying and made contact with him."

Pippa allowed herself a quiet "Good for Bee."

"After that they met regularly, Dad and Bee. Things got a bit garbled then, but the general gist was that after some years he actually stopped drinking. Got himself a job as a driver, and a small flat, and went on from there. Well, it wasn't quite as straight forward as that. I gather there was some slipping and slithering along the way, but gradually he got himself straightened out with the support of some self-help organisation."

Pippa could contain herself no longer. "But that's absolutely marvellous. Can she arrange for you to meet?"

73

"That's the odd thing. Bee is worried that if I turn up I might upset the apple cart, turn back the clock and all that."

"After all this time?"

"Mm. I gather it has been quite a struggle. And he's re-married, someone in the same self-help group. I gather there are quite a few health problems, too."

"I still don't see why you couldn't make a very tactful approach. Perhaps write to him. Or ring him if we can get the number."

"Bee wouldn't tell me. She really seems to be worried that my turning up out of the blue might throw him. But I've found out where he lives. Bee mentioned that he'd become obsessed with computers and I discovered him and his new wife, Laura. On Facebook. From this I worked out where they are and checked with Directory Enquiries. They live in a cottage in a village just out of Weymouth. The Facebook entry was also full of stuff about birdwatching. Seems they go over to a place called Radipole Lake, one of the RSPB nature reserves every week-end."

Pippa made a decision. "Let's go and look him up then," she said.

"Mm," Jude said, looking doubtful, then more positively, "I suppose it'll be a chance to give the campervan an airing too. In fact, it's quite odd really. When I was a kid I had a mega crush on a girl who was into birds, but I was far too smitten with her to take much notice of them. She was called Beverley and I called her Bev the Beaut. You know how Aussies love chopping the ends off words."

"Hm. I see I still have a lot to learn about you yet," Pippa said.

2

They checked out the camp sites in the area and found several on the coast near Weymouth. One in particular was quite close to the Radipole Lake Nature Reserve, so they booked in for three nights the following week. It was while Pippa was shopping next day that Jude took a puzzling call.

"Someone called Greta Schmidt rang. German by the sound of it. Wanted to speak to Professor Eastman's daughter."

"How weird. She rang a couple of years ago, just after Father died. What did she want?"

"She didn't say. Or leave a number."

"Not much I can do about it then." Pippa shrugged, partly in helplessness, partly to shake off a sense of unease.

They arrived at the Weymouth camp site by late afternoon. After they had registered and found a pitch in the quietest corner of the site, they set off to find the address where Jude's father now lived. It turned out to be a cottage next to a small supermarket in the middle of the village. A couple of hundred yards down the road was a nice-looking pub called The Mariner.

"How about having an evening meal here," Jude said.

"You're not anticipating your Dad will suddenly walk in and there will be a sudden and instant recognition and reconciliation?

"Of course not," said Jude, who clearly was. "If he's not drinking he's not likely to be a pub regular, is he?"

"There are non-alcoholic drinks."

In the event, it was a pleasant meal uninterrupted by more than a casual friendly greeting from a trickle of locals who had come in for a pint. Returning from the loo, Pippa paused to ask the barman if he knew Bob and Laura Jamieson. Apparently only slightly. Bob and Laura were a quiet couple, kept themselves to themselves. Laura Jamieson was involved in a lot of charity work and sometimes came in to ask if they would put a collecting box on the bar. And occasionally they came in for a meal.

"What's the betting that tomorrow is the one Sunday he doesn't go over to Radipole?" Jude muttered when Pippa reported to him.

"We could go and knock on his door now," she said.

On the way back to the car, they did a detour up the High Street. They stood on the narrow pavement opposite the cottage. A warm glow of light came from the front room, and there was a gap where the curtain had not been pulled across.

"Don't!" Jude said as Pippa crossed the road to peer through it.

She came back in a few moments and reported a cosy atmosphere. She was about to enlarge on this when, without warning, the cottage door opened and a slim older woman leaned out to put a milk bottle on the doorstep. She glanced across at them, called pleasantly "Good evening," and went back into the cottage.

They had already been to check out Radipole Lake which was almost part of Weymouth itself, and only a short walk from the harbour. There was a big public car park by the entrance to the reserve, and they made sure they were there early next morning. The small café that formed part of the Visitors' Centre had just opened, so they ordered a coffee and a bun and sat at one of the open air tables watching the coming and going.

Pippa asked, "So did the object of your boyish desire manage to teach you anything about bird watching?"

"Not a lot; except I took rather a fancy to the magpie-lark, not unlike our own magpie. Bev said it usually paired for life and was one of relatively few species that sang a duet with its partner."

"Never heard that."

"Yeah, well, nor did I. Apparently they sing a half-second apart, so I guess you needed to be more expert than I ever was, though Bev swore she could tell there were two."

"Well, I guess we could both do with a bit of guidance." Pippa got up and strolled back into the Centre. A few minutes' later she came back with a book for identification. "They recommend this one for beginners. And there's a blackboard listing the kinds of bird we are likely to see."

"We haven't got binoculars," Jude pointed out.

Pippa delved into a pocket and brought out a small pair. "I found these in Dad's Studio. That's one of the surprising things I found out about him. He loved growing things, and he watched birds."

Jude took them from her and tried them out, fiddling with the small wheels to adjust them to his eyesight. "Hey, that's really good," he said focussing across the car park.

"It's feathered birds you're supposed to be looking at."

He readjusted the direction and focus to a nearby reed bed. "Ah, got you. Blue tit." He handed her the binoculars, "Look how pretty it is."

"I do know what a blue tit looks like," Pippa said, but had to agree that through the binoculars it took on a whole new allure.

Jude grabbed the binos back. "There's a little chap I haven't seen before. On top of that reed."

"There are only about a million reeds," Pippa pointed out.

"Yes, well. It's a little brown job. The trouble is most of your birds are little brown jobs."

"True, not to compare with your gaudy Aussie parrots and rosellas and humming birds and …."

"This one had an eye stripe. I'm sure it had an eye stripe." Jude began fumbling through the book she had just bought. After a while he said excitedly, "There, that's the one. Look."

She peered over his shoulder. "Moustached warbler … breeds in southern Europe. I don't think so."

"It's a sedge warbler," offered a woman at the next table. "There is a likeness, but your friend is right. I'm afraid a visitor from Southern Europe would have brought the twitchers here in their droves."

"Twitchers? What kind of bird is that?"

She laughed. "A human one. It's what we call someone who'll travel hundreds of miles just to tick a new bird off their list."

Jude grinned. "We're rather new to this."

"We all have to start somewhere." She gathered up her own book and binoculars. "May I suggest you do the circuit anti-clockwise, the light will be better. And look out specially for the bearded tits. There are a lot about at the moment. And when you get to the hide keep a special watch for little egrets. They've started wintering here, and I hear a couple of them have arrived already."

"Did you ever think there was so much to know about birds?" Pippa asked.

"No. And strictly speaking that's not what we are here for. Remember?"

3

They set off into the reserve, along a narrow path between banks of reeds. After a couple of hundred yards, Pippa said "There doesn't seem much about. Except reeds, and more reeds."

Jude looked up at the sky as a formation of geese passed overhead, honking. "There's plenty of noise coming from the reeds. I guess it needs rather more patience than we're giving it. Just stop for a while." Further down the path a couple had stopped and were pointing and peering into the reeds.

"Look there's something," Pippa said. "Right down in the reeds. Coming up now. Ssh. Don't move. Oh damn, it's gone."

"No, it's just moved over. I've got it. Oh, it's gorgeous."

"Where, where?"

He handed her the glasses. "Third reed on the right," he said helplessly.

"Got it, got it. He's gorgeous. Your little brown job with the eye stripe. Look at the markings on his breast." Pippa passed the binoculars back and grabbed the book. After a moment she read out "Sedge warbler – breeds commonly in reed beds and swamps … underparts streaked – supercilium distinct … resembles moustached warbler…." She paused to give Jude a hug. "Aren't we good? Bev the Beaut would be proud of you."

"Are you getting hooked?"

"Could be. Perhaps we could start feeding the birds in the garden."

"I could make a bird table."

"We could buy a bird bath."

Jude grabbed her arm. "Ssh. There's another of those sedge warblers."

"Where? Oh yes, I've got it. No it's not. It's got a black head." Pippa began scrabbling through the book. "There," she said triumphantly, "There it is. It's a reed bunting."

They ambled on, came to a seat, sat down.

Jude started studying the book more carefully. "You see how all the birds are divided into families, and there's a map showing where you are likely to see each species." He flipped over a few pages. "Ah, now I see why it couldn't have been a moustached warbler. See, you find it all along the Mediterranean coast."

Pippa produced a leaflet she'd picked up from the Visitors' Centre. "Let's see what we're likely to find. Look here's a booming bittern."

"Blooming bittern?"

"Booming. Apparently that's the noise it makes which you are more likely to hear than actually see the bird." Pippa read on. "Except you're not likely to hear it now." After a while she said, "Oh and here is the little egret that woman was telling us about. Isn't it pretty, and look it's got yellow boots." Jude peered over her shoulder and saw the slender white bird had indeed got feet that were yellow spreading up its legs.

They wandered on, came to a parting of the ways.

"Anti-clockwise she recommended," Jude said taking the right branch of the path. "If we follow this circuit we'll come to a viewing point, then further on a hide. We could have our sandwiches there."

The viewing point turned out to be a series of fence-like barriers with viewing slits at various heights so that you could look through to open water. A couple were already surveying the scene.

"Anything interesting?" Pippa asked. "We're very new to this."

"Mm. 'fraid not," the woman said. "It's getting close to the middle of the day and they tend to tucker down around now. But we've just come from the hide and there are some great views of the egrets."

"Then we might as well move on."

Surprisingly the hide was empty when they reached it. They found seats down one end of a long row of viewing points, and lifted the narrow panes of glass that separated them from the outside world.

"Wow," said Pippa. You didn't even need the binoculars to see the group of little white egrets that pottering about in shallow water only a few metres away from the hide.

"Yellow boots and all." added Jude.

They took their time, getting their fill of observing the graceful birds, breaking off to explore a varied duck population: widgeon, teal, shoveller. With their lack of expertise, it took quite a while, until Jude announced complainingly "I'm starving," and Pippa delved into the knapsack for the sandwiches she had prepared and put in the fridge the night before. They ate in contented silence and were on their second sandwich when the door opened and a man and a woman entered.

The man said "Good'day," with a twang that was unmistakably Antipodean, and Jude went into a paroxysm of choking.

They recognised the woman who had put out the milk bottle the previous evening. She was trim in a pair of jeans and anorak, a contrasting scarf drifting round her neck. "Hello," she said. "Anything interesting about?"

"Interesting to us," Pippa said, "but we're newbies when it comes to birdwatching. There are great views of egrets."

"Aren't they just beautiful?" She paused to focus her binoculars on them. She turned to the man. "There are seven or eight of them, Bob," then looked across to Pippa to explain, "Bob's sight isn't so good these days. But he's absolutely ace at recognising bird song and often identifies a bird before I've even seen it. So where are you from?"

"Oxfordshire," Jude said. "Not so much marshland around there."

"Why am I getting an Aussie twang?" the man, Bob, asked.

"We've spent quite a lot of ..." began Pippa, then "*Ouch !*" as Jude trod on her foot.

"I'm from Western Australia," Jude said. "Just visiting." He collected together the picnic rubbish and stuffed it into a plastic bag. "C'me on, Pippa. We ought to be going."

As they rejoined the path, Pippa asked "So what was all that about?"

"The guy's half blind, for heaven's sake. I wasn't about to say 'oh and by the way, I'm your long lost son'."

"So what now, then?"

"Dunno." Jude suddenly looked crumpled and defeated. "At least I know where to find him now. Let's go and do your stuff in Finland and think about it when we get back."

Crossing Europe, September 2010

1

Over and over again, Pippa questioned Jude about that brief meeting with his father. No, he had not recognised him. He was nothing like the memory he had. He remembered him as a much bigger brasher sort of person, but then he had only been a small boy himself and he had rarely seen his father sober.

"It seems such a shame after all those years," Pippa insisted. "You need not have blurted it out. We could have gently eased the conversation round. Talked about my father. Said how much you had missed yours...."

"For Chrissake, Pippa, give it a rest. That's precisely the point. I didn't miss him. It was a bloody relief to see the back of him." And to Pippa's surprise and dismay, Jude burst into tears. They were in the garden, doing some cutting back before their trip. Jude threw down the pair of long handled secateurs he was using and slumped on to the lawn. She squatted down beside him.

"Sorry, lover. I shouldn't have kept on about it. It just seemed such a shame after all those years and all your efforts."

Jude rummaged in his jeans pockets, found a handkerchief, blew his nose. He said, "I suppose that's the point. While I was doing the research, I found myself reaching back to any memories I had. Some of them were rough, but there were some good ones, some bloody good ones, and I concentrated on those. Especially when Dad took me fishing on the Swan. I guess he'd had enough to drink to be happy, but not violent. I remember those times as really peaceful. You know how things are when you're a kid. If something boring happens you think it's going to go on for ever. And if you're having a great time, you can't imagine it ending. So I let myself think we could be doing this every day for ever, only next day he was that different person again. When he was fishing, he looked so strong and handsome and as if there wasn't any problem in the world he couldn't

82

tackle." Jude blew his nose again. "I couldn't see anything of him in that frail old man we met, and I suddenly realised there was a whole chunk of my life I would never get back."

Pippa stretched out a hand to twine her fingers through his. This wasn't the moment to say that he might never retrieve the past, but might contribute towards a future. "I'm sorry," she said again. "Let's finish off out here, and I'll go and throw some lunch together."

Soon after they had returned home, an email came from Liisu saying that she would be in the south of Finland for the first half of September, staying with a cousin who lived in the country about an hour's drive away from Helsinki. If it suited them, they could join her. She suggested that she should meet Pippa and Jude in Helsinki. How about midday on 5th September on the steps of the Cathedral? They studied the map of Helsinki. The Cathedral looked easy enough to find. She also sent a couple of photographs of herself, sitting on a bench outside a log cabin, which she described as the house where her cousin lived. She was attractive in an outdoorsy sort of way, and in one of them she held the hand of a small boy.

"I wonder if it's her little boy," Pippa mused.

"None of your business," suggested Jude. But Pippa asked in her next email. The reply came *No, he is a small cousin. My Eero is far away, but sadly his father was a devil man.*

"I think that means 'mind your own business'," Jude said.

They started preparing for the journey straight away. Aristotle watched it all implacably. Pippa took Jude into her father's studio in the garden and they went systematically through the contents of the cupboard, selecting all the diaries and translations they felt might be relevant, including her grandfather's original diaries in the hope that Liisu might understand Russian. Jude agreed that the translations made by her father brought history vividly to life. Sometimes Aristotle followed them in and ended up curled up on a shelf in the cupboard in which Pippa had found her father's diaries. It became clear that this had once been a regular haunt.

They settled for a day crossing from Harwich to the Hook of Holland in the first week of September. Aristotle followed them back and forth as they loaded the camper van, then sat on the window ledge of their neighbours' house wistfully watching them drive off. The crossing was blessedly smooth which did not prevent Pippa from sitting in a window seat, her eyes firmly fixed on the horizon which she had learned was a sure-fire preventative for seasickness. Soon after disembarking they joined the European motorway system and headed for a campsite on the outskirts of Arnheim.

Neither of them had anticipated their journey across Germany via the autobahns would be anything but tedious, but at least it was fast. Pippa giggled at each exit as it was marked 'Ausfahrt', and Jude got grumpy over major hold-ups on the outskirts of Düsseldorf and Hanover. But they did the whole thing in little more than three days. They camped for one night in Germany, another in Sweden before heading for the ferry crossing from Stockholm to Helsinki. At the camp sites, Pippa went on reading her father's translations and became increasingly puzzled.

"It's really odd," she told Jude. "The Winter War between Russia and Finland lasted from November 1939 to March1940. Then there was an uneasy truce and war broke out again in the summer of 1941. In the meantime, Father had been born in December 1940. As soon as the second war seemed imminent, Grandfather Josef packed his wife and tiny son off to Sweden."

"Well, surely that's natural, isn't it? He didn't want them caught up in another war."

"That's what I thought. But then Josef disappeared. Father had kept some of the letters he wrote to his wife Annikki, once she and the boy had settled in Sweden; and then again when they had moved to England. That was through some Quaker organisation. That's when they settled in the Midlands and Father was sent to a Quaker School."

"So when did your grandfather disappear?"

"The last letter in the file is dated April, 1943. The following year, the Finns were forced into another treaty. Part of this demanded that the Finns expelled the Germans from their soil, but the Germans had no intention of going quietly. They retreated through Finnish Lapland, burning everything as they went. After that nothing. Father's records show that his mother, Annikki, made many attempts to contact Josef by letter or by telephone as soon as the war was over. The only clue she ever found was from one of Josef's neighbours who said she had last seen him when he was on his way to see the authorities about something in the spring of 1943, but he didn't know what. At that point it was still some months before Annikki left Sweden for England."

"And at that stage your father was still only a toddler."

"He was three or four. Once she got to England, Annikki made a life for herself, with Quaker help. Of course she kept on trying to trace Josef, but in the end even she gave up. She was a wonderful seamstress and never short of work. The Quakers paid for Father schooling and because he was brilliant, he got scholarships to some posh independent school and went on to university." Pippa stopped and sat looking down at her Father's notes on her lap. "I wish I'd know him better."

"Well you're getting to know him now, and hopefully Liisu will be able to fill in a lot of gaps."

The weather was good for most of the trip, and especially fine on the day crossing across the Baltic to Finland. The northern evenings were still quite long, and they stood out on deck watching their leisurely progress, first through the sprawling archipelago off Sweden's coast, gradually darkening to black humps on a luminous sea. Perhaps these huge skies and landscapes were in her genes, but Pippa felt the strangest sense of coming home.

"It's really odd," she told Jude.

"Perhaps you were an Eskimo in an earlier life," he suggested.

"Lapp not Eskimo," she retorted. "And according to the guidebooks they prefer to be known by their own name for themselves: *Same.*"

"I stand humbled."

"That'll be the day." But Pippa was aware of a sense of elation she had not felt for a long time, as though she were on the brink of something important happening.

2

Yawning noisily, Jude took himself off to bed. Pippa stayed on deck until the cold drove her into one of the bars where she had a nightcap before following him. But she couldn't sleep, and was up again as the twilight brightened to dawn over the distant silhouette of Helsinki. Jude joined her as they nudged between islands stirring into life. They watched in silence as clusters of buildings dissolved into individual ones, and above them they could distinguish the soaring cupola that marked the Cathedral.

The ferry had slowed down and progress was down to a crawl as they nosed through narrow straits, noting the increase in traffic as they approached the mainland. They could hear the hum of motor traffic now, mixed in with the medley of sounds that added up to human activity.

It was full daylight now, the low sun catching the pastel-washed buildings on the harbour front and glint of the Cathedral's cupola.

"Oh look, look," cried Pippa, pointing, and Jude saw too down on a nearby shore a wooden platform built at the water's edge where women were scrubbing carpets, then laying them out in the sun to dry.

"I'd have thought hoovering would be simpler," Jude commented, ever the devil's advocate.

"Oh, you!" Pippa was too enchanted by it all to be really cross.

It felt as though they had slowed to a standstill but, no, just perceptibly they were edging closer to the blur of structures that now recognisably indicated a major city. They began to distinguish the huddle of market stalls on the harbour front and the busy-ness of market holders and shoppers. A riot of colour marked a corner of the market given over to flowers. Through binoculars Pippa saw other stalls piled high with forest fruits or crisp vegetables; others displaying baskets, brushes, birch whisks, ladles and other sauna equipment.

"Oh, look, look!" she cried again, and this time she was pointing to a flotilla of little boats drawn up along the harbour, selling fish or vegetables freshly brought in from the islands.

"Are you planning to get off this vessel?" Jude asked at last, and reluctantly Pippa left the deck rail to join those assembling near the companionways that led to the car decks.

In a later email, Liisu had advised them to leave the campervan at the terminal and go on foot via the market to the Cathedral. They were off the ship in no time. Pippa was even more delighted with the market at close quarters, but was equally anxious to meet the cousin of whose existence she'd had no inkling only a few months earlier. Firmly holding her hand, Jude pulled her passed the stalls' temptations, across a main road and down a narrow street that brought them out on to the spacious square dominated by the Cathedral. Already at this early hour, office workers had paused to sit on the broad steps and lift their faces to the sun.

Among them, sitting alone was a woman with corn coloured hair, a smart, casual denim suit and striking scarf swirling round her shoulders, her face also lifted to the sun. Pippa and Jude approached her quietly, stood for a moment watching her. Pippa especially. The way the sun caught the woman's cheek bones, and the slight upturn of her mouth as she greeted the sun provided a combination that for a moment caught Pippa's breath. The "Oh!" of recognition escaped from her involuntarily.

The woman opened her eyes, put a hand up to shade them from the sunlight. "Cousin Pippa," she stated rather than queried.

Pippa sat beside her. "Now I understand," she said. "When I first saw you and the way you sat and the half smile - I knew where I had seen it all before. You are *so* like my grandmother, only happier." She took Liisu's hands in her own. "Now I understand why Father fell for you when you were a little girl."

"And I thought it was because of my beautiful mind," Liisu said dryly, and they all laughed, banishing any tension.

Jude sat down too and there were introductions.

Liisu said, "I suggest in the first place we go to market and have coffee. In Finland it is always coffee time, and there we make plans." So moments later they were in the market again, and Liisu was preventing Pippa from buying a mountain of bilberries "because they are free in the woods where we pick them," so she contented herself with buying a sauna brush instead.

The coffee was thick and black, Liisu drank hers through a lump of sugar she held between her teeth, and Pippa tried to do the same but only succeeded in choking. Liisu rummaged in a bag and brought out a map. "Now we make plans. I think it is easier if I travel with you and show you the way. But first we go to my apartment where I have to take things my cousin needs, and we can have some more coffee."

"In Finland it is always coffee time," Jude said dutifully. "I wonder you all don't become gibbering wrecks."

"I am ready when you are," Liisu said placidly, looking anything but a gibbering wreck.

Her apartment was on their route, in Espoo, among the earlier of Helsinki's many modern suburbs. Her apartment block was one of several in warm-toned brick, scattered about a natural setting of granite and trees as though the buildings had grown out of the very soil.

"Why can't we create suburbs like this?" Pippa wondered aloud.

"Because you have too many people and not enough land," suggested Liisu.

The apartment itself was quite small, but made more spacious by the lack of dividing walls, so that the well designed kitchen area filled the short end of an L shape, while the longer side was the living room, a huge window completely filling one wall. The remaining walls were covered by original paintings of Finnish land- and seascapes. While Pippa and Jude admired these and the real landscapes beyond the huge window, Liisu was already making coffee. A few minutes later they were sitting at a low ceramic table by the window sipping the excellent brew.

Liisu said, "We have so much to tell each other, but it is better we wait until we get to Suojärvi when we shall very much time."

"Soo-oh-yarvi," mimicked Pippa experimentally. She frowned. "That sounds a bit like the place Grandfather Josef mentioned in his diary, when he was recovering from his wounds."

"That was Suolampi," Liisu said. "And it means Swamp Pond. Suojärvi means Swamp Lake, and they are quite near each other. Suojärvi is where my cousin lives, though there is no swamp now. Nearly every place name in Finland means something to do with nature."

"Helsinki?" queried Jude.

"Except Helsinki. There are always exceptions." Liisu opened out the map she had taken from a drawer. Pippa and Jude had bought quite large scale maps but nothing like this which showed an amazing network of rivers and ponds and lakes seemingly endlessly opening out into each other until, right at the edge of the map water seemed to cover everything.

"That is Saimaa," Liisu explained. "A series of enormous lakes that cover much of the middle of Finland." She leaned forward, pointing with a pen. "This is the route we shall follow now, east out of Helsinki, then a little north-east till we come to this small town and only a few kilometres away is my cousin's summer house."

"Presumably if she's your cousin, she could be my cousin too?" Pippa suggested.

Liisu wrinkled her forehead in thought. "You are right. She is the daughter of your Grandfather Josef's sister, so she is also your cousin."

There was a pause while a far away memory tugged at Pippa's mind: her own dying mother referring to Father's younger cousin.

"Yes. And like Josef, she married a Finn, Heikki. But she stayed in Finland. In fact, come to think of it, our family has done more for Fenno-Russian relations than the rest of the country put together." She pointed to the map. "In the winter she and Heikki live up there in the Saimaa area; in fact they will be closing the summer house up in a few weeks' time." She left them to drink more coffee and study the map while she went to collect up the things she was taking for her cousin.

"Have you noticed the colours?" Pippa said, gazing out of the window. "I mean foliage colours."

"You wait till you get to the north." Liisu looked up from her task of folding blankets into a large holdall. "I may have told you we have a special expression - *ruska-aika* - for it there. It means russet time, but the colours are everything from crimson to orange to lemon. It is all the undergrowth of berry plants, as well as the trees, and the bushes on the tundra."

Pippa sighed. "Why do I get this feeling I have already seen it before, that I have come back to a familiar place."

89

"May be it's because of all those diaries you've been reading. Your grandfather's for a start," suggested Jude.

"But that was describing the Winter War - everything was frozen, no colour but white."

Liisu paused in what she was doing. "Now you are really making me curious. Your grandfather - you mean grandfather Josef? Remember he was my relative, too – though probably once or twice removed." She pulled a strap tight round the hold-all. "Please no more talking, or we shall never get to Suojärvi!"

Finland - early September 2010

1

Jude did the driving and Liisu the navigating. Helsinki's suburbs merged as seamlessly into the countryside as the city had merged into the suburbs. There was water everywhere. Pippa gave up trying to decide whether she was looking at bay, inlet, lake or open sea. Conversation was mostly limited to road directions, but on one of the longer straight stretches Pippa asked, "Tell me more about this cousin we shall be staying with, Liisu. You said she was the daughter of my grandfather's sister. My mother mentioned that she thought Father had a young cousin, but for some reason he didn't want to make contact."

She took some moments to reply. "That's right. This sister, Maga, was much younger and adored her brother. When she learned he had settled in Finland, she turned up one day. Bag and baggage as I think you say. That was some time after your grandmother Annikki had left for Sweden with her little boy, and sadly after grandfather Josef himself had disappeared. Maga's baggage, by the way, included a baby called Margarit. It is Margarit you will be meeting, who is now married to Heikki."

"Your extended family seems to be getting more complicated by the minute," Jude observed.

"It's getting a bit overwhelming," Pippa said. "Father always seemed such a lonely man."

"With a mixed background of Finn and Slav, that is likely," Liisu said. "I think Maga did write to him when he was in England, but she had no reply." She leaned forward, "Slow down Jude. At the next crossroads we must turn right."

A few miles later they passed through a small community which Liisu announced was their nearest shopping centre and asked Jude to stop. She returned with a bouquet of three roses. In Finland, she explained, you never visited without taking flowers, any more than you never visited without being offered coffee.

And then they were there. Suddenly Jude was instructed to turn left on to a barely visible forest track and they jolted gently between tall pine and shoulders of granite. The track divided a couple of times, then between the trees they distinguished the distant glint of water, and beside it a cluster of wooden dwellings. By the door of the largest of them stood a woman with grey hair, her ample form wrapped in an enormous apron. They stopped the campervan, jumped down and went towards her. Pippa looked at this new relative and felt her throat contract. Female and rotund Cousin Margarit might be but there was no mistaking that she was relative of the stern man Pippa had called Father: similar blue eyes and straight gaze; similar widow's peak of thick hair thinning towards the crown; similar mouth whose smile lit the entire face - so rare in her father but now illuminating Margarit's.

2

She came forward arms outstretched. "No English," she said and continued in a torrent of Finnish from which Pippa distinguished 'Jooseppi' from time to time.

Liisu moved in to embrace her and quieten her down while they began to unload the campervan. Pippa stood a little apart, a little stunned by the beauty of the spot and the sense of homecoming. Almost without realising it she moved away from the group and walked down to the lake shore. There was a small wooden cabin here, a sauna bathhouse she guessed. But it was the lake that took her attention, stretching to a distant shore, ringed by forest with an occasional break in which she could make out a small cabin or bathhouse. All of it contained in the kind of silence you can hear, suddenly broken by the clatter of waterfowl taking off from a nearby bay, and then the low hum of an outboard motor as a small boat nosed across her line of vision.

A voice muttered and she saw that Margarit and Liisu had come to join her.

"She's complaining that the lake is getting crowded," Liisu said, and when Pippa turned to look at her, she saw she was serious. Liisu went on, "We've had this summer place for about three or four generations. When we first came, we were the only house to be seen. Now look."

Pippa looked. The average Brit would regard this as virtually uninhabited. An Aussie would not. It all depended on your criteria.

"*Kahvia! Kahvia!*" came a call from the house. Even Pippa recognised this as a summons to coffee, this time by Heikki, Margarit's burly husband.

A flowerbed luminous with nasturtiums extended round one side of the house and there was a wooden table and several benches where the coffee had been set out. Further introductions were made. Heikki had a beefy handshake. "Little English, but understand some words," he announced.

While they had coffee, Liisu explained the lay-out of the little community of cabins that had grown up here over the years. Pippa and Jude were to have the small cabin about fifty metres from the main house. The loos were earth toilets in a separate little building near the sauna. There was also a tap from which you could fill bowls with lake water for washing. The sauna was lit most evenings.

And what about Suolampi. How far is that?"

"It is about 10 kilometres through the forest. We shall go soon," Liisu promised.

"I could stay here for ever," Pippa said as they humped their things into their own cabin.

"You might think differently in the dark depths of winter with a couple of metres of the white stuff on the ground." Jude commented

"As opposed to 100 degrees-plus in a parched landscape?"

"Mm. How about we live in the here and now. What do you make of cousin Margarit? I saw your look of amazement."

"It was the resemblance to Father." Pippa noted his raised eyebrows. "I know, I know you knew him as a difficult old curmudgeon. And so he could always be. But when he smiled, it lit his whole face, like it did Margarit. And those blue eyes …"

"Yes, I did notice those."

They pottered about, unpacking the necessities. Jude broke in, "I'm not too sure about this sauna business."

"What's the problem?"

"I thought you and I would be having one together, but I gathered I go in with the men - well, man, since there is only Heikki; and you with the women."

"I gathered the same. So?"

"I'm not baring my all to a stranger."

Pippa burst out laughing. "Don't tell me you've gone prudish!"

Jude looked sulky. "That's all very well, but at least you'll be with Liisu who speaks English."

"You mean you don't like being naked in a foreign language?"

Jude gave up and slid his backpack under the bed. "I'll miss all the gossip."

"Well," Pippa pushed her pack next to his. "There's no way you can have sauna with us, so you'll have to get used to the idea."

In the event, Jude was wrong. Obliged to communicate in another language, Heikki dredged up a remarkable amount of English, and the whole procedure of being initiated in to sauna etiquette was so absorbing that Jude quite forgot his nudity.

"First you go to sauna," Heikki explained. "When enough, you come out to get cool. Then in sauna again. As many times as wish. It is good to throw water on hot stones." He indicated those on top of the stove in one corner of the sauna. "Water make sauna feel very very hot. Must be careful. After enough sauna, run to lake." He noticed Jude's expression. "All OK. No one see." No one interested, his tone implied. "Then back to wash room here and mix hot water with cold and wash. You will see, it is very fine."

Jude decided that the simplest thing was to follow what Heikki did, and soon they were sitting each on his own towel in the sauna, Jude on the lowest rung because it was cooler there, Heikki on the top one. After a while Jude stopped feeling that it was quite absurd to be sitting stark naked with a total stranger and ventured, "So how did you meet Margarit?"

"Her mother Maga, she come to Finland after war to find Josef. But he already gone."

"Gone where?"

Heikki screwed up his face in an effort to find the words. "Difficult. He was taken. I think Liisu explain better. Maga has Margarit with, but then she very small baby. Maga was very unhappy. She wrote to Jooseppi - Pippa's father - he not reply. Maga became ill and then she die."

Jude surveyed the slicks of sweat spreading over his body, feeling the pine scented heat saturating into every pore and remembering what Pippa had told her about an unknown Russian aunt whom her father had refused to contact.. "That's terrible. So who looked after baby Margarit?"

"That was Josef's - mother - how do you say?"

"Mother in law?"

Yes, mother in law. Father in law was angry man, but mother in law very kind. Then as she get bigger, Margarit goes to school. And there we meet."

Jude turned to look at him. "You are childhood sweethearts?"

But that was a bit too much for Heikki. Hiding his incomprehension, he took a ladle of cold water and flung it on to the hot stones. The temperature seemed to soar, burning Jude in every corner, stinging his nostrils, his lungs, his eyes. He picked up his towel and fled.

The towel wrapped round his waist he sat on a bench on the balcony of the sauna house. Though it would be daylight far into the evening, the sun was low now and the light on the lake created a texture of light and fluidity that was quite magical. Jude sat watching its subtle changes, aware of a deep contentment. After a while Heikki joined him, bringing two bottles of beer.

"Now drink," he said. "Enough sauna for first time. Tomorrow longer."

When he had finished his beer, he wandered down to the jetty, and Jude followed him. The coolness of the lake was delicious. Jude swam out some distance into the lake, glanced back at the shore, but Heikki had already swum out further and they drifted back together in companionable silence.

When they went in to wash. Heikki stoked the sauna stove up with more wood. Then they took it in turn to scrub each other's backs.

95

Apparently that was a sauna tradition too. As he dressed, Jude was aware of a combination of physical tiredness and mental alertness similar to that he used to feel after a full day of particularly good surfing.

"Thank you, Heikki," he said as they left the sauna house.

"You are welcome," Heikki responded, clapping him on the shoulder.

The women folk had just returned from a walk and were brewing more coffee. Heikki called out a greeting as they approached and there was a murmured chorus of *kiitos*, which Jude recognised as 'thank you'.

"He said *terveisiä saunasta* - greetings from the sauna. That is traditional," Liisu explained.

It seemed there were a lot of traditions associated with the sauna.

3

Over coffee, Liisu also announced that while the women were having sauna, Heikki would be preparing his speciality for supper: *poronkäristys* or reindeer stew. Jude's task was to peel a minor mountain of potatoes and wash the salad. No domestic chore could have been more pleasant as Jude took himself, the potatoes and bowl of water down to the lakeside. Heikki came to join him just as Jude was finishing and an outboard motor droned in the distance.

Jude shook his head in disapproval as he said, "This lake is getting far too crowded," and Heikki grinned his appreciation.

The reindeer stew was delicious, gamey in flavour, but tender in texture. The three women had returned scrubbed pink and glowing from the sauna. Beer flowed freely. After his third, Jude turned to Liisu. "While we were having sauna, Heikki mentioned that by the time Maga arrived here from Russia, Pippa's grandfather Josef had already been taken. What did he mean?"

"Ah." Liisu finished her mouthful, put down her fork and said slowly, "It is rather complicated."

96

"Everything about her Finnish connections turn out to be complicated," Jude observed.

"I will try and explain. When Josef came here and little Jooseppi was born, he became a Finn and changed his name to Itäinen or Eastman. He learned to speak Finnish very well, though always with an accent, so when the Germans came - that time when they were our allies against the Russians - no one ever questioned his origins. Then during the Continuation War, things changed. The hatred against the Russians was very great. The Germans had suffered terribly as they retreated - perhaps as badly as the Russians had suffered when the Germans advanced…."

Liisu broke off and Jude looked puzzled. "But what has that to do with anything?"

She sat up straighter and looked at him directly. "It has everything to do. All over Europe there were slave camps where the Slav people were worked to death. Someone … someone must have told the authorities, for suddenly Josef was told to report to an office in town. We never saw him again. But the Germans are very thorough, and after a lot of research, we found a record that Josef had been sent to a big transit camp in Germany."

There was silence round the table. Pippa had stopped eating and listened, her eyes fixed on Liisu's face. She had heard of the slave camps, seen some of the grainy newsreels in documentaries, and the skeletal, hollow-eyed figures that lived in them. Never in her worst nightmares had she thought they could be connected in any way with her. Into the silence she asked at last, "Do you know to which camp he was sent?"

It was Margarit who answered in a great flow of Finnish. Liisu translated, "When the war was over, Margarit's mother Maga went to Germany to try and get news. Germany was then divided into several areas of authority - the British, the American and the Russian - and some were more helpful than others. We have to remember that the whole of Europe seemed on the move at the time, with displaced people trying to get home or find news of loved ones. Maga managed to establish several negatives - that is the camps where Josef had not been, including thank God Belsen." Liisu paused a moment. "Then Maga fell ill herself. She had left Margarit in Finland with Josef's mother-in-law and had to return. And soon after she died. But she did make notes of all the places she had been and Margarit still has them."

"Then," Pippa said firmly, "We shall finish her work and go to the ones she did not visit." Her voice was quite wobbly and Jude leaned over and took her hand.

Pippa sat up suddenly and said, "The diaries …" and disappeared. In moments she was back with her grandfather's diaries, her father's translations of them and the letter she had found. It was the latter that caught Margarit's attention. She leapt to her feet, exclaiming loudly.

"She says this is in her mother's writing," Liisu translated.

They all turned to watch as Margarit pulled out two sheets of paper from the envelope, scanned them, exclaiming "Oh, Oh," several times and then looked round at them all, the tears streaming down her face. Then she picked up the two sheets of paper and began slowly translating them into Finnish.

Liisu translated again. "She says it was written by her mother Maga soon after she arrived in Finland after the war and found Josef was missing. She had always hero-worshipped him, and now she wanted to make contact with someone who could tell her more. Somehow she had heard that Josef had been sent to a slave camp in Germany and she was desperate to have more information. So she wrote to Annikki. It looks as though she opened the letter and could not read it. We'll never know why she did not ask anyone to translate it for her. Or may be by the time Pippa's father was old enough, it was too late to do anything."

"Or maybe it wasn't too late," Pippa said slowly, "and he managed to find the camp where Josef was sent."

It was Jude who said, "But if Josef was sent to one of those awful camps, someone must have told the authorities that he was Russian. Who would do a thing like that?"

It was Liisu who answered without hesitation. "That is just what Pippa's father, my Uncle Jooseppi, came to find out. I think it was about 1970 - I know I was very young. I also know that it was the thing that hurt Margarit the most: that Uncle Jooseppi did not come to see her but travelled directly to Kittilä to find the truth."

"And did he find it?"

"That is the big question. The facts are that a short time after he left to go home to England, a body was found on the shore of a lake a few miles away. The body of a man called Kalle who had once worked with my father's family in south Finland. Kalle had married a local girl called Kirsti. There is a story that she was also in love with your grandfather Josef, but no one knows the truth of that. The fact is that Kalle hated all Russians. In fact his father was German, his mother Finnish, and she had sent him to her relatives in Finland before she died and when his father joined the army. His father eventually died from wounds he received on the Russian front. So Kalle stayed in Finland and married Kirsti. Then, when our father moved north to work in Kittilä, and he eventually inherited the farm, Kalle asked if he and Kirsti could come and work for him. After a while Kalle got his own property and became a reindeer herdsman: a person who knew too well the nature of Lapland to get lost or have an accident in the wild."

Pippa's mind had been working over time. "So this Kalle was German. Do you remember his surname? Did he have any children?"

"He adopted a Finnish name, Pajalainen. 'Paja' means smithy." Smithy – Smith – Schmidt. Could there be a connection with a girl called Greta Schmidt? Pippa's mind went into overdrive. Liisu went on. "No, for some reason he and Kirsti never had children. It might have been a happier marriage if they had."

"How did he die then?"

"He was found by a lake some miles from his house. It looked as though he had fallen into the lake and then crawled out of the lake and died of exhaustion. A boat was found capsized in the lake. But because he had broken neck, some people have other ideas."

"They think Pippa's father killed him?"

"I tell only the facts," Liisu said. "I leave others to weave stories. I was only a child then. And I had a good place in my heart for Uncle Jooseppi. My father may have some views, but he has not spoken about them." Later, when they were having coffee, she said, "You know, it is not so far from here to Suolampi, the place where my aunt Annikki found your grandfather Josef in 1944. It is only about 10 km through the forest."

99

"What do you want to do, Pips?" Jude asked later that evening when they had retired to their cabin.

"I want to be in six places at once." Pippa looked at him, troubled. "I want to go to Suolampi to see where grandfather Josef nearly died. I want to know why Father ignored his cousin Margarit and went straight to Kittilä. I want to check out all the slave camps in Europe and go to Kittilä to find if Liisu's father knows about this man who died." She gave a helpless shrug. "But there are many scores of camps and it's over half a century ago."

"There won't be scores. Anyway, Maga had already checked a lot and Margarit has the list. We need to do a web search." Jude sat on the bed beside her and put his arms round her. It was the sort of hug that goes with deep caring and Pippa let herself be enfolded by it. The hug went on for a long time.

Eventually she said, "This bed is a bit narrow for this kind of malarkey."

"How about this kind of malarkey, then?" Jude asked, lying lengthways along the bed, lifting her over him and beginning to unbutton her shirt.

Perhaps because of the tensions of the day, their love-making seemed to reach new depths of mutual caring and afterwards, Pippa wept with huge gulping sobs that gradually subsided, until she collapsed on top of him and said, "That's better." She noticed that Jude's eyes were moist. "You really do mind, don't you? About Granddad Josef and what Father did."

"I care about you," Jude said. "And yes, I do care about Josef, because he sounds like a hell of a guy and he's your granddad."

Pippa slid off him, adjusted her clothing, said, "I guess a sauna would be a really good thing, now."

"Yeah, though much as I like old Heikki, I'd swap him for you any day." Jude sat up. "But before we get back into the day's normality, let's make a decision. Firstly, we go to Kittilä, meet the rest of the family and do some nosing around. Then we go to Germany and suss out the slave camps or what's left of them. There'll be archives that's for sure. You know how damn'd thorough those Jerries were."

"Is that really what *you* want to do?"

"I need to know the end of this story as much as you do. And after that, perhaps we could go and find the end of mine."

Finland : mid-September 2010

1

That evening, after sauna, Pippa and Jude told their friends of their tentative plans. They understood immediately how important it was for Pippa to find out about her father. When she understood what was happening, Margarit said she was sure she could help, for her mother had left a lot of notes about her attempts to find her brother Josef. Then she had added that it was Maga's strong instinct that the most likely place to get more information would be the camp at Fallingbostel in western Germany in the Hanover area.

"That's a huge help," Jude said. "And as far as I remember, we pass quite close to it on our way home."

They agreed that Liisu should travel north to Kittilä with them, which meant waiting a few days as she had some things to do first in Helsinki. She would book their places on the car-sleeper to Rovaniemi and, in the meantime, Pippa and Jude would wait in Suojärvi.

It proved to be an idyllic time. With Liisu away, conversation with Margarit and Heikki was inevitably limited so they were left to their own devices, walked miles along tracks through the forest, marvelling at the subtle changes of tints as the undergrowth of berry plants increasingly patterned the forest floor with every tone from lemon to deep gold and pink to crimson stained with the creamy patches of lichen. "Though wait till you see the Lapland colours," Liisu had said more than once.

Pippa also took up her yoga practise, neglected for too long. She got into the habit of going down to the jetty before breakfast and going through a simple routine of stretching and balancing poses. One morning she became aware of someone nearby and looked round to see Margarit doing the same balancing exercise, standing on one leg, the other foot up in her groin, hands raised above head. Margarit smiled serenely without losing her position. "Make happy head," she said, which Pippa thought summed up much of yoga nicely. After that the two women met most mornings, communicating through their yoga practice and smiles.

Then one day they decided to find their way to Suolampi, where Liisu's family had had their family farm and where Pippa's grandfather Josef had slowly returned to health.. Heikki said he knew the way, Margarit got a fine picnic ready for them to take with them. They left straight after breakfast for the days were already noticeably shortening. After a sharp frost overnight and under a deepening blue sky the colours were more vivid than ever. After a while their chorus of 'look at that's … ' "and have you seen's…' gave way to silence as they ran out of adjectives to do justice to the barrage of foliage colours that assaulted them at every turn. It was an easy trail and they made good time, even allowing for a couple of stops to watch a formation of cranes heading south, and a pause for coffee.

Suddenly Heikki said, "Here we are," as they topped a gentle rise and saw the glint of water between trees. They made their way down to the shore. Obviously the vegetation had changed many times since 1940, but Pippa found herself trying to imagine the scene in the depths of winter and to picture how Grandfather Josef had ended up in his near-fatal situation.

As though reading her thoughts, Heikki said, "I have been here in winter. No colours. Only white and black. Your grandfather, he fall asleep. Then came snow and freezing and his leg was trapped. He not strong enough to make free."

"Bloody hell," Jude said. "Can you imagine."

"And then," went on Pippa, "our grandmother Annikki came out of the forest like a fairy godmother and rescued him. And if that hadn't happened, I wouldn't be here." It was a mighty sobering thought.

"And nor would I. I can really understand how your dad was fascinated by cause and effect."

Pippa looked at him in surprise. "Explain."

"Well, how the combination of incidents or coincidents trigger events that have effects for decades, centuries to come."

Heikki pointed across the lake. "You see where is big new house? Before that was farm of Liisu's family. In a barn Josef stayed and became well. Now all is different. City people come and make holiday houses and bring much people and noise."

They had their picnic sitting on rocks and tree stumps. It was too cold to linger long and they set off for Suojärvi as soon as they had finished. On the way back, Pippa noticed the colours less. She thought of her grandfather, probably quite close to death at that stage, and the young woman who had found him and whom she had only known as a gentle old woman. And now she wanted more than ever to learn about the Josef who had never been allowed to grow into an old man.

The next day Jude suggested they went into the nearest town to do some research. They found that the local library also acted as a computer centre where they could book some time to go on line. They began with entering 'Concentration Camps in World War Two', but the list was so considerable that they changed it to 'Slave Camps'. The plethora of names and their localities was almost as confusing.

"Let's try Fallingbostel," Jude said, typing in the word.

"Oh," Pippa said, as a new page came up informing them that there were over 130,000 references.

"No probs," Jude said, clicking on Fallingbostel Military Museum, and in a neat table before them appeared a chronicle of events, summarising the history of the camps during the war. Or rather camps.

They read that a camp, Stalag XIB, had been established within a barrack camp in 1939. By May-June 1941, Stalag XID/321 had been established next to it, designed to take 30,000 Russian prisoners. Described as 'subhuman' by the Germans they were put into the compound and left to fend for themselves. Huddled together in front of the screen, Pippa and Jude read how the numbers in the camps fluctuated and conditions worsened. From November 1941 to February 1942, the numbers were decimated by a typhus fever epidemic. In all about 300,000 Soviet POWs died in the camps.

"Could Josef have been one of them?" Pippa wondered aloud.

Jude was still reading. Soon after the epidemic, Stalag XID/321 was disbanded and taken over by XIB. It was doubtful whether conditions were much better as more and more POWs were brought here from other camps. Conditions were made worse by the removal of mattresses and bed boards from prisoners' accommodation in reprisals for alleged bad treatment of German POWs in Egypt by the allies.

"You couldn't in your worst nightmare imagine what it was like, could you?" Jude said. There were quite a lot of photographs, black and white records of an aerial view of the camp, men huddled together in a barrack, and two skin-and-bone figures sitting on bunks. He read further. "Look, it says after the camp was liberated, the remaining Russian prisoners went berserk, looting and raping, and the Brits put them back in the camp for safe-keeping until they could be repatriated." He paused. "I guess Josef wasn't among them by then, or he'd have come back."

"I still need to go there. See what it was like."

Jude was still exploring the website and clicked on a new heading. "Yes, I understand that and here is something that should help: look, a marked trail round Fallingbostel. What a weird idea, a guided walk round a concentration camp."

They stopped to print out the pages they had been reading before returning to Suojärvi. Margarit had been cleaning out the main cottage; Heikki was peeling more potatoes.

"Liisu telephone," Margarit said. "She ready after two days."

So in a couple of days they could be on their way north. Pippa was aware of anxiety combined with anticipation. She looked out across the lake, still as a mirror and reflecting back every small puff of cloud. It had been a wonderful interlude. But it was time to move on.

They did not leave quite as quickly as Pippa had hoped. A close friend of Liisu had been badly hurt in an accident, so she had delayed their departure by a couple of days so she could spend some time with her. As she sensed Pippa's impatience, she said, "You could use the time to explore the city, especially the South Harbour. Your father loved it there."

So every morning they took an early tram into the city centre from Liisu's flat, strolled down the leafy Esplanaadi to where the market stalls and boats were waiting on and by the quay with their rich displays of fresh fruit and vegetables, fish, handicrafts, knitwear. Usually they stopped at the same coffee stall for breakfast and to watch the world go by, but especially to take in the scene of pastel buildings, which included the Presidential Palace and City Hall, and up one of the narrow streets the Cathedral with its broads steps where they had first met Liisu - a week, good God, only a week ago.

2

It was on the third morning that Pippa caught Jude looking at her, his head slightly on one side, smiling.

"What?" she asked.

"*Rakastan sinua.*"

She looked exasperated.

He pushed over to her the little pocket dictionary they usually carried with them. "Look up *rakata* - spelled 'r', 'a', 'k', ..."

But Pippa had already found it. "'To love'", she read, and looked uncertain. "What's brought this on?"

Jude said seriously, "I've recently found myself trying to imagine life without you. And it's unimaginable."

Pippa looked thoughtful, closed her eyes. After some time, Jude said "Well, for goodness sake say something."

She opened her eyes. "I was just trying it out. And with the same result." She suddenly giggled. "I do believe that after all this time I've fallen in love with you."

"And you think that's funny?"

"Well, don't you, after so many years? I mean clearly we must have liked each other, and several absences have helped the heart grow fonder. But love in the 'death us do part' - well, no, that wasn't on the agenda."

"So what shall we do about it?"

"Do we need to do anything just now? Here's an idea. How about we both sort out our pasts, then we go ahead and plan our futures."

"Sounds good," Jude said. After a moment he asked, "Is Aristotle part of the package?"

"Absolutely," Pippa said.

When they returned to the flat that evening, Liisu was in much lighter mood. "My friend is making good progress. I was beginning to think I must stay in Helsinki. But I am happy I can leave with you tonight."

They had to be at Helsinki railway station a couple of hours before departure. Liisu went with Jude to the appropriate area for getting the vehicle loaded on to one of the two-tier carrier-wagons. Liisu had already checked that the campervan just came within the height restrictions. Pippa waited for them in the cafeteria sipping black coffee and wondering what Father would have made of it all. She felt a wave of sadness that she had not persevered more in getting to know him; then recalled incident after incident when he had been peremptory, dictatorial, unforgiving. Except for occasional incidents and that weird dream where they had come close to an understanding and he had assured her of protection from any malevolence from the body in the cupboard. Had she had a premonition that he had some dark secret? She shook her head in exasperation at her own fantasy, gulped her coffee and was glad to see Liisu and Jude making their way towards her.

They boarded the train. The sleeping compartments were quite small: two couchettes one above the other, a narrow passage and the door into a tiny loo/shower facility. Liisu said she hated eating in a swaying restaurant car and had made a delightful picnic of open sandwiches, pastries, yoghurt and fruit. They ate while they waited for the train to leave, which it did on time, creaking and creeping through the Helsinki suburbs. It never seemed to get up a great speed so there was plenty of opportunity to observe Finnish domestic architecture in its innumerable variations on the theme of wood, concrete or brick - most of it set among a natural backdrop of trees, meadow or granite bedrock.

Liisu was sharing her compartment with a stranger, so she stayed with Pippa and Jude until she stifled a yawn and said she'd better go before she fell asleep on the spot.

When she had gone, Pippa said "I can't believe we're actually on our way to whatever it is we are going to discover."

Jude was sitting on the top couchette, legs dangling over the edge, gazing out of the window at the decreasing number of habitations and increasing number of trees. "We may not discover much. It was a long time ago."

"Well at least Uncle Matti, Liisu's father, will have some information - after all he was there."

"Mmm." Jude slid down and went into the shower room. "Sorry, love. Liisu's weariness must be catching. I'm bushed. I'll have a quick shower and turn in."

When he had finished, Pippa followed suit and by the time she came out Jude's lanky form was prone on the upper couchette. He opened an eye. "Love you," he said.

"Likewise."

She got ready for the night, fished a book out of her rucksack and settled down to read. But her head was too full of unanswerable questions and projected outcomes, so she switched off the light and settled down to sleep. And surprisingly did. When she next checked her watch, it was two o'clock in the morning and a dark grey light glimmered round the edges of the blinds.

From time to time she got up to peer out into the night: dark shadows of forests, sometimes a broad clearing, a cluster of buildings, and the occasional pinprick of light. Eventually she got dressed and sat on her couchette peering behind the blinds. As dawn faded from fiery red and orange to pastel shades and daylight began to filter across the scene, Pippa stared enchanted by the kaleidoscope of colour. Liisu had been right. The quantity and intensity of it was beyond anything she had seen before.

"You're awake," said Jude's voice and he swung down to sit beside her, pulling the blind up so that they got the full impact of the colours. "It's surreal. The one thing we don't get in most of Oz are autumn colours. I thought those in the UK were pretty amazing. But this…."

They were due in to Rovaniemi a little before seven o'clock. Pippa went out into the corridor to give Jude more elbow room and found Liisu there leaning on a rail by the window.

"You were right about the colours," Pippa said. "Jude is quite drunk with them."

"Not too drunk to drive I hope!"

108

It took a while to get unloaded at Rovaniemi, then Liisu directed them on the short drive round the city. It was only a few kilometres south of the Arctic Circle and was set by a fast-flowing river.

"That's the Ounasjoki, the Ounas river - the same river that goes by Kittilä. Our house is quite close to it. Turn left at the next junction and we'll come back to the city centre and get some breakfast."

"This city is so modern."

"That was not exactly by choice. In the war, one of the terms of our peace treaty with Russia was that we must send away all Germany army. They retreated north into Norway destroying everything...." Liisu broke off. "Stop here, Jude. This is the main hotel and we can have breakfast looking over the river."

An hour later they were on their way again, soon crossing the Arctic Circle, sometimes following, at times crossing the Ounas river. The scenery was quite flat, the forests never far and mostly crowding to the very roadside, though Pippa noticed that the trees were substantially smaller and the forest floor substantially brighter than in the south. Then, after an hour or so, they began to see hills ahead - low bare-topped rises above the dark forests.

"Over there is Yllästunturi - 'tunturi' means fell. It is a favourite place for skiing and hiking." Liisu said. "We often go there, though I prefer the fells further north at Pallastunturi."

And then they passed the sign of 'Kittilä' marking their arrival at their destination. It was clearly a flourishing small town, with a main street lined with shops and roads leading off into residential areas.

Liisu directed Jude through several turnings, then they were heading away from the main part of town along a track through meadows leading to the river. Ahead was the kind of house that had become very familiar to them as they travelled through the Finnish countryside: wood-built, painted deep red, with steps leading up to a porch. And standing at the top of the steps was a tall, sturdy-looking, white-haired elderly man. He stayed where he was, waiting for them as they parked the campervan and made their way up the steps. His whole being seemed contained in stillness except for his blue eyes that twinkled like a child's and an expression that said, wordlessly, 'I am very glad to see you'.

"*Isä!*," exclaimed Liisu. "I hope you have been looking after yourself, Father."

"Welcome home, daughter." The twinkle belied the formality of his words.

Liisu did the introductions, and her father shook hands with them in turn, holding Pippa's for several moments as he looked at her and said, "I never think I meet Jooseppi's daughter."

The house was one that had survived war destruction, with an annexe added "to cater for the extended family," Liisu explained. "Father thinks I have not done my duty in this way. But Eero is working in the Far East and now I think it is late for me to extend the family any more."

Pippa found herself wondering why Liisu had not married again. Too independent? The next moment, Liisu gave her the answer. "I had a wonderful man. He was in peacekeeping for United Nations. Killed while keeping peace in Africa."

Pippa touched her shoulder. "That's terrible Liisu."

She nodded. "Many things are terrible. Like your grandfather being taken to slave camp. Like your father having a sick head. Without terrible things, perhaps we do not find wonderful things to compare. For example, after my man died, I was mad for a while and lived for a short time with a devil man. The result was my Eero"

Pippa squeezed her shoulder, far from sure whether she could view tragedy in so detached a fashion. "Where is your Eero?"

"He is making good money in Japan and has a nice girl friend. Soon I shall have a Japanese granddaughter and will go there and see her."

Pippa and Jude had been put in the annexe, with a large room with two narrow beds and an adjoining shower.

"They do go in for narrow beds," Jude grumbled.

"And I thought it was my beautiful mind that attracted you," Pippa said sadly.

"That, too."

110

From the house, a track led across rough ground to a sauna bathhouse by the river and continued along its banks a short way to a grove of pine and birch. "That is our favourite place," Liisu said. "Father likes to go fishing here. As children we would swim or practise in our canoe. Now they say they will be building houses there. Everything is changing so quickly." She looked towards the low rise of the fells. "Not so long ago, all that was wild country. Now there are many hotels and holiday houses."

"Good for the economy," suggested Jude.

"Yes there is that. But not so good for the soul."

The following day Liisu said she would show them Pallastunturi, her very favourite fells, a couple of hours drive to the north. Although there was a hotel there, there had been no major developments and you could still walk for miles through landscapes that hadn't changed much since the last Ice Age. They left early, stopping for breakfast en route, and turning off the main road to follow the winding minor road up to fells.. The autumn colours had brought a lot of visitors but under such huge horizons it did not take long to lose them as Liisu led the way along a trail to the top of a fell called Pyhätunturi, which she said translated as Holy Fell. From its slopes they looked down on the scattering of buildings of the hotel and its annexes. Liisu pointed to a pile of flattened rubble. "Those were the ruins of the original hotel, destroyed when the Germans retreated into Norway."

The magnificence of the scenery silenced them. Here on the open fells much of the growth was of the dwarf variety - dwarf birch, dwarf willow, dwarf berry plants, repeating the same brilliant colours of the south but in miniature form of greater intensity in a carpet that glowed in the autumnal sun. It was a slow gradual climb culminating in a short steep stretch before they came on to the rounded fell-top with its cairn of stones. Though they were at no great height, the expansiveness of the view gave the impression of being on top of the world.

Pippa squatted by the cairn. "I can understand why Father loved it here."

"He liked especially this place," Liisu said. "My father brought him here first, but he told me he returned many times. Uncle Jooseppi said for him it felt like a holy place."

111

"How odd," Pippa said. "I didn't think Father did God."

3

"What did Matti say about the body that was found after your father's visit? Jude asked that evening when they returned to Kittilä.

"There hasn't been a chance to ask him yet," Pippa said, which was true but only up to a point. She knew there was an element of procrastination about her delay because once she knew the facts she could not un-know them and might have to adapt her whole way of thinking about the Father she was beginning to think of in a new positive light.

After breakfast next morning, she went in search of him. Liisu said he had gone to the place by the Ounas where he liked to fish, and Pippa followed the track, glimpsing him as he sat on a tree stump by the river. He was not fishing, but had a piece of wood in one hand and a knife in the other and was whittling away at it, pausing periodically to gaze out over the water. He looked up and smiled as she approached, and patted a neighbouring tree stump.

"Come and share this place with me Pippa. It is where I have all my big thoughts."

She sat beside him. "I want to ask you about Father, Matti. But first please tell me about my grandmother Annikki. She died before I was born, and I only remember a photograph of a white-haired lady who always looked sad."

The old man smiled and shook his head. "And I remember a beautiful young woman with long light hair that she tied back on her neck." His hands described a bun. "Remember she was nearly ten years older than I. I was schoolboy. And she laughed very much. In spite of war and that our father was often angry."

"Why was he angry?"

"Some people are so. Then Annikki found Josef by the lake. I came home from school and there was very bad feeling. Later Annikki took me to meet him. He was asleep and his face so white like snow, I think he is dead. But he opened eyes and smiled when

112

Annikki said who I am. It was very nice smile. Then later she has Josef's baby." He sat quietly as though he was conjuring the scene up in his mind. Then he began to work again at the piece of wood in his hand and went on. "One night very late Annikki come to my room and woke me. She said that Josef had told her she must go with little Jooseppi to Sweden where they would be safe. I understand why you remember her as sad. .She never saw her Josef again."

"Why did he want them to go?"

"It was very bad time. The German army was retreating in Russia. Many died, were sick. They hated Russians and Russians hated them. All had done terrible things. Josef wanted Annikki and his son to be safe. He should have gone with them, but I think he hoped to get back - to Russia to see his parents and it was easier from here."

"And do you know what happened?"

The old man looked sad. "I cannot tell you much. I was still at school when Josef went away. Then after war I go to university and then north to work for my uncle here in Kittilä on his small farm. When he died, he leave farm to me. I never saw Annikki again."

Pippa was silent for a long time, trying to imagine what it must have been like for her grandmother never to see her brother again. Then she asked "But you did see Jooseppi?"

He nodded. "Yes, he came here. It was 1970. You were few months old. He looked very much like his father, except Jooseppi was an English gentleman, not rough soldier like Josef. By then I was married and Liisu was small girl. Jooseppi liked to play with her - then he looked much younger. And she followed him everywhere because he tell her stories."

Pippa thought sadly that he had never told her stories.

A selection of extracts from post-war letters between Kalle in Finland and his friend Hans in Germany, and from Kalle's diary (translated from German into English)

July15th 1948

Dear Hans, I am sorry I have been such a bad correspondent for so long. Life has become very complicated. I also feel for you and the problems that you and your family face now the war is over. But we Germans are strong and we shall overcome.

I will try and explain. It had been my hope to come home, but now I have learned that my father died from his wounds on the Russian front, there are no family ties. It would be selfish to add another mouth to feed when there are so many shortages. Annikki's brother Matti has moved to Lapland in northern Finland to work on his uncle's small farm. I have asked if we can go and work for him there. I am hoping this may offer Kirsti and me an opportunity for a new life. It would be a fine opportunity to get away from the bad memories here, and perhaps good for Kirsti and me. There are still no babies, and sometimes Kirsti is not interested in trying to make any, so I have to persuade her. Annikki has written many times wanting news of Josef, but we cannot tell her anything. She and Jooseppi are now in England where he has become, she says, a proper English boy, now going to school.

If we go to Lapland, perhaps you will visit us. I think little Heinrich would enjoy it there. Yours, Karl.

August 15th, 1948

Dear Hans – Great news. Matti's uncle has offered me a job in Lapland. We leave in two weeks. Any chance you can visit us? You remember how spectacular the autumn colours are here? Yours, Karl.

September 12th 1948

Dear Hans -What wonderful news. Of course you and young Heinrich will be more than welcome here at the end of the month. The colours will be magnificent and the mosquitoes long gone.

114

What a pity that your wife cannot come, but I understand if her next baby is due in October, it is better she stays at home. Yours, Karl.

October 15th 1948

Dear Karl - Thank you, thank you dear friend for your welcome and the wonderful time you gave us. Little Heinrich speaks of nothing else and wants us to move to Finland! He asks all the time why we can't live by a lake and have a boat. I thought your Kirsti was so good with him - it is a shame that she does not have her own child. As for us, we are so happy with our new daughter.

You seem very settled in your work, but I think we know each other well enough for me to say that I felt there was some tension between you and Kirsti. Perhaps it would be good for you to spend some time back in Germany. There are some Finnish companies in Hamburg who might be glad to give you work - one especially which makes furniture. Yours, Hans.

Over the next months there is intermittent correspondence concerning the possibilities of Karl moving to Hamburg.

April 2nd, 1949

Dear Hans – There has been a major development. Last month Matti's uncle died and Matti has inherited the farm. He is offering me a small piece of land on which there is an old house I can renovate, and raise a small herd of reindeer. I think I must make the best of this opportunity. Perhaps it will make things better between Kirsti and me. Yours, Karl.

January 4th, 1950

Dear Hans, - The New Year is a time for new beginnings, so here are my plans. Over the past months I have been training a young man to look after the reindeer so that I can take some time off to visit Germany. At this time of year Kirsti always stays with her brother in Rovaniemi, so I am planning to come to Hamburg. If I could stay with you for a short time, I will find an apartment which I can lease for perhaps six months and get some employment. I would like to come early in February if that is all right.

I think I need a change. Yours, Karl.

In subsequent correspondence, Hans confirms Karl may stay with them, and tells him of a job with a Finnish furniture manufacturer for which Karl successfully applies.

January 10th 1951

Dear Hans, - It is just a year ago that I was planning my visit to Germany. What a wonderful time that was. It made me realise that for the past decades I have been stagnating, trying to become a Finn and this I can never be.

Please look after my dear Greta - I miss her very much. I had forgotten how it is to have such a relationship with a woman. Since my return, I have changed some things in my relationship with Kirsti. I think she needs to be examined for our lack of children. What a fine boy your Heinrich is. If he would like to come for a holiday he would always be welcome.

I hope to return. The Finnish company for whom I worked in Hamburg said they would be glad to have me back, especially in the months before Christmas. This would be good for me as it is the time that Kirsti stays in Rovaniemi. I will think about it. It could make all the difference to me, and perhaps to my marriage. Yours, Karl.

Over the coming years, Karl spends several winters in Germany and has a deepening relationship with Greta.

March 5th, 1962

Dear Karl - It is three weeks since you left - your fourth winter in Germany. The children miss you and want to know when their Uncle Karl is coming back, especially Heinrich. I think he hopes to come and spend a holiday with you in the next year or two. And of course Greta especially misses you, too. Yours, Hans.

September 10th 1965

Dear Heinrich - Yes, you and your friend will be very welcome to spend some time here during your Christmas vacation from University. Your father says you are studying engineering and doing very well. I really have missed my times in Germany. Since Matti began to be ill, it has been necessary for me to stay here and help run the farm. But I hope to come back in the winter of 1966. Yours, Karl.

September 10th 1965

Dear Hans - It will be so good to have young people in the house over Christmas. We still have no children. I have a good mistress in the nearby town. You will understand that a man has needs and she fulfills them very well.

I plan to come back to Germany for another winter next year. Yours, Karl.

September 12th 1965

My lovely Greta – I imagine you know that Hans' son Heinrich is coming for Christmas. How I wish it could be you. I ache to see you after so long, but Matti's illness has given me a lot of responsibilities.

I will do everything in my power to come back next year. Your own Karl.

December 21st 1965

Dear Greta - I am bewildered and angry. My friend's son Heinrich tells me you have a child. How can this be? Why did you not tell me you had another lover? I cannot see you again. Your broken Karl.

January 10th 1966

Precious Greta - You have made me the happiest man in the world. What a New Year gift! But why did you not tell me before that you have borne me a son? And already he is two years old! I was angry that neither you nor Hans told me, but I understand that you planned to do so on my visit last year and it is unfortunate that I have not been

117

able to visit Germany for so long because of Matti's illness. I shall come without fail next autumn. Your devoted Karl.

March 7th 1967

Dear Hans, Perhaps you can understand why I am in low spirits since my return to Finland after the happiest time in my life. It was like a miracle when I went to Greta's apartment and there she was, as beautiful as ever, with my small son! Don't you think he has my nose? Of course I have said nothing to Kirsti, but my mind is all the time trying to find a way for me to spend more time with my precious family. Yours, Karl.

June 15th 1968

Dear Hans - You are a genius. Why did I not thinking of inviting Greta and little Karl to come here? It will be terribly difficult to keep my hands off her, but Kirsti is often away and we will manage. And I think she will enjoy little Karl - he is a really sweet boy. I am sure she will believe that story that they are your close friends for she has an uncomplicated mind, and to make it even more believable you will pay us a visit during their stay. But please do not be too friendly with my Greta! I can't wait for the autumn.- Yours Karl.

November 4th 1968

Dear Hans - I thought the visit was a great success. Did you really think Kirsti was a bit suspicious? She has not said anything to me. What a relief that she had to spend a few days in Rovaniemi so that we could be a proper family for a short while. And then I shall be back in Germany this time next year. Yours, Karl.

November 25th 1968

Dear Karl - Perhaps I was wrong. It was the way Kirsti looked sometimes, but she is a strange woman. Have you considered leaving her and moving back to Germany? This could be the best solution. Yours, Hans.

January 5th 1969

Dear Hans - Yes I have considered it very often. But I have to say that I am a little anxious about taking this step. The Finns are very proud and I think might make trouble for me, especially Kirsti's brother Pentti who adores her and has rather a violent temper. But I shall continue to think about it. - Yours, Karl.

June 4th 1969

My lovely Greta - I am devastated that I cannot come to Germany next winter. Matti has to have a major operation and I must stay here until he has completely recovered.. Please believe that I shall come without fail next year. I should tell you that I am thinking about coming permanently so that you and I and little Karl can be a proper family. In order to do this I must fulfil my commitments here and then I can sell our home and make a new start with you. - Your loving Karl

There follows intermittent correspondence making plans for Karl's forthcoming move to Germany, until March, 1970, when it ceases. From then on both Hans and Greta write regularly asking for news.

May 15th 1970

Dear Karl - Still no news. Surely something must be wrong. Yours Hans.

May 25th 1970

Please, please write, my love. Little Karl is all the time asking for you. Please write.– Your own Greta.

June 1st 1970

My love - There have been some problems, including a fire at Matti's farm. I am exhausted. . The situation is also quite bad between Kirsti and me. Then I overheard a conversation between Matti and someone on the telephone. It sounded as though it was from abroad, probably England. I couldn't believe what I was hearing: that Jooseppi, Josef's son is planning to come here in the summer.

I have decided that I will come to live in Germany as soon as possible. Yours always, Karl.

June 15th 1970

My beloved - That is wonderful news. Why do you worry about this Jooseppi? Do you want me to come to you? Little Karl keeps asking about you. Your loving Greta.

June 15th 1970

My wonderful wife – You cannot understand the loathing I have for Josef and his son. Their people are responsible for the destruction of all that I hold dear, and now I fear this Jooseppi comes to make trouble. Don't worry. I am ready for him. Then we have the rest of our lives together. – Your adoring Karl.

There follow several messages from Greta begging him to be careful.

July 28th 1970

My beloved - Again no news of you. Both Hans and I are worried. He is thinking of making a visit to see what is happening. Your worrying and loving Greta.

Finland : late July 1970

Matti Itäinen was fishing from his favourite spot on the banks of the Ounas river when he heard the stranger approach. He knew it was a stranger from the amount of noise he made with his footwork and his grunting.

"Good morning. You are Matti Itäinen?" a voice asked in good but accented English.

"I am. And you are?"

"Hans Müller, a very good friend of Karl Schmidt who worked for you. I think he called himself Kalle."

Matti pulled in his rod and turned to study his visitor: a well-built, good looking man of his own generation. The sort, he guessed, that would expect you to jump to attention if he asked you something. "I imagine, Mr. Müller, you have heard the news of Kalle's death?"

"I heard reports in Kittilä. They say that Karl drowned in a lake. The Karl I knew would never put himself in a position to drown in a lake. I would like more details."

Matti pulled in his gear, but left it there. He did not intend to be long. "Let's go to the house and discuss it over a good cup of coffee."

A few minutes later, the two men faced each other across the kitchen table. "So what is it you know?" Matti asked.

Hans summarised the correspondence he had had with Karl, his friend's relationship with Greta and their son. As though in justification he commented, "I understand his wife Kirsti is cold."

"It is not a subject we discuss," Matti said. "I think there were some problems."

"I would like to meet her."

It seemed better to prevaricate. "She is away with her brother. On a cruise I think."

"Then I would like to see the place where it happened," Hans said. It was not a request, but a statement.

"That is possible. I will come with. You will need other things - coat, boots. There maybe rain after much dry weather. I can borrow to you."

They went the following day. Though overcast, it was dry but fresh and Hans was glad to have the borrowed gear. Matti drove by a different route to avoid the risk of passing near Kirsti's house in case she chose that moment to appear.. It was a rough track, but passable and went within a few hundred metres of the lakeside scene of the accident. He noticed that his passenger made no comment about the pleasantness of the scenery but kept his eyes fixed on the track ahead.

He parked the car between two birch trees and led his visitor up over an embankment to the lake shore. It was a quarter-mile walk to the site and they walked in silence, heads down against the increasingly strong wind across the lake.

Then, "Here," said Matti. They stopped by a point below a tumble of granite. Pebbles and stones gave way to a strip of sand at the water's edge.

"He drowned here?" Hans said in amazement looking at the gentle slope of the beach and the peaceful lake.

"His boat it was a kilometre from here," Matti explained. "There was strong wind. Perhaps he hit rock. Then he swim, but he has wound on head and lose strength."

"He was a very strong man," Hans said in a tone that expressed *I don't believe a word of it.* "And look at these marks by the lake. You say it has not rained?"

"No, not since the - the accident."

Hans was examining the disturbed soil, including a couple of clear footprints. He looked at them for a long time, then he turned to look at his own footprints at the edge of the water where there was still some dampness. "Look. See these footprints are same as my boots. Your boots. How is this possible?"

"I have been here once or twice – with Kirsti's brother and the police." He did not mention it had not been necessary to wear boots.

"But you said it has not rained since this so-called accident."

"I lent my boots to Jooseppi," Matti said before he could stop himself.

"The son of that Russian soldier?"

"He does not live in Finland. He has nothing to do with accident."

Hans went on standing there, looking down at the footprints. "It is question for police to decide. I am not satisfied with this story. I must find the truth for little Karl, Karl's son."

Finland/Germany : late September 2010

1

So Kalle/Karl did have a child in Germany.

There was silence while Matti went on working at his piece of wood and Pippa thought about what he had said. Finally she asked, "Can you tell me anything about this man who died when Father was here."

The old man gave a big sigh as though he knew the question would come. "Pippa, I would like so much to help you. I can only tell you facts. This man was called Kalle. He was there in south working for my father when Annikki found Josef and brought him to the farm. Father was very angry. He hated Russians. Kalle also. His mother was Finnish and sent him here as a boy but died soon after. His German father is in army, died from wounds on Russian front. He still had friends in Germany and went there many times, sometimes staying to work there for some months. One of his friends, Hans, came soon after Kalle died. This Hans tells me that Kalle - or Karl as he call him - had a young son in Germany."

Pippa leaned forward, clasping her hands, her eyes bright with interest. "But this is amazing, Matti." She told him about the phone calls from Greta Schmidt, and he nodded. "Yes, that was his name. It is possible she is granddaughter."

Suddenly there was a whole new range of possibilities. Pippa asked, "Was it this Kalle who told the Germans that Grandfather Josef was Russian?"

Matti raised his shoulders. "It is possible. Someone tell them for sure. And one day Josef is gone. I do not know details, but I come home after school one day and say I am going to see Josef. And father say he is no more there. When I ask where he is, father cannot say. Or will not say. Then after war I inherit the farm in Kittilä from my uncle and Kalle ask if he can work with me. He comes with his wife Kirsti who also knew Josef and Annikki. After some time Kalle gets some land and few reindeer."

124

Pippa watched his hands as he whittled away at the piece of wood. "It's a duck," she said. "What you are making."

He smiled. "Yes, it is *mergus merganser*. It comes every spring to Ounas river and makes many babies."

Pippa could not postpone her question any longer. "And do you think Father killed Kalle?"

"Pippa, I do not know. Your father came that summer in 1970. I was very happy to see him. He asked many questions. He asked about Kalle and said he must go and see him. I tell him it is not good idea because everything happen a long time ago, and no one can be sure, but Jooseppi say he must go. Kalle, he is living then in the forests some miles from Kittilä, with his wife. Jooseppi is away two, three days and when he comes back he is strange: somehow excited and rather happy. I ask what happened, and Jooseppi say that Kalle is away so cannot see him, but it did not sound like truth."

There was a long silence. Pippa went on watching Matti working away at the merganser's head. At last she said, "Then they found his body," making it a statement not a question.

"Yes, they find Kalle's body in a small lake. He has wound on head and his neck is broken."

'His neck was broken' -The memory of her long-ago dream and her father's voice repeating 'I told you Philippa, there is no longer any need to be afraid' was as vivid as if it had just occurred. She asked, "But why did they think Father had anything to do with it?"

Matti stopped whittling again, and stared into the distance, elbows resting on his knees. "I think you are like Jooseppi, you like to know truth, Pippa."

"Yes, I do."

"It was very dry that summer. When we go a few days later with Hans, Kalle's friend from Germany, we see several boot marks by the lake. They were from boots I borrow to your father when he go to see Kalle. After he sees the footprints of my boots, Hans goes to tell police, but after much dryness there comes much rain and no more footprints. And Jooseppi is already back in England." He raised his eyes to meet hers. "I am sorry Pippa, but it was so."

"No," Pippa said. Her mind rejected absolutely the idea that the new perception of her father, gradually emerging from her recent investigations, was capable of cold-blooded murder.

Matti remained silent, absorbed in refining the head of his carving.

"What sort of person was this Kalle?" Pippa asked at last.

The old man shrugged. "I cannot say he was a fine person, but a good worker like many Germans. He worked for my father in the south. A little younger than my sister Annikki. Kirsti, his wife, was a girl from Karelia who came to live in our village. After Winter War, Russia takes Karelia and Kirsti cannot see her family, only her brother who was in Finnish army; so she was glad to have Kalle as friend first, then husband. Soon after the end of the big war, I went up to work for my uncle on his small farm here, near Kittilä. It was great surprise when my uncle dies to find he has left farm to me. Kalle asked me if he and Kirsti could come and work for me. I knew he was good worker, so I take him. After some time he get own land and small herd of reindeer.

"He and Kirsti live in the forest, very lonely place. Kalle drink a lot, but so do many Finns. Because of this he was rather popular. Many people feel sympathy even though he is German because he lose father in war, and his wife was cold. He say Kirsti will not make babies with him, will not give him sons. Of course I do not know truth of this. He had a German friend, Hans, who visited sometimes with his son and I think this made Kalle restless. Later Kalle went to Germany a lot. This Hans came here soon after Kalle's death. As I told, he say Kalle has child in Germany."

And this son may have had a daughter called Greta.

"Is Kirsti still alive?"

"Yes, she lives and is - how do you say when someone likes not to be with people?"

"A recluse?"

"Yes, she is recluse. I have not seen her long time. She still lives in small house in middle of woods. Some say she is witch. She has a brother, Pentti who lives in Rovaniemi. He wants her to live with him, but she doesn't like."

"Perhaps I could go and visit her."

"She likes not to be with people," Matti said again. "But you can try. At home I show you on map where it is."

But it was not to be. Overhearing their discussion about Kirsti on their return to the house, Liisu said, "You can't speak with Kirsti. She is in hospital. No one knew she was ill until her brother went to visit her and found her unconscious. She is very sick with cancer, in hospital in Rovaniemi."

Matti asked "And where did you hear this?"

"At the small post office in town. Her brother Pentti was there sending a parcel. After the operation Kirsti will stay with him and his wife. She can't live alone for some weeks."

Matti nodded. "Yes, Pentti loves very much Kirsti. He always look after when she allows. He hated Kalle because of his drinking."

"Perhaps he killed Kalle?" Pippa suggested hopefully.

"Pentti was in Rovaniemi with his family at the time," Matti said. He looked at Pippa sadly, knowing she was trying to find an alternative, however unlikely, to clear her father's name.

The news that they would not be able to see Kirsti for some weeks was a major blow.

"So now what?" Jude said to Pippa when they were alone.

"Well, we can't stay here weeks. I need to earn some money and there's Father's house to clear before we can put it on the market. And what about Oz? You can't expect your partner to run it alone indefinitely."

"Yes. And then there's Dad."

Pippa raised her eyebrows. "So you haven't given up?"

"Of course not. Even less now that I have seen how things have developed for you. It's made me realise that I knew my father even less than you knew yours. I'll just have to take things very slowly."

She came over and put her arms round his neck. "So this is what we do," she said. "We leave in a few days time. We stop in

127

Fallingbostel on the way home. Then as soon as possible after we get back, we'll make a trip to Weymouth."

Jude pulled her close, nuzzled the crook of her neck. "That's just what I had in mind"

Pippa drew back gently. "There's one thing I haven't mention because I know you'll say it's my overactive imagination...."

"Try me."

"Well it's this absurd picture I have in my head of Kalle lying there with a broken neck. It is so much like the body I saw in the cupboard .... in the dream. Remember I told you?."

"Overactive imagination isn't in it, my sweet. Are you saying you are psychic? Or your father was? Or what?"

"I'm saying it's all very odd that I seem to have had déjà-vu without knowing there was something to have déjà-vu about."

"You're becoming even more weird than your cat," was all Jude could think of saying.

The Itäinens completely understood their plans.

"Come back in Spring," Matti said. "Then you will see a very different landscape."

"And Kirsti will be home again. In any case she usually spends part of the winter in Rovaniemi," Liisu added. "But I shall miss you."

2

Over the next few days they went into town and booked places on the overnight train back to Helsinki for the following week. They also booked a passage on the ferry from Helsinki to the north German port of Travemünde, a couple of days after their return to Helsinki. Liisu wanted to stay in Kittilä a couple more weeks, but she came with them to Rovaniemi and saw them on to the train.

"How odd that a complete stranger can soon feel like an old friend," Pippa commented as the train slid into the northern night.

128

"Mm, but having all those connections helped."

Liisu had lent them the spare keys to her flat in Helsinki and they spent a couple of days re-organising their luggage, buying maps and planning their return route. They also returned to the Fallingbostel website and printed out details of a 9-km walk round the camps.

And then Jude chanced on a video clip. It only lasted five minutes but, when it was over, they both sat in silence for a long time before Pippa murmured, "Play it again."

It was the story of a young Russian woman who had recently learned that her grandfather had perished in Fallingbostel. The clip showed pictures of him and of his daughter, the searching girl's mother. It followed the granddaughter's arrival in the small German town, walking between the neat houses of the present-day community, then flashed back in stark black and white to the camps of the 1940s. The sound was in Russian as the girl described her journey, but there were subtitles in English. Starkly the text told them that the Germans had regarded the Slavs as sub-human so no preparation was made for the prisoners who arrived in their many thousands. The men were left to dig trenches in which to try and create some makeshift shelter and under the bitter conditions of winter scores died every day.

Later the camp was hit by typhus which spread like wildfire through the crowded but more acceptable conditions of Stalag XIB, the prisoner of war camp, and infinitely more so through the adjoining slave camp of Stalag XID. Later still the survivors were worked to death logging in the forests to get materials to build more barracks. The girl's grandfather eventually died on 19th January, 1943, the fact tidily recorded on a certificate with his name, photograph and number.

"Good God," Jude said. "Did they have a certificate for every one of those tens of thousands of dead?"

Pippa did not reply and when he turned to look at her, he saw a tear rolling down her cheek. At last she said, "Will it ever end? Paul Pot - Ruanda - Srebrenica ....."

Jude continued ".... Ireland - Iraq - Afghanistan ..." He squeezed her shoulder. "You can't take on the pain of the world, sweetheart. Just try and be part of the cure for some of it."

Pippa sniffed, blew her nose, nodded. "I guess the guy that runs the museum is trying to do just that. Did you notice it said that some Russians have been writing to him asking for samples of the soil to be sent to them, so their dead fathers or sons can return at least symbolically to Russian soil?"

"Yeah, and the girl took some home with her, for her mother."

Pippa went on staring at the computer screen. "But why were the Slavs regarded as subhuman?"

"Why did the Aussies look down on the Aborigines, the white South Africans on the Blacks, the English on the Irish, the Protestants on the Catholics?"

"Yes, but they didn't treat them worse than animals."

"Certainly not worse than animals. We love our animals, treat them like four-legged humans. But I'm afraid you're wrong. There may not have been extermination camps but there are plenty of ways of degrading people."

It was too difficult to unravel. Pippa sighed. "Do you suppose Father went to that place in search of Grandfather Josef?"

"From what I have learned of your father, I think it is highly likely. May be that's what sent him on that mission of revenge, to find out who had told the authorities your grandfather was a Russian."

"If he did go on a mission of revenge."

"Could be we shall never know."

"Oh, I have every intention that we shall know," Pippa said.

3

It was a 27-hour crossing to Travemunde, and with it they left the bright colours of *ruska-aika* and returned to the wet drabness of a mainland Europe autumn.

"I don't suppose there'll be that much to see at Fallingbostel," Jude warned Pippa as he pulled out on to an autobahn.. "It was nearly three-quarters of a century ago."

Pippa was studying the papers they had printed off the Fallinbostel website. "Yes, look there are several camps: Stalag-this and Stalag-that." For some reason she had been expecting a predominantly industrial landscape, but in due course they came to rolling farm country, studded with woods.

When she commented on it, Jude said, "Yes, but don't forget that all this is part of the Luneberg Heath, and it's a popular walking area."

"Come to think of it, Luneberg Heath rings a bell. Something to do with school and World War Two."

"Yeah, it would. It's where the Germans signed an unconditional surrender and ended the war."

"Clever clogs. Doesn't that make it even more ironical that so many people died here uselessly? Still, as you say, it's a popular walking area," Pippa went on wryly, "And we even have a guided walk to prove it, though I don't suppose you meant that kind of walk. Anyway, the description of the walk makes it clear that there aren't many traces of passed horrors, just some foundations, memorial plaques and cemeteries. But it still feels right to be going."

The map of the walk also made it clear that the camps were set a mile or two outside Fallinbostel in the village of Oerbke which had largely expanded over the remains of the camps. Instructions for the walk began from Fallingbostel railway station, so it made sense to find a guesthouse near there. They found a family-run *gasthaus*, checked in and went in search of a meal. As they strolled through the neat and peaceful streets of the town, Pippa mused "It's really hard to think of this is as the scene of so many horrors."

"Isn't that the seminal problem of being human? That we don't learn from past mistakes. We hurry on to obliterate the ugliness we have created so it doesn't stop us creating it again?"

"That's pretty defeatist."

"Yes, well most people don't want to wallow in ugliness. People like your Dad who wanted to try and understand how we get like this so we can avoid the repetition are few and far between. I don't see too many signs saying 'this way to the slave labour camp', do you?"

After breakfast next morning, they set off for the railway station and from there, instructions in hand, followed as far as they could the trail of Grandfather Josef. It began at the station itself, on one of whose walls was a memorial to the Soviet prisoners of war who, after long forced marches, had completed their journey to Stalag XID in cattle trucks. From here the trail led under Autobahn 7 and about half an hour later they came to a sign pointing to what their printed account described as the Cemetery of the Nameless, the mass graves and final resting place for multi thousands. On the way they crossed wasteland between the autobahn and the gardens of new houses. The concrete foundations of some of the barracks were still visible, but it needed a lot of imagination to translate these into serried rows of barracks covering a considerable area. Later the path went past the sewage treatments work, over a small bridge, then uphill towards the entry to the Cemetery of the Nameless.

It covered a vast area and included a collective grave for 30,000 unknown Russian prisoners of war.

"It's like walking on green sponge," Pippa said. "An anonymous green sponge. Do you think we could put up one of those small memorial stones, like in war cemeteries, perhaps in Daerley churchyard?"

"Dunno, but we can ask."

Jude moved on and then realised Pippa had not followed him. When he turned, she was delving into her bag and produced a small bowl. Then she leaned down and scooped enough of the green sponge to fill it.

"I reckon I'm entitled to my own bit of Fallingbostel soil," she said. Jude did not need to ask her where the bowl came from as he had noticed it on a shelf in their room at the b. and b.

There were also over a hundred memorial stones commemorating the dead of other nationalities. Near the exit, the Polish Memorial stone was inscribed *1939-1945 May your mortal remains Become the seed of Freedom for all nations.*

"God help us all," muttered Jude.

"Since when did you start doing God?" Pippa asked.

"Spirit of the Universe, not old-man-in-the-sky."

Was there a difference, Pippa wondered?

132

A short while after leaving the cemetery, they came to the area known as Marquartsfeld, the site of Stalag XID where grandfather Josef had survived, if only just, for the several months of his incarceration. Only a few remnants of barracks remained. Pippa stood staring at them, trying to get a sense of association, but she felt nothing other than a deep sadness for the totality of unimaginable suffering this place had witnessed.

There was not a great deal more to be seen, except for the sole building that survived intact, the clean white delousing centre. The minds of those intent on delousing men who were imminently going to die of cold, starvation or overwork, beggared belief.

"I want to go home," Pippa said, and Jude did not try to dissuade her.

Oxfordshire/Weymouth : November-December 2010

1

For the first days after their return, Aristotle followed Pippa around like a shadow.

"That cat is seriously weird," observed Jude.

"That cat is seriously special," Pippa countered.

It took several days to get sorted out, wade through an accumulation of mail and even email that had collected since they last checked it in Helsinki. One was from Liisu lengthily saying how much she missed them and also reporting that Kirsti had come through her operation. Well, that was a relief. Their experience of Fallingbostel had only strengthened Pippa's determination to clear her father's name and Kirsti would be a crucial element.

They both found it difficult to settle. The few weeks away had been so packed with new experiences and new acquaintances, not to mention a barrage of unpalatable facts, that life back in Daerley Green felt unreally normal. Jude in particular was restless.

"Why not go back to Weymouth and have another go?" Pippa suggested.

"No." He shook his head. "It doesn't feel the right time. And I can't tell you why."

"Procrastination, that's why. I know that's annoying, but I think it's true. I just wondered whether it might be easier if you could talk to Laura on her own first."

Jude started shaking his head again, then stopped. "You know that's not a bad idea. Sort of neutral territory." His enthusiasm for the idea visibly increased. "Yeah, I'll go over to Weymouth for a couple of days and get out from under your feet."

"I quite like you under my feet, but heaven knows there's enough to get on with here." Jude left next morning so that 'I can't be accused of further procrastination'.

134

2

He had not driven very far before he began to regret the decision. Pippa had a way of nudging him into actions that he would otherwise have postponed, perhaps eventually forgotten. This business of living with another person in a totally committed way took some getting used to. Of course they had been together for a very long time, but not in a committed way. They had each lived their own lives, coming together regularly to have fun, do some housekeeping, have sex. But it was Joseph Eastman's illness that had precipitated this closer commitment.

Still, it was a sunny if crisp day in early winter, the countryside was looking good, and he made excellent time. He had decided to stay at the pub close to Bob and Laura on the principle it might be easier to find an opportunity to catch her on her own, and as luck would have it, his room looked out on to the main street, almost as far as the bend on which their house stood.

"Hello," Jim, the owner-barman had greeted him when he came in. "You're beginning to be a regular." And, yes, he did have a single room free on the first floor.

"Come to see Bob and Laura?" Jim asked next. Damn it, the man had too good a memory.

"No," Jude said. "I have some business in the area, though I might look them up. Better not mention it though, in case I run out of time."

In order to give himself some breathing space, he decided next morning to pay a visit to the Radipole reserve. It wasn't a week-end so hopefully he wouldn't bump into his father. It would also give him head space to think of Pippa and their visit there together. On a week day morning in late November, the reserve was almost deserted. Jude paused for a coffee at the Visitors' Centre before setting off to retrace the path he had followed with Pippa some weeks earlier - and, God, what a lot had happened since then!

He had not walked far down the track before his attention was taken by a flurry of activity as a group of small birds came from behind him and obligingly landed on reeds a short distance ahead.

Though fidgety, they remained in the same location and he soon got a good look at them through his binoculars: his best view yet of a party of bearded tits. *Wish you were here,* he informed Pippa in his head. He continued at a leisurely pace, pausing whenever there was a break in the reeds and an opportunity to scan more open stretches of water. There was a glimpse of a massive flotilla of surface feeding ducks, which he identified as pochard, and a smaller group of one of his favourites, the small neat teal, with its flashes of green.

At one of the viewing stations, he paused to eat the sandwiches he had bought at the Visitors' Centre. There was less to see here, so he went on to the hide where he'd had his first and only encounter with his father. The hide was empty. He installed himself on one of the benches, opened the window slit and surveyed the watery scene before him. There was precious little activity, though he exclaimed appreciatively as the azure flash of a kingfisher crossed his line of vision. He got out his identification book and checked it against the list of recent sightings he had copied from the Visitors' Centre. A grey heron lifted off from behind a reed bed and drifted down to land again in shallower water not far away. There it stood, motionless enough to be a statue until in a flash of movement it lunged forward and retreated again with a silvery fish in its slender bill, carefully positioning it so it could be easily ingested.

"Great," Jude said. Almost at the same moment he was aware of the door of the hide opening behind him and caught an unusual movement out of the corner of his eye. In a moment he had framed it in his binoculars and followed it as it sped low over the water. "*Wow!*" he exclaimed, as only half certain he said, "My first ever bittern."

"A bittern it certainly is," said a pleasant female voice behind him, and he turned to find himself looking into the amused grey eyes of Laura Jamieson.

"Hello," she said, then echoing the barman, "You're becoming quite a regular."

"That was absolute magic," Jude said. "Wait till I tell Pippa about that."

"I see she's not with you," Laura said, settling down on another bench and adjusting her binoculars. "Any more than Bob is with me. He's in a rare foul mood. He doesn't often get on his pity pot these

136

days, but when he does there's no shifting him. Anyway, enough about that. Is there much out there?"

"Nothing unusual, at least not for someone like you." Jude said. "No, Pippa couldn't make it this time. I had some great views of bearded tits earlier. I know they're common if you live round here, but for a newbie like me they are magic."

"Bob likes the bearded tits. He usually hears their chinky sound before I've spotted them. He's amazing."

There was silence as they continued to scan the scene. Laura murmured "Pintail," and a bit later, "I love those chunky shovelers," and by following the direction of her binoculars, Jude saw them too.

Then, quite unexpectedly , Laura said into the silence, "Is it really coincidence that we keep bumping into each other?"

And without thinking it through, Jude put down his binoculars, stared out at the reeds and said, "No, not entirely. You see, I am Bob's son."

3

"Oh Good God!" exclaimed Laura. And burst into tears.

Completely at a loss, Jude moved over to the bench where she was sitting. How did you comfort a virtually unknown elderly woman? After all, she was his stepmother. He patted her shoulder and said, "I'm so sorry. That was crass of me."

Laura sniffed, blew her nose. "Yes, it was rather. Your father does the same: blurts things out without stopping to think."

"Yes, well I don't know him that well."

Laura's expression softened. "No, of course you don't. And I imagine such memories as you have you might want to forget."

Jude became aware of approaching footsteps and voices and said quickly, "Shall we find a quiet corner while we try to catch up on the past thirty years or so in private?"

Laura nodded. They collected up books, binoculars, a box of half-eaten sandwiches and were ready to go as the door opened on a group of newcomers. They strolled back towards the entrance, Laura leading. She walked briskly, neatly, stopping as they came to a seat. It overlooked an opening in the reeds with views across an expanse of water.

"You start, Jimmie," Laura said.

"I never did like the name Jimmie and changed it to Jude when I went to Uni. I imagine Dad will be mad."

"You'll find he's a very different Dad from the one of your memory."

He nodded, then gave her a sketchy resume of his life, his meeting with Pippa.

Laura looked puzzled. "But what on earth made you decide to look for your father after all these years?"

So Jude explained how they had begun their journey into Pippa's past, and how it had triggered a need to know more about his own.

"He'll be so proud of you." Then she gave a sudden deep sigh. "Oh dear."

"That sounded heartfelt."

"The truth is," Laura said, "I'm not sure how ready he is for this."

"Mm. You may find this hard to believe, but that's why I'm taking this so slowly. It's why I really hoped to have a chance to speak to you first. Your Aunt Bee was very much against my making contact."

"Yes, she would be. But then she had to deal with Bob when he was still a very sick man."

Jude leant forward and looked out across the water. A few water birds were silhouetted against the glitter of the water, but he didn't do duck silhouettes yet and he just noted the sight and soundlessness of the scene. He said, . "Could you start at the beginning, please?"

"Well, you must realise that there was a very long gap between Bob leaving you and your mother, and our first meeting. Of course, we've talked about it a lot. It's not a pretty story, but in brief he spent some time in London, living rough. During that time he teamed up with two or three other street people who had good contacts for getting seasonal work in East Anglia. So off they went to pick cabbages or potatoes or whatever it was the season for. They got basic lodgings and food, and it was probably a life saver from the point of view of their health, but of course all the money they earned went into a communal pot for a massive drunk when they got back to London, until they ran out of money and went back on the street. Until the next lot of seasonal work came along."

Jude, resting his head against his clasped hands, felt his fists tighten. It was not what you wanted to hear about your own dad. "Go on," he said.

"Bob lost track of how long this went on for, but it was some years. Then one of the team heard of work available in Devon, so they all headed in that direction, thinking that it also had the advantage of being good cider country. He has no idea how long they were there. Seasons came and went. He remembers being in hospital on several occasions, but not why. Once or twice he ended up in a police cell, and again doesn't remember why."

Jude unclasped the hands behind his head and leaned forward to cover his face with them. Into them he said, "I had no idea it got so bad." After a moment he removed his hands and looked at Laura. "But why did he go on doing it - the drinking, when it must have been obvious that it was killing him?"

"Because he was sick, Jude. Addiction is an illness, however hard you may find that to understand."

"An addiction or an excuse?"

She went on as though she had not heard him. "Finally he woke up in hospital again. This time he was so sick there was no way he could leave. In due course, he found he was in a hospital in Weymouth, and distant bells began to ring in his memory. It gradually came back to him that he had a brother John and the last time they were in touch, he had been living in Weymouth. One of the nurses checked, and he still was. So the hospital contacted him. John did not come, but Beatrice, your Aunt Bee, did. John had heard echoes of Bob's adventures and didn't want anything to do with him, but Beatrice persuaded him that Bob should stay with them at least until he had recovered. Once Bob started feeling really well, the inevitable happened, and John threw him out. Beatrice helped him get a small flat and a small job to pay the rent. She's quite a remarkable old girl, your Aunt Bee. Not only that, but she also happened to know of a recovering alcoholic called Dizzy and put the two in touch with each other. Dizzy eventually persuaded Bob to come to one of the meetings of his self-help group and he's been going ever since."

Jude leaned back in the seat again. "But how did you get to know him."

Laura smiled. "I was a member of the self-help group."

"I see," Jude said. Then, after a moment, "Jeez.. But that means ...."

Her smiled widened. " Not all sweet old ladies are what they seem, Jude. Yes, I am a recovering alkie too.

At last Jude managed, "Seems Aunt Bee is not the only remarkable old girl." He held his head. "I think I have information overload."

"I'm not surprised. Let's go back into town and have some tea." Laura took his hand. "I hope you'll understand if I don't suggest that you come and meet your father today. I'm not sure he's ready for it. Or that I am come to that. We all have a hard time getting into recovery, but I guess it was particularly difficult for Bob because he was carrying such a load of guilt regarding you and your mother. Beatrice managed to trace some news of her through friends of friends, and it helped Bob a lot to know that she had done so well in Perth, and that she even had a good partner for some years before she died. But there was never much news of you."

"Well, the last thing I want is to trigger a relapse. Don't worry Laura, take as long as you like to think about it. And if it's not meant to be, I think I can live with that."

It wasn't until he had returned to the pub, collected his things and was on the way back to Daerley Green, that Jude began to feel the real emotional impact of the day's events.

1

For some reason he found it difficult to share the depth of his mixed feelings with Pippa. The puzzlement she expressed about Bob's continued drinking echoed his own; all the same he was irritated by it.

In fact, he was as restless as ever, if not more so, and then events made decisions for him. At breakfast time one morning Pippa answered the phone and handed it to Jude. "Someone called Rosanne, sounding as Aussie as they come."

She noted his startled look and the monosyllabic one-way conversation, which started with "Oh God!", then continued with a series, "Of course," "Yes I'll let you know," "Mm," and "Yes," ending with "I'll call you back tomorrow morning our time." He returned the receiver to the kitchen wall bracket, looked at Pippa and said "Bloody hell! Poor old Craig."

"Tell," Pippa said.

"Craig's been in a road accident. Quite bad. Broken bones. Rosanne is his current P.A. and sounds as if she might be a bit more. They need me back to keep the business going for a few weeks - one of our busiest times."

Of course it was the height of summer Down Under, and Christmas fast approaching.

"Obviously you must go. You can book on the computer."

"I hate leaving you."

Pippa smiled. "Yeah, and I'll miss you. But it's a good time. I still have a load to do here. You are at a loose end, in fact as useful as a distracted rabbit."

Jude didn't argue and booked himself on to a flight in two days' time. Pippa drove him to the airport. The house seemed horribly empty when she got home. But Aristotle was already installed on the bed.

She looked at him from the door. "He's right, you know. You *are* seriously weird." Then she went into the living room, sat down and made long lists. She had decided to clear the house as far as she could. There were still papers to go through, and these she collected together in her father's erstwhile study downstairs. There were a few good pieces of furniture which she arranged to have sold at auction. For the rest, she would call in a second hand dealer and tell him to take away all but some bare essentials for living.

It was Pippa's plan to stay in Daerley Green until the house was sold, and it was not a good time for selling. In an odd way it seemed to be the final act she could do for her parents: make sure that the new owners were suitable, though how she was to judge this she was not clear. In the meantime, she was thinking of renting a flat in the middle of the village and setting up a yoga class in the village hall. Beyond that she could not think.

The next day, she began to make enquiries about a short-term lease in the centre of the village. The folk of Daerley Green were more than average travellers and she soon heard through the grapevine of friends of friends a few times removed who were imminently going to seek warmer temperatures for the rest of the winter. They had a ground floor flat round a corner from the market place: three rooms, tiny kitchen, shower room - ample for her and Aristotle. And immediately available.

Aristotle was less convinced. For a week after she had moved in he kept disappearing and returning to his old home from which the neighbours scooped him up and brought him back; finally he realised that if he wanted food he had to stay with Pippa. Happily the three flats which had been made out of the one house shared a small garden. Happily, too, Aristotle had not forgotten the lessons learned from his youth when he discovered that the rural nights can hold unexpected terrors for a lone cat. He soon learned that a window in the kitchen left loose could be eased open. Pippa hoped that two-legged wanderers would not make the same discovery.

Jude rang to report that Craig had visibly cheered up when the reins had been taken out of his hands. He reckoned he would be away a couple of months, at the most three. Pippa put a notice about her yoga classes in the Post Office and within a fortnight had half a dozen enquiries. There was no point in starting before Christmas, so she booked one of the rooms in the community centre from the New Year,

142

and got out her yoga library to start serious preparation for the forthcoming classes.

As she worked out a number of routines, Aristotle sat on the windowsill watching, then washing himself and, in the process, achieving ever more elaborate contortions.

"OK," Pippa laughed, ruffling his head. "But you just try doing this," as she walked away carefully emphasising her two feet.

Accustomed to the greater space of Father's house, she had to admit that the confines of a smaller flat had its disadvantages. Aristotle, too, had problems in adapting. One evening as Pippa hauled a pile of her father's papers into the living room and plonked them on a small table by her favoured armchair, Aristotle made a tentative leap on to her lap, landed on top of the tottering pile of papers and knocked the lot, with table, to the floor.

"Oh really," Pippa exploded.

"Miaoul," protested Aristotle and fled into the bedroom.

It took a while to retrieve the scattered papers and there was no hope they were in the rough date order she had put them in. Pippa settled back in the armchair, took a folder off the top of the pile, and opened it. On the top was an envelope containing a letter.

Dearest Kirsti, it began. Pippa checked the date line: September, 1942

2

Dearest Kirsti - My heart goes out to you and the bad situation in which you find yourself. I wish my Annikki were here for she always knows the best thing to do. I have several messages through Red Cross she is safely in Sweden and that she and little Jooseppi are well. I pray God I can join them. But about you. Annikki was always afraid about Kalle's temper. Everyone knows that he has had a hard time, coming to live here after his Finnish mother died, then his German father away on the eastern front. But Annikki's family especially helped him and she hoped that when he married you things would be better and it was so for some time.

Pippa paused in her reading and stared across the room. So it was true that her grandfather had had a friendship with Kalle's wife all those years ago, when he first came to Finland. But how then did this letter come to be in her father's possession if grandfather had sent it to Kirsti? She sorted through the papers again and found an envelope addressed to her grandmother. Scrawled on the outside were the words: *To my sister: Letters of Josef Itäinen.* Presumably Matti had found them and sent them to Annikki. But why had her father translated them? Had he hoped she, Pippa, would find them one day? She would never know.

She read on : *The main problem is when he is drinking. Then his mind goes back and dwells on all the bad things in his life, especially this terrible war which has devastated the lives of so many in Finland, in Russia , in the world. But you do not need a history lesson, dear Kirsti. The fact is that he has become more and more sure it would have been better if he had returned to Germany, and perhaps it is true. He is always calling someone call Hans, but they speak in a German dialect I do not understand. We must be careful about meeting, you and I, because above all Kalle hates all Russians. I will think about all you have said and write to you again.*

Pippa spent some time searching for further messages until she found a very short one: *Thank you for your support. Kalle is going to Helsinki at the end of next week. He will be away for several days. I will wait for you.*

She read the correspondence through again. Did this mean that her grandfather had been having a secret affair with Kalle's wife? Could that have been the cause of a violent row between her own father and Kalle in 1970 resulting in the latter's death? She said a loud *"No!"* at the thought. Austere her father had certainly been, but he was no killer. He was a man who watered plants and fed wild birds. And even as she thought it, she knew it was a *non sequitur.* Anyway who was talking about affairs? Kirsti had simply asked Josef to go and see her.

As she shuffled through the papers looking for the rest of the correspondence, she noted that Aristotle had slunk back and was watching her from the windowsill.

"All right, Totty. We all make mistakes." He began washing his chest with long, languorous movements of head and tongue.

144

Her search only unearthed a few more letters, mostly expressing Kirsti's unhappiness and Josef's reassurance. A last letter from Kirsti explained how Josef came to be in possession of the correspondence. *My most Precious Friend,* she wrote *With great reluctance I am returning your letters. How often I have wished that I met you before I met Kalle, but it was not to be. And I know how you love your Annikki, and I love her too. But at the moment you are the only thing that gives my life meaning, and now I will not have even the comfort of your writing. Of course I agree that it is safer they are not where Kalle might find them.*

Pippa sat for a long time with these last expressions of Kirsti's distress between her fingers. What a difference between the generations. Could one imagine a modern-day Josef, his wife away, resisting the temptations so readily available? And what a relief it must have been to Kalle when his potential rival, and a hated Russian at that, had been removed from the scene. Had that been his main motif in making the authorities aware of Josef's presence? If so, her father would have been well aware of it with all this evidence in his possession. Had that provided a main motif for his return to Finland in 1970, to pay off an old score? Or to meet Grandfather Josef's old love? She remembered how hurt Margarit had been that Father had not deviated even a few hours from his main mission to travel north.

"It would be good to have Jude here to chew it over with," she told Aristotle. But when Jude rang that evening, it all seemed too complicated to explain.

"It's forty degrees plus," he told her. "Everyone's booking for somewhere cool. Except for the Poms who are arriving here in droves."

"They're forecasting snow here."

The snow began a couple of days later. When it showed no sign of abating, Pippa decided to move back to the house. It was essential to keep the place habitable for any potential buyers, and it was a relief to have more space. Aristotle was confused but pleased. When she opened the door to nudge him out, he looked at her as if to say *and how am I supposed to dig a hole in this stuff?* He would return through the cat flap very shortly after, presumably mission accomplished as he never made a mess in the house.

It snowed and it snowed. Because their small cul de sac was off a minor road off another minor road, no clearing was done except by the more vigorous members of the neighbourhood, and even then it was impossible to move the car from the drive. A couple of neighbours offered to clear the campervan of its thick white cloak, but Pippa had no immediate need to drive out of the village. Indeed everyone was being urged to avoid any road journey that was not absolutely necessary. And she could walk into the village centre.

The enforced restrictions provided an excellent opportunity to get down to some serious planning of her New Year yoga classes and to get herself in trim for them. These were occasionally interrupted by calls from Jude gasping in Queensland's highs of the upper 40s Celsius. Aristotle's sleep was likewise occasionally interrupted by being unceremoniously tipped out into the snow. On one occasion he did not return and Pippa spent a frenzied day scouring the snow for his paw marks. In the end she gave up trying to distinguish them among the Oxford Circus of animal tracks across the garden, until she finally noticed a set heading for Father's garden studio. She eventually found that Aristotle had somehow gained ingress - presumably sneaking in when she had gone to fetch some papers - and was asleep on one of the shelves in the cupboard; he was squashed awkwardly between the files, his nose resting on a pile of Father's notebooks.

Pippa stood watching him for a while, awash with relief. When he tried to stretch and found he couldn't, Aristotle peered at her through slitty eyes.

"You did that purposely to worry me," she told him. "You monster."

"*Miaoul*," said Aristotle.

It was a curious Christmas. Robin and Marion had planned to come and spend it with her but, after horrendous newspaper reports of motorists trapped overnight in their cars, they all agreed that it was an unnecessary risk. Pippa did a foray into Banbury and bought some unaccustomed titbits for herself and for Aristotle and they both stuffed themselves into a stupor in front of a succession of television repeats. Jude rang three times on Christmas Day. On the last call he announced that Craig was making great progress and should be back in harness around the end of January.

"Probably coming home in Feb," he said.

146

It was the best Christmas present she could have had, especially the way he referred to 'coming home'.

3

On Boxing Day she put on a pair of boots and trudged down to Whirling Wood on the outskirts of the village. From the trampled snow it was clear that quite a few people had braved the conditions and over a number of days the snow had begun to melt then re-frozen, then been covered by fresh layers. Walking was hard work, but the wood was beautiful, the skeleton shapes of the trees at their best, and a noisy throng of fieldfare squabbling up in the trees. It was a steep slippery pull back up to the village and she let herself into the house, stamping cold feet and chiding Aristotle for being unable to put the kettle on.

And then for no reason she could think of, she sat down in the living room fielding a flood of memories of Christmases past, all of them silent, none of them really memorable except for their immemorability. She and mother had made the best of it, usually indeed going for a tramp down to Whirling Wood. No doubt that was what had triggered the nostalgia. Father merely sat in his study, writing or doing some research. Once she had wondered how on earth her parents had come together. It was only as she grew up that she began to understand. Mother, a bright and intelligent child, had escaped from the tedium of a house in which culture was regarded as only suitable for those with time on their hands. Pippa's grandparents had been salt-of-the-earth country folk, the product of generations of salt-of-the-earth country folk. They were baffled by thelr only daughter Frances and the ideas for self improvement that had finally drawn her to London. There she had got a job as a typist, then secretary, and taken evening classes to fill the woeful gaps in her knowledge. And in a library one evening she had met Joseph Eastman, looking for a researcher and quickly recognising her bright intelligence.

Had she ever regretted it? According to her mother, no. She was in thrall to Joseph Eastwood's brain, had continued to help him with his research until her life had been taken over by the demands of first Robin, then Pippa. In any case, she had made it clear that there

147

had been great changes in Joseph after his visit to Finland in 1970. Prior to that he could have moods that were positively skittish, though it was hard to imagine. As the children grew up and needed her less. Mother had developed her own skills as Pippa had discovered when she found her small but thriving greetings cards self-publishing enterprise. By then it was too late to do anything about her own contribution to her mother's isolation. If she had not headed for Australia at the first opportunity, her mother's path would undoubtedly have been less lonely. But the young do not usually think of such things.

Pippa thought back to those few days she had spent with her mother before she died. She had never given it much thought, except to feel grateful that at least she had been there. But now she realised what a precious time it had been and the sense of companionship that had grown in the lengthening silences. Who was it that had said the most important thing you can do for another person is to help them die? Christ? Mohammed? Buddha? Probably all of them. Looking back, she thought in some small way she had helped her mother to die. Undoubtedly she had helped her father even more, only he would not have been aware of it.

Something soft and warm intruded itself on to her lap.

"Oh Aristotle," Pippa said, and buried her face in his fur and cried as she had not yet cried since either of her parent's deaths. The large cat circled her lap, alternately rubbing the 'good' side and the bumpy side of his head against her.

Her mobile rang and she reached out for it. Jude.

"I wish you were here," she said because it was the first thing in her mind.

"So do I." A small pause. "Are you OK? You sound odd."

"Feeling a bit sorry for myself. Just sitting here thinking back over the past."

"Try thinking about the future. You can do something about that. For a start, how are the yoga class bookings going?"

"Mm, ten enquiries so far. I'd say six of them were serious. A couple want private lessons, and the other four hopefully will provide

148

a nucleus for a class, though I'll need more than that to make it viable long term."

"Where will you do the private ones?"

"Here. It makes sense as I have spare mats and blocks. Not sure what I'll do when I move back into the centre of the village. You couldn't swing a cat in that flat, not even Aristotle."

"Well, you'll need to keep the house warm for prospective buyers, so why not keep the private lessons there? You could have the heating on low and boost it a couple of hours before classes?"

"Yeah, I think you're right. Pippa giggled. "Do you know, Jude, that you and Aristotle have a lot in common?"

"Huh?"

"Seriously. You both intuitively seem to know when I need cheering up."

"For heavens' sake."

"He's curled up on my lap as we speak. Though I think I'd rather it were you."

"Now you're talking," Jude said. Then he went on, "There's something else I want to talk to you about. You may have read about floods in Queensland. I'm in Brisbane at the moment, staying with one of Craig's friends who runs a shop here. Even if the floods reach here, I am perfectly safe, and I don't want you to panic. I have more friends who live inland on higher ground so can always stay with them. And lots of people are keeping an eye on the cottage in Murwillumbah."

"Is there anything I can do?" What a stupid question.

"Yes, don't panic. It's created mayhem for the business. Everyone's cancelling trips here and wanting to get away. I may have to stay a bit longer to sort things out."

It was about the last thing Pippa wanted to hear just then. She ran her fingers through Aristotle's fur a bit too vigorously. "Miaoul," he protested.

"What's that?"

149

"Aristotle says hello and stay safe." Pippa gripped her mobile. "And I say it, too. I need you, Jude." Had she ever said that to anyone before?

"The feeling is mutual," Jude said in a voice that sounded just a little wobbly. "I'll ring again tomorrow."

Oxfordshire/Weymouth : January 2011

1

Friends invited Pippa to see the New Year in with them and she accepted. There had been enough introspection. The friends lived in a flat overlooking the market place and as midnight approached they went to join most of the rest of the village holding hands in a multi-layered circle. Someone let off firecrackers and when Pippa got home she found Aristotle burrowed under the bedclothes.

In due course he came to sit on her stomach as she lay on her back, hands behind head, staring at the ceiling and noticing some cobwebs as she began to plan 2011. Nothing further could be done with regard to her father's history until Kirsti had recovered from her operation. There was little she could do concerning Jude and his Dad until the former returned from Australia. The only thing she could and should get on with were her yoga classes and the sale of the house. Not much she could do about the house, either, which was in the hands of Hedges and Waters. What a splendidly rural name. Which reminded her that a couple from Hampshire were coming to view the place in a few days if they could get here. So the best idea was to focus on the yoga classes.

The room in the Community Centre was booked for Monday and Thursday mornings, and she had worked out an outline for each class. They were all beginners which helped. All women, but that was par for the course. For some reason Brits had decided that yoga was women's stuff, contrary to all evidence of its long history. Quite different from her classes in Oz where she had several men. Odd.

She would have to give serious thought to the viability of running two classes a week though. It was well known that exercise provided one of the most popular of good intentions among New Year resolutions which often did not survive the month of January. It might have been better if she had made her charges for a course of so many lessons rather than charging on a pay-as-you-go basis. Well, too late now. Anyway, in the immediate future money was not a major problem. She and Robin would split the proceeds of the sale of the house between them. Robin had insisted that she should take a higher share of Father's investments and their income because of the time she had devoted to him, and she had allowed herself to be persuaded. Those last months had not been easy.

. By now, with the more valuable pieces of furniture sold and most of the remainder taken by second hand dealers, the house felt like a hollow shell, except for the kitchen, study, living room and the dining room, the latter now turned into their bedroom. Upstairs the emptiness echoed. Throughout the proceedings, Aristotle disappeared temporarily and when they were over, he found a box formerly used for storing root vegetables in the conservatory and claimed it as his own. It was only gradually that he re-established his position at the end of the bed.

But she was allowing her mind to butterfly, and mindfulness of the moment was one of the first tenets of yoga training. She examined her state of being: back slightly stiff from lack of movement, very warm patch on her stomach created by Aristotle's presence, and a bit of a blank in her mind concerning the yoga classes. Very gently she eased Aristotle off his perch, got out of bed, did several stretches, and headed off to Father's study where she kept her yoga books and notes.

2

Pippa did not take to the couple from Hampshire who arrived with the man from Hedges and Waters soon after breakfast a few days later. They did not look like housing estate people - not even highly desirable executive housing estate people - as Mrs. Hampshire made quite clear early on.

"We've decided," she explained to Pippa as they stood in the living room, "that we want to do a lot of travelling while we are still young enough to enjoy it."

Pippa indicated that she agreed this was a good idea.

"So," Mrs Hampshire continued, "We are selling our home, which is rather a fine listed building, and plan to spend any proceeds on all the travelling we have not had time to do while we were building up the business."

Pippa did not ask what the business was but said it seemed a pity they would not be spending so much time in Daerley Green which was really a very nice community.

"Oh I'm sure it is," Mrs.H. said. "But you know we are not really community people."

Pippa began to wonder what kind of people they really were.

"There is, of course, an excellent golf club only a few miles away," the man from Hedges and Waters said. He obviously knew more about them than Pippa did.

They toured the downstairs and the garden. Mr. Hampshire made nice noises about the condition of the house and the upkeep of the garden. It was on the way upstairs that Mrs. Hampshire began to sneeze uncontrollably. When at last she could speak, she said "Do you by any chance have a cat?" at which point Aristotle came out of an empty room to peer at them through the banisters. *You're a devil cat,* thought Pippa. *So you don't like them either.*

Mrs. H. gave a little shriek. "Oh dear, I am *so* allergic to cats. We'll have to go Robert."

"Perhaps you could come back another time," the man from Hedges and Waters said, not very hopefully.

Six people turned up for Pippa's first Monday morning yoga class, including one man. He was someone called Pete whom Jude had befriended at The Trumpet and who came along to see what it was all about, as well as get news of Jude. Ages ranged from late teens to late seventies and much of the lesson was spent discussing the concepts of yoga and how they could be applied to the individual. Two of the older ladies had physical limitations and it was agreed that Pippa would devote her Thursday class to those who preferred to practise the postures in a sitting position. News of this spread quickly and in the following three days she had four more enquires from three women and another man currently living in Freshfields, a retirement home on the other side of the village.

It would mean extra work, adapting the postures to sitting positions, but Pippa was delighted. Pete, who was currently out of work, offered to pick up the 'oldies' for their Thursday session. The two private pupils came at different times on a Wednesday. By the end of January, Pippa had settled into a comfortable routine, her lessons planned ahead for the foreseeable future, and both Monday and Thursday classes attended by a steady hard core of six each. Aristotle took quite an interest in the procedures, and having checked that no one was allergic to cats, Pippa allowed him to stay on his windowsill perch.

And something else had happened.

It was Pete who asked her casually one day whether she was on Facebook. Pippa had never been very keen on social networking on the internet and said so.

"May be you should think about it," Pete said. "A lot of it is rubbish I agree. I mean who cares what anyone has had for breakfast? But with something like yoga, I'd have thought you could get in touch with other teachers, swap ideas, may be even get up some more local interest."

Pippa said she would think about it, then put it out of her mind until one week-end when she had finished checking her email. Perhaps Pete was right. After all, it had helped Jude trace his Dad. No harm in looking anyway. Registering was straight forward enough and having done so she entered 'yoga classes' in the search panel which led her to an option allowing her to enter details of her own. Pippa brooded over this for a moment before deciding it needed more thought prior to announcing these to the world.

For a while she amused herself entering different subjects or names into the search panel. To her amusement she found Robin's page. Funny, he had never said. But then informing his sister was probably not the first thing that would have entered his mind. She glanced at the messages on his wall (wall? as in graffiti?) and then added to them *Hello Brother - Jude is in Oz at the moment. Give me a call.*

And then she remembered Jude's comment about his father's page on Facebook. In view of his lack of eyesight presumably Laura checked it and kept it up to date. Indeed, there was a picture of the two them: she had binoculars clamped to her eyes and he had a hand on her shoulder.

For a moment Pippa hesitated before reading the messages. It felt rather like eavesdropping, then she realised the absurdity of the thought. The messages would not be there for all to see unless it was intended. A lot of them were exchanges with fellow bird watchers amongst which references to booming bitterns featured prominently. There was also an amazed reference to something called a lesser yellowlegs that had drifted across from North America to a local sewage farm. And then Pippa's searching gaze homed in on the name Jimmie.

The message was from someone called Dorrie. It expressed delight at Bob's recovery, said it was sure his first wife Anne would have been thrilled too, and ended up with *I often wonder what happened to young Jimmie.* The response from Bob was *I used to wonder daily, but now I guess it is better to get on with what remains of my life and leave him to his.*

Jimmie? Oh, of course, that was Jude's real first name.

3

Pippa read the messages through several times. The latest date line was quite recent - in the New Year of 2011, that time for past regrets and new beginnings. Jude would not have seen it. She scrolled back through earlier messages, spasmodic over the passed years, until she reached the first one: *Bob, what an amazing surprise. I was thrilled to get your message and learn that you are recovering. Yes, it's a shame that Anne did not live to see it, but in the end you were better apart. I guess poor little Jimmie was the one to be most affected and I pray he has found his way through.* Pippa paused in her reading, amazed that such matters were being discussed so openly, then reading back she noted that nowhere was it mentioned from what Bob was recovering. Dorrie continued *It is understandable that you should wait until you felt secure in your recovery before you contacted old friends, and I am so glad that you regard me as one. I'm afraid it is too late for me to think about a trip to Europe, but perhaps you and Laura might think about coming here.*

Pippa scrolled back to Dorrie's most recent entry: *I often wonder what happened to young Jimmie.* Then she clicked on Dorrie's rather blurred photograph and was immediately taken to the older woman's profile. It confirmed that she, too, was a Ten Pound Pom, had arrived in 1966, in the same year as Jude had been born. Later she had become an English teacher and moved around the Continent, now living in Western Australia. Had she been in touch with Anne, Jude's Mum, before she died? Among her details was her email address. Pippa paused for another few moments, then clicked on it and started:

Dear Dorrie - You won't know me, but I am a friend of Jimmie - or rather Jude as he calls himself now. A rather special friend, I hope. How we came to meet is a very long story, but I have just seen your message to his Dad, Bob, and I wanted you to know that Jude is OK. He and I have been living together for some years, first of all in Australia where we met, and currently in the UK. Jude did try and make contact with his Dad but only recently learned that he is in recovery and also blind. He is afraid it might upset him if he suddenly turns up, so we are not rushing into things. In the meantime we are doing some research into my father's life. He died some months ago, and it is an even more complicated story which I will tell you if you are interested. Jude has spoken about you and how much his Mum depended on your friendship. Did you get to meet her when you moved to W.A.? With best wishes, Pippa Eastman.

Pippa glanced at her watch. It was nine o'clock in the evening - the early hours of tomorrow in Western Oz.

A reply was waiting for her as soon as she booted up next morning. *Dear Pippa - you will never know what joy you have brought to this old heart to know that Jimmie/Jude is well and has such a lovely-sounding partner. Please tell me more: how he looks and what he is doing. And the long story about your father, too. I have plenty of time on my hands these days. I attach a photo which may amuse you. Your new friend, Dorrie.*

Pippa clicked on the attachment. It was of a young woman holding up a baby. The young woman had fluffy auburn hair and was not Jude's mother as she had seen pictures of her; so it must be Dorrie.

The baby had its eyes wide open in surprise and a little rosebud mouth shaped in a perfect 'o'. Presumably Jude, though she could not pretend to find a resemblance.

She spent much of the morning replying to Dorrie's message. It was surprisingly therapeutic as well as quite useful in putting her own thoughts in order. She also realised how far they had come in uncovering her father's and grandfather's stories, though she did not dwell too long on grandfather Josef's final days in Fallingbostel. Once she had sent the email off, she checked through her notes for the following week's yoga classes. One of her private pupils was doing particularly well and she spent some time adapting some of the more advanced poses so that they would stretch her capabilities. One of her Thursday sitting class had also progressed sufficiently to join the Monday class. It was not that she had achieved phenomenal physical progress but had overcome some mental blocks which had prevented her from doing what she was capable of doing. Yoga was as much a question of flexibility of mind as of body.

A week after her first contact with Dorrie, Pippa had a message from her that gave her a lot to think about. *I hesitated about sending this,* Dorrie wrote, *but I think you and especially Jude have a right to know. His Dad is not too good. Laura sometimes puts things in her emails that I guess Bob has not entirely agreed on. Mind you, I have had to learn to read between the lines. It must be something to do with the Stiff Upper Lip thing you Brits have that you can't come right out and say you're not having an easy time. I gather Bob has had a fall. Laura says it is nothing serious, but I gather he is housebound so I guess it is serious enough. From your emails I gather that Jude is away. It might be an idea, if he is not too far away, to suggest he makes himself available to return if necessary. If he, too, could only loosen that Stiff Upper Lip, I know Bob would rejoice at the thought of seeing his son again.*

Pippa read it through a couple of times, then sat staring out at the garden beyond Aristotle's silhouette on the windowsill, his tail resting on a radiator.. The snow had gone except for the odd scrap where the winter sun could not reach.. The garden's drabness matched her mood.

"So now what am I supposed to do, Totty?" Aristotle's tail flickered in recognition of even this travesty of his name.

157

She felt suddenly angry with Jude for having put her in his position, but it was a brief anger for the absurdity of such blame was instantly apparent. It just felt a terrible responsibility. But it was impossible properly to judge the situation on the basis of supposed facts acquired third hand from the other side of the world.

There really was only one sensible thing to do. It would be at least four weeks before Jude would be back in the UK. If there truly were a crisis, she was sure he would return earlier, but she could not put that sort of pressure on him if Dorrie's assessment as to Bob's condition was inaccurate. She checked her diary. There were yoga classes on Monday, Wednesday and Thursday of the following week. If she left immediately after the Thursday morning class, she could be in Weymouth by early evening. The neighbours would look after Aristotle and she could be back by Friday lunch time.

Over the next few days, the enormity of her decision and what it might lead to became ever more daunting. But she really could not think of an alternative.

4

It felt very odd to be driving the campervan without Jude. Pippa worked out a cross-country route which eventually brought her to the A303 for a straight run through to Dorset. She had decided against using a campsite at this time of the year and found a bed-and-breakfast place a short walk from the harbour. On the drive down she had thought through the various options of how to make contact with Bob or Laura. Preferably Laura. The only solution she had come up with by the time she had settled into her room was to go for a drink at The Mariner, the pub near the Jamiesons' home.

The bar was relatively quiet on that mid-week early evening except for an intermittent trickle of people coming in to order fish-and-chips, the pub's take-away speciality on a Thursday. Pippa ordered a glass of red wine, then asked "I wonder if you know some acquaintances of mine, Bob and Laura Jamieson?"

"Yes. In fact, Laura's likely to be in at any moment. She usually comes in for Thursday's fish and chips, especially since Bob since been poorly."

"I do hope he's improving."

"You can ask her yourself." The barman was grinning at someone beyond her. "Good evening Laura. How's the old man? This lady has been asking after you both."

Suddenly it was all happening too quickly. Pippa recognised the slim older woman immediately, found herself looking into her questioning grey gaze. "Oh, it's you!" was the old lady's unexpected response. "Your partner was here only a few days ago." Well, a month ago actually.

Pippa gave a small laugh. "Sorry, it must almost seem as though we are stalking you. But there *is* a reason."

The barman interrupted. "I assume you want the usual, Laura. Be ready in a few minutes."

"Thanks, Jim. Just for me this time and I may as well have it here. Bob's meeting an old mate this evening."

"Could you come and share my table," Pippa said. "And I'll try and explain why we keep popping up in your life. I was really sorry to learn your husband was crook …. er, poorly. These Aussie expressions are contagious."

Laura smiled. "Aren't they just! My first husband must be having a quiet a chuckle wherever he is now. I used to be a bit of a pedant when it came to the purity of the English language - as if there ever were only just one! But how did you know Bob was poorly? He was all right except for a bit of a cold when your Jude was here."

"I had an email from Dorrie."

"Ah Dorrie. What a whirligig of a world we do live in!" Laura said wryly.

Well, at least she had a sense of humour.

Pippa chose a table in an alcove away from the door and the bar. Settling herself, she said, "The fact is that Jude was called back to Australia. Something to do with his business. Of course he had told me about his visit here and about meeting you. It left him quite … quite mixed and unsure of what was the best thing to do. So in a way the small crisis in Australia was well timed. I think he told you something about the research we've been doing into my father's past, and our visit to Finland?"

159

"Yes, he did. I gather your grandfather was a Russian and married a Finnish girl. Quite an unusual mixture," Laura said.

"He may not have told you, though, that I was also trying to prove my father was not responsible for the murder of a rather unpleasant man."

"No he didn't tell me that. I probably didn't give him much chance with all the things I was unloading on him. I imagine he gave you an idea of all that?"

Pippa nodded. "And to tell the truth, I probably wasn't very helpful. I just couldn't … still can't understand why his father went on drinking when it always got him into so much trouble."

"Most people have a problem with that." Laura put her hands on the table and sat staring down at them as if they held the answer. "Put it like this. Imagine, your every nerve is screaming for release from anguish and the only thing you know will achieve this for certain is the one thing that caused the anguish in the first place."

"It's very hard to imagine."

"Yes, because it doesn't happen from one day to the next. For most people it's a gradual process: initially a harmless sop to help with a problem, to help you sleep, to get you through a difficult patch ….." Laura was so absorbed in her attempt to get her point over that she did not hear the barman call, "Grub's up, Laura." Pippa went to fetch it, and as she put it in front of her elderly companion, she looked up startled. "I *am* sorry Pippa. It is so very difficult to explain."

"Well, you're doing rather a good job, so eat your fish and chips and take it for granted that I sort of understand. And while you eat, I'll give you a resume of our Finnish adventure." She had just about completed the tale when Laura pushed her plate away and said, "Can't manage any more."

"Well, have a break and tell me how you and Bob first came together. It was at a meeting I understand."

"That's right. Bob had been living rough for years and in and out of hospital, when his ever-to-be-blessed Aunt Bee put him in touch with one of our group, who brought him along to a meeting."

"So what happened?"

160

"He was in a very bad state I gather. I was away and didn't meet him for a couple of weeks, and he was still in a rough state then. Argued a lot and thought we were all talking rubbish. Then he stopped coming for a while, and came back even worse. It was terrible. Then one evening he burst into tears and said he'd had enough."

"So you tamed him?"

"Well, we all did.. But I'd retired and probably had more time to listen than the others. He got into the habit of coming round to my place for coffee, then staying on. He had a lot of stuff from his past to work through, including the way he treated Jude's mother and the fact that he had completely lost touch with his son."

Pippa was silent, absorbing what Laura was telling her and thinking how strange it was to be learning such things from a near-stranger.

"He never tried to make contact?"

"He did eventually get in touch with Dorrie and learned Jude's mother was OK, had a partner, and Jude himself was OK. So he made the decision to leave them in peace. But I know it still bugs him from time to time."

"Do you think he's ready to meet Jude."

"I don't know, Pippa. I really don't know. May be I'm being over-protective, but the trouble is I know how bad it can be if you go back out there." She paused a moment, then gave Pippa one of her direct looks and said, "How would you feel about coming to one of our meetings?"

To be truthful, she felt aghast. "But won't they mind?"

"No. We have open meetings for relatives or people who are interested, and there's one tonight. I came here early to get something to eat first. You would be made very welcome. It might help Jude to understand better."

Pippa made a decision. "OK," she said.

The meeting began at eight o'clock. Laura arranged to pick Pippa up after she had had something to eat, but it turned out she wasn't feeling very hungry either and struggled through half a lasagne. She really wasn't sure what to expect, but whatever it was it wasn't the group of people of all types and ages she saw chattering noisily in the church hall where the meeting was held. One or two people glanced at her curiously and smiled. Laura announced she'd brought a friend of Bob's who 'isn't once of us. She's a civilian.' 'It's what we call non-alkies' she explained to Pippa who hadn't yet got used to this spritely old lady being one them.

She went on to explain that one of those present would lead the meeting, talking about his or her own story, and then it would be open for anyone to chip in. The speaker turned out to be a man in young middle age, perhaps about her own age. Pippa's eyes widened as his story unfolded. It was hard to believe that someone who had been through lost jobs, a broken marriage, a succession of hospitals and even a spell in prison could be sitting there looking so cheerful and 'normal'. Though she was now beginning to wonder what 'normal' was.

In due course various people responded to the man's experiences, some clearly identifying with them, others not but still sharing the hell of isolation he had gone through. Someone asked Pippa if she wanted to say something.

"At the moment I'm busy being gob-smacked," she said. "But one thing I don't understand is that you all talk of the first drink as doing the damage, when it seems to be the tenth or umpteenth."

There was a murmur of appreciation round the room. "That's the mistake we've all made in our time," the speaker responded. "If you think about it, there can't be an umpteenth if there isn't a first."

Pippa thought about that during the rest of the meeting and as she drove back to Weymouth, having promised to keep in touch with Laura. What on earth Jude would make of it all she could not imagine.

162

Oxfordshire : early February 2011

1

"Where the hell *are* you?" he demanded in a string of ever-more urgent-sounding messages on the answer-phone.

She caught him on his mobile as he was returning from visiting Craig in hospital.

"I needed a break and spent a night away with a friend."

"Hm." Thankfully he did not ask which friend, but returned to an old hobby horse. "If only you'd get a mobile, there wouldn't be a problem."

"OK, OK. I give in. I loathe the nasty, intrusive things, but I give in."

"They do have an 'off' button."

"OK, OK. How's Craig? And how are the floods?"

Jude's tone lifted. "Craig is doing great. And we had a bad couple of days with the water rising, but now we hear we're getting compensation and we should be back to normal within weeks."

"Was there a lot of damage?"

"No, there was a brilliant forewarning system, and we managed to move all the computers and files to the upper floor before the water got into the ground floor."

"Presumably you'll have to stay until the office is up and running again?"

"No, my sweet. That's what I've been bursting to tell you for the last twenty-four hours. Craig has made such good progress that all he wants is to get back into action. Of course, he'll have to take it easy, but I suspect Rosanne will make quite sure that happens. No doubt those two are an item. I feel quite envious."

"I thought we were an item."

"Yeah, but several thousand miles apart makes for a pretty fragmented item."

"There is a remedy."

Yeah," Jude said again. "And I'm taking it. I'm booked to get back on Tuesday week."

When she had put the phone down, Pippa grabbed Aristotle and waltzed round the room with him, ignoring protesting *miaouls*. When she released him, he fled under the furthest corner of the bed. Pippa folded herself into a meditation pose and went through a series of breathing exercises to calm her mind and focus her concentration for the impending class. It was not until after it was over and she had returned the furniture to its normal position that she allowed herself to lounge in an armchair in a distinctly non-yogic sprawl and think about Jude's revelation.

The news of his imminent return was fantastic. She had been aware of missing him dreadfully, but even then the level of her joy at the news of his unexpectedly early return took her by surprise. Jude, she realised, had now become a major, perhaps the most major thing that had happened to her. It brought its own complications, most immediate of which was the way she had deceived him however much it might be in his own interests. She knew instinctively that he would not take kindly to her attempt to mastermind his affairs, however good her intentions. She also knew that trying to cover it up would set the worst possible precedent for their future relationship. There had been far too much covering-up in her life or, when that failed, escape in order to avoid whatever the conflict might be. This time it had to be faced.

And it was then that she was struck by the realisation that there really was no one with whom she could sit down and freely discuss this dilemma. Back in New South Wales and Queensland there were one or two Aussie women friends, but even they were more likely than not to shy away from what they might regard as a Serious Problem. Or if they weren't, she had never needed to put it to the test. Her time in the UK had been spent being a dutiful daughter or a professional adviser. Her brother Robin would probably say impatiently, *why don't you just come out with it? That's what sharing partnerships are for.* And he would be right. Heaven knows, by now they'd had a great deal to share.

164

But she still did not relish the prospect.

Jude's arrival was at the usual unsocial hour of many long distance arrivals in London Airport. She identified a camp site within a few miles of it and arrived in the early evening of the day before. It was impossible to sleep with her mental preoccupations with her visit to Weymouth and what Jude's reaction would be to it. So perhaps it was not so surprising that after the first vigorously satisfying hug, she avoided the issue by bombarding him with a barrage of questions on his journey and his time in Australia. Finally, he broke in with "Whoa, whoa. Let's rein in that runaway mind of yours and start again somewhere a bit more peaceful." Pippa suggested a break for coffee, but he was anxious to get home and by the time they had retrieved the car and rejoined the motorway, the build-up of traffic was enough to require her full concentration.

By then, Jude was glad enough to give her a run-down of all that had happened, how well Craig had recovered from the accident, how business was beginning to pick up, and a graphic account of watching the flood waters rise up the steps and into their office.

"It must have been terrifying."

"Well, worrying certainly. But the authorities did a really good job of keeping us all in the picture, so we had good time to get all the essentials out of harm's way." By now they had switched from the M4 to the M40 and were on the borders of Oxfordshire. Jude looked out at the winter landscape, gave a grunt of satisfaction, and said, "Your turn now."

"Yes, well, it wasn't the most joyful Christmas I've ever had and the weather as you know broke a lot of records. Aristotle hated it."

"Never mind about Aristotle. What about you? Something's wrong."

"What makes you say that?"

"When you babble like that, like you did at the airport, it's usually a cover-up for something."

Pippa thought, *when you are close to someone you get to recognise things like that. Worry made her babble, it made Jude clam up.* "Yes, well, like I said it hasn't exactly been a fun time. Though the yoga classes are going really well."

"Pippa!"

She turned to look at him briefly. He looked good and she was so glad to have him back. "Yes," she admitted. "There is something, but I need a bit of time to explain."

"I'll give you time," Jude said.

2

In the end the decision was taken out of her hands. Once home, they dumped Jude's luggage in the hall, had breakfast and were heading for the bedroom when Jude said, "Just check the answering machine." It had always been one of the first things he did when he returned from an absence.

Apparently there was a message. Jude listened to it, then re-played it with a puzzled frown. Then he pressed the re-play button again and handed Pippa the receiver. "Someone called you last night."

He continued to watch her as she listened to a pleasant, half-familiar voice saying "Hello Pippa. Laura here. I so enjoyed talking to you and it was brave of you to come to the meeting. I can't remember when you said your Jude was getting back, but the more I think about it the more sure I am that it would be good if he and I had a similar chat. Give me a call and we'll fix a date when he's back."

Pippa went on staring at her feet. "Oh," she said.

"Yes, 'oh'," repeated Jude. "So that's what you've been putting off telling me about." He took her by the hand, back into the kitchen.

So, sitting at the breakfast bar, looking him straight in the eye, Pippa gave him an account of how she had made contact with Dorrie, learned the news of Bob's affliction, made the decision to go to Weymouth.

Jude interrupted briefly with "Fancy, dear old Dorrie," "You poor lamb, what a decision for you to have to make," and finally, "That was pretty brave of you."

"That's not all. I went with Laura to one of those meetings of the self-help group they both belong to. That was pretty gob-smacking to realise Laura was in recovery too. But I must say I have a bit of a different take on it after going to that meeting."

Jude took her hands in his. "That was amazingly brave of you to do that."

Pippa stared at him. "You mean, you're not mad at me?"

"For trying to be helpful?"

"So what will you do?"

"I'll go and see Laura, of course."

Then Pippa took his hand and led him upstairs where they made love and she cried great sobs until all tension had been wept away. That evening they discussed future plans, changed them, re-discussed them and changed them again. It was clearly too early to return to Finland which would currently be in the depths of winter and Kirsti would not have had sufficient time to recover from major surgery. Jude seemed set on continuing Pippa's quest to clear her father's name.

He tried to explain. "I'm sure there is going to be a good outcome to this. With my Dad, with all he's been through, I'm not so convinced that it's a wise idea to pursue it any further."

"You mean I should have left well alone?"

"No. Maybe, yes. I don't know. I'm very muddled. Not even sure it's right for me, let alone him. That's why the only immediate solution is for me to go back to Weymouth and get a feel of the situation for myself.." He hesitated before adding, "And I think on this occasion I should do it alone."

Pippa agreed, adding "Though it would make sense to check things out with Laura first." She wondered why things needed to get so complicated just when they were on the verge of being the best they had ever been? She had a thought. "How about Dorrie?. How about asking her? She's been in touch with your Dad, knew him in the old days. Her opinion would be worth a lot. Anyway now I've come clean, I can show you her emails, including a picture of her."

She went off to rummage in a drawer and came back with some print-outs and the photograph. Jude studied the latter for a long time.

When he looked up his expression was warm with affection. "Apart from the grey hair and a few wrinkles, she hasn't changed. It must have been an awful pain having to keep an eye on me during term time, while Mother was doing her course or until she got back from work. Dorrie - she was Auntie Dorrie then - taught me all sorts of card games, and of course she often let me win."

"She never married?"

"There was a guy, but like Dad he wasn't too keen on commitment and disappeared before things got too heavy. I think Mother gave her a lot of support at the time."

"Did they keep in touch once you'd moved to Perth?"

"Oh yes, she visited us several times. But I'm ashamed to say that by then I was part of gang and loath to miss out on the action."

"And what about Bev the Beaut?"

"She eventually headed for Queensland, married a Pommie of all things and, after a brief pang of regret, I forgot all about her." He paused. "Anyway Dorrie will have the latest news about her, for sure."

They waited until next day when they could choose a time when it would be a sensible hour in the evening in Western Australia. Pippa dialled the number and said, "Hi Dorrie. This is Pippa ringing from England. There's someone here who would like to speak to you."

She handed the cordless receiver to Jude who said in a wobbly voice, "Hello Dorrie. This is Jude … Jimmie here. Pippa told me you've made contact and I can't believe I'm talking to you after all these years." There was a pause while he listened for a long while during which Pippa slipped out of the room. From the living room she heard the intermittent murmur of Jude's voice, the long pauses while he listened. Then there was an explosive "Good God, but that's only a few miles from here. Twins did you say? Of course we'll look them up." After another silence, the door opened and Jude came in still holding the receiver. Into it he said, "Mm. It's got rather complicated. Pippa thinks I should make contact, but frankly I'm scared: not just of what it might do to Dad after all these years, but what it might do to me." There was another longer pause before he said, with a slight laugh in his voice. "You could be right, Dorrie. You always were the wise one. Yes, I'll pass you back to her."

To Pippa, Dorrie said, "Jimmie … Jude … can tell you what all that was about. I just wanted to repeat what I said to him: when you're back in this part of the world there'll be serious trouble if you don't look me up."

"Try keeping me away," Pippa said. "I just can't wait to hear what your Jimmie got up to when he was a little boy." She rang off and handed the receiver back to Jude. "Well? So why is Dorrie the wise one?"

"She pointed out that one of the reasons I'm putting off seeing Dad is that I'm worried the meeting won't come up to expectations I've been harbouring in my subconscious all these years." He grimaced. "Some people might think that was psychobabble."

"Others might call it the voice of experience. And what did she have to say about Bev the Beaut?"

"Well, that's amazing. She's actually living only a few miles from here on the outskirts of Woodstock. I've got her number and email address. Married with twins. Teaching somewhere in Oxford. Husband into marketing and away a lot."

"So presumably that will be our next social engagement?"

3

That evening they sent off an email: *Dear Beverley - I hope you have retained some not-too-unpleasant memories of a small boy called Jimmie back in Adelaide. He remembers you very well. He has changed his name to Jude and is now rather large, and temporarily living just a few miles away at Daerley Green with a lovely lady called Pippa Eastman. Dorrie Grey gave us your email address and we'd love to come and see you. Yours, Jimmie/Jude.*

The reply came within the hour: *Dear Jimmie/Jude - How could I forget such a little horror? Seriously, I remember we had a lot of fun, even though I never forgave you for that awful nickname you gave me. It's hard to think of you as a big boy with a lovely lady, but I'd love to see you both. How about a light supper next Wednesday? The boys will be at football, and my Dan is away at a seminar, so it will be peaceful. With affectionate memories, Beverley.*

169

The cottage was at the junction of two minor roads near a bridge, about three miles outside Woodstock. It looked like an old cottage with some new appendages, not yet completely finished. In the yard at its side some free range chickens scratched about, and in a field opposite a small flock of sheep peacefully grazed.

Jude surveyed the scene with interest. "Must say I never thought of Bev as a typical Good Lifer."

The cottage door opened. Their hostess had clearly been looking out for them. Pippa found herself being appraised by enquiring eyes in a squareish face, framed by thick chestnut hair in which there were a few flecks of grey. "Good Lord," said a voice with an unmistakeable Aussie twang. "You have grown into a big boy, and you do have a lovely lady."

The cottage was low-ceilinged, small-windowed, cluttered, cosy. Beverley waved an arm at the untidy evidence of male youth. "Order is impossible in the presence of young teenage boys," she said, "Even if I were an orderly person, which you might not remember I am not, but dear Dorrie could certainly confirm."

"I only remember being terribly in love with you," Jude said solemnly.

"A state which you quickly outgrew I seem to remember," Beverley smiled. "Or at least you had by the time I visited you in Perth by which time you had other more absorbing interests. But let's not bore poor Pippa with that. Come in and crack a bottle of wine."

The cottage door opened into a kitchen from which a short passage led into an equally cluttered and cosy living room. There were a lot of books, many about Australia, which they leafed through while Beverley fetched glasses and a bottle. As she poured the wine, she asked "So what triggered this journey down memory lane?"

"How about you fill us in first on how you come to be living just a few miles away," Jude said.

"Well, I think you know I went in for teaching? I started off in Adelaide, then went east and north and ended up in a junior school in Queensland, where I met this dishy Pom, Dan, who had come over on a year's exchange scheme. The year turned into two, then three, and we ended up as an inseparable item, and I followed him back here.

170

His folks are from East Anglia, but then he got promotion to the company's Oxford office so we moved here."

"What does Dan do?"

"He's in IT. But perhaps more relevant to you is his passion for history." Beverley got up, went across to the bookshelves, drew out a book and handed it to Pippa: *Europe's Fault Line by Joseph Eastman.* When Jude mentioned your name was Eastman, it rang a bell. And now," Beverley said firmly, "Let's get back to memory lane."

"You explain," Jude told Pippa. So Pippa explained as succinctly as she could how they had both been drawn into delving into their respective histories, giving a brief summary of the unanswered questions surrounding her own father's past.

"Complicated," Beverley commented. She turned to Jude. "I suppose I'd better learn to call you Jude now. And I suppose I can guess what's led you down a similar path."

"You know about Dad?"

Beverley raised her wine glass. "First let's have a toast to friends reunited." She took a sip. "Yes, Dorrie told me what a tough time your mother had, though I didn't meet her again until after your dad had left. Then a few months ago, Dorrie emailed and said she was in touch with your dad, Bob, and his second wife through Facebook. Apparently he was losing his sight and feeling a bit low and she wondered if I could go and see him. So I did." She paused for another sip of wine. "He wasn't at all what I imagined, and I liked him a lot."

"What did you imagine?"

"I suppose someone rather brash and loud...."

"Which was how he was," put in Jude.

"Well, he certainly isn't now. He's not exactly frail, but looks a bit shrunken. I suppose we all shrink a bit as we get older. And quietly spoken. And his Laura is a darling."

"You're right there," Pippa said.

Beverley was clearly taken aback. "You've seen them?"

Pippa gave a resume of their encounter at Radipole. "Then Jude got cold feet, and we left. But since then I've been back and met Laura. Jude was away in Oz at the time."

171

"I was scared it would all go wrong," confessed Jude. "How do you tell an old guy you're his long lost son, and what a pity he can't see you any more?"

Pippa looked exasperated. Beverley said, "There are more subtle ways of introducing yourself, Jude. And you're going to have to do it, you know. He has such deep regrets about the way you must remember him."

"He does?"

"Couldn't stop talking about it. Though I did notice he tended to do that when Laura wasn't in the room. Perhaps it was easier to talk to me because he didn't really know me in those bad old days. But he wanted to know every last detail of how you were when I knew you, and was tickled pink when I told him about Bev the Beaut. Look, I'll leave you to talk things over - help yourself to more wine - while I throw some supper together. Then I want to hear more about where you live in Oz and what you do. And about Pippa's Dad."

By the time they had finished their next glass of wine, Beverley had the barbecue set up just outside the conservatory door and great smokey meat smells were wafting into the cottage. They ate in the conservatory: chicken, steaks, sausages, a range of salads, followed by a selection of cheesecakes. By the time they left, they felt they had known each other half a lifetime.

"You'll come over to Daerley as soon as Spring shows its hand," Pippa said. "And bring Dan. It would be great to meet one of Father's fans."

"Wasn't that great?" Jude said as they turned back on to the main road.

"Yes, it was. You know we're going to have to give serious thought about what Beverley said about visiting your Dad?"

"Mm, and I think what she said has helped to make me ready for it."

"We'll check diaries when we get home."

But when they reached home, there were two messages on the answering machine, The first was from Greta Schmidt. *I must see you,* it said. *I shall be coming to England in a few weeks and will call you.*

172

"This woman is getting really persistent," Pippa said. But the second message abruptly catapulted them into new priorities. A message on the answer-phone from Liisu told them urgently to call her at the first opportunity. Kirsti had had a relapse and had only a few weeks to live.

Oxfordshire: February 2011

1

"It's a bit late to call," Pippa said. "Finland is two hours ahead, so it'll be nearly midnight."

Jude was already dialling. "Liisu said it was urgent."

Pippa went to get the cordless phone from the kitchen. Liisu answered almost immediately. "Oh, I am so happy to hear your voice," she told Jude. "Though it is a bad situation with Kirsti. They found some days ago that she has these secondaries, and nothing can be done, except to keep her as comfortable as possible. They are moving her from the hospital in Rovaniemi to a special care home in Kittilä. She asked for this as she has more friends here, though I think it is not so many."

"Do they know how long she will live?"

"Some weeks, they think."

Pippa said, "I can't possibly bother her at such a time."

"You can," Liisu said firmly. "You must. I saw her in hospital in Rovaniemi and told her about you. She is so happy to know that Josef's granddaughter has been in Finland and says she has to see you before she dies. She says she has important things to tell you."

Jude said, "We'll discuss it and do everything we can to come. Liisu, thank you for letting us know. We will contact you as soon as we have made plans."

Pippa followed him into the kitchen. "It's impossible Jude. There's the house to sell and someone due to see it next week.. There's your Dad. There are my classes. It's impossible."

He put his arms round her. "It's not ideal, but it's not impossible. We can ring round your yoga students, no problem. The house is on the market, and the agent has the keys. And my Dad is my problem." He led her back into the living room, pushed her gently down on to the sofa, poured her out a stiffish Scotch.

"There is one solution that might help," he added as he sat down beside her. "If you went to Finland and I went to Weymouth it would (a) save money, (b) mean that I would be here most of the time." As Pippa opened her mouth to object, he said, "No, I'm not keen either; but it would partly solve the difficulties."

"It will be awful to be without you in Finland."

"It will be awful without you in Weymouth."

"And how will you manage with Aristotle?"

"We could both make an effort to like each other a bit more." As though he had overheard, Aristotle padded into the room, sat down, curled his tail round and surveyed them. Then he padded over to Jude and sniffed his shoe.

"Mm. Perhaps you could even take some of my yoga classes."

Jude bent down and scratched the animal's head. "I think Aristotle might be better at that."

Pippa did some visualising and giggled. "Oh dear, I'm beginning to see it all happen in spite of me." She took a sip of whiskey. "It's going to be hellishly cold in Kittilä at this time of the year," she said, and Jude knew she was half way towards agreeing with him.

They didn't get much sleep. By the time Pippa had sipped her way through the whiskey, she was complaining of thirst and demanding tea. Jude made them both a mugful and they migrated to the computer where they found that currently flights to Finland were far from full. Pippa printed out a list of her yoga pupils who would need notifying of a temporary cancellation of classes. Jude made lists of all he needed to know if prospective buyers came to look at the house. Around 2 a.m., Pippa was busy explaining to him which of the fences they were responsible for, when her voice began to slur and she fell asleep mid-sentence. Jude tucked some blankets round her and then sprawled in an armchair until he became so stiff he took himself off to bed, followed by a puzzled Aristotle.

175

He was awoken at nine o'clock with a cup of tea and Pippa standing over him, looking at Aristotle curled up at the foot of the bed. "Now I've seen everything," she said.

2

It turned into a busy day. First there was a call from Hedges and Waters announcing an afternoon visit in a couple of days' time, the same day as another viewer was coming in the morning. Next they checked the airline schedules to Helsinki again and printed out possible flights in late February and early March. Then Pippa located the deeds of the house, marking 'her' boundaries and responsibilities. At this point, while Jude was making coffee, the phone rang.

"Liisu," exclaimed Pippa. "Yes, I *am* coming." She reached across for the print-outs of possible flights and began reading them out. Then she stopped, listened a while and said, "OK, yes I understand. And yes, early March would be better for me, as long it doesn't risk being, you know, too late." She listened some more. "OK, that's fine. I'll go ahead and book. And it's good to know you will be there, too. Sorry, what was that?" Then a laugh, "No, there's no way I shall be bringing the campervan."

To Jude she explained that Liisu was tied to Helsinki until the end of February, sorting things out for Kirsti and fulfilling her own commitments, but that she planned to travel north on March 1st and suggested that ideally Pippa arrived two or three days later. They could stay at her father's place which was only a short walk from the rest home. "And she recommended that I leave the campervan at home."

"Yes, I gathered that, and I might have had something to say if you had left me bereft of four wheels, not to mention the agony of anxiety at the thought of your slithering your way across the Arctic." Jude poured out two mugs of coffee and handed her one. "Anyway, if you're not going until early March, we've got a couple of clear weeks."

"That's a great relief. It means I can finishing sorting Father's studio and clear out the garage. And with a bit of luck the snowdrops will be up."

"And what am I doing?"

"Helping me. And thinking about what to do about Dad."

"Mm." They supped their coffee in silence for some moments before Jude said suddenly, "Have you actually thought what you are going to do when you have sold the house?"

Pippa looked back at him silence for a few moments. "To be honest I find it very difficult to think beyond Finland and Weymouth. But I have planned to the extent that I will keep the flat in the village at least until the owners come back and that won't be until May."

"And will there be room for me as well as Aristotle?"

Pippa looked thoughtful. "I guess so, given your new rapport. Or if necessary we can find a bigger flat. But you have to decide what you plan to do, too. I mean what about your business and Craig….. "

"Not to mention us. You're right," Jude said. "Impossible to think of anything beyond Finland and Weymouth."

After coffee, Pippa left Jude with a list of telephone numbers of her students, and set off herself for Freshfields. Six of her pupils lived there, two of whom had graduated to the Monday class, the other four still in the Thursday one. As soon as she explained that there was a family crisis in Finland, they understood and even promised to get together once a week to practise the simpler poses. By the time she'd had coffee with three of them and returned home, Jude had contacted her other pupils who likewise had said they would continue to practise in her absence.

"So what's next? How about lunch at the Trumpet?"

Over tomato and basil soup, warm crusty bread and a couple of glasses of house red, they fleshed out the list of tasks needing attention.

"My priority is clearing out Father's studio," Pippa said. "A lot of it was done when I was sorting out his translations of Grandfather Josef's diaries. But there are stacks of journals that can be thrown out and papers that need checking in case I overlooked anything of importance."

"OK. While you're doing that, I'll check the upstairs and make sure it's as presentable as possible for the next viewers. It's the day after tomorrow, isn't it?"

177

"Yes, two lots. And the first thing of all is to book my flight."

Pippa spent the afternoon in the studio in the garden. Initially there was quick and satisfying progress as she strung up piles of old journals and humped them into the kitchen for recycling disposal. Later, progress slowed down as she dumped several box-files of papers on the desk and began to go through them. Many of them were old bills and receipts, all of them signs of her father's deteriorating mental state for once he had been meticulous at throwing away 'out of date rubbish'.

Her first astounding discovery was contained in a worn school exercise book. It consisted of copious notes in her own childhood writing, with a few sketches, and some quotations from the Finnish epic poem of the *Kalevala*. The next moment she was catapulted back into the dream she'd had in which she had discussed with her father the way in which the music of the Finnish composer Sibelius so precisely made sound images of the Finnish landscapes and of that epic poem, a copy of which she had found in his study.

"But I thought I had dreamed all that," she said aloud, turning the pages of the notebook which provided proof that her dream had been based on reality. After a while, she put the exercise book aside and made herself return to the box of papers.

There were letters from former colleagues, sometimes raising some abstruse point on the historical evidence for some statement he had made in a paper or talk. She spent time reading these, drawn into this other world which had dominated her father's life and she found herself wondering how he managed to extract himself from it to participate in the day-to-day trivia of family matters. But then he never had participated in them much. Once again she thought how solitary a life it must have been for her mother, especially once first Robin, then she had left home.

And then she found a letter in her mother's writing. It was dated 1983

"Dearest Joe - Today we have been married fifteen years. To most people we must seem an ill-assorted pair, you with your serious preoccupations with the past, and I with my irrepressible silliness which used to irritate my mother so. But we have learned to understand each other - or perhaps it is an instinctive empathy that needs no effort of understanding. We have come to know what the

178

modern young call how to give each other space. Though I do not
comprehend or wish to enter those complex journeys that take you into
distant scenes and centuries, the fact that you are there within the
same four walls pursuing your passion gives me the greatest comfort.
I think it is the same for you that I have come to express my silliness in
ways that I can share with others in the form of greeting cards. We
are so fortunate. All the same, just now and then, I need to hear or
express a few words to give our love substance. So I say to you now:
rakastan sinua, Jooseppi. -*Your Frances always*

And underneath, in her father's neat hand: *minäkin rakastan*
sinua – Jooseppi. I love you too.

Rakstan sinua - I love you. The words Jude had said to her on
Helsinki market. Pippa felt a tightening of her throat. "Get on with it,
you stupid woman," she told herself, but she put the letter aside to
keep.

When Jude came in with a tray of tea, she showed it to him.
"I'm sorry I didn't know her," he said. "But there is a lot of her in
you."

"There is?"

"Silliness, certainly. But I guess there's quite a lot of your Dad,
too."

Pippa's eyebrows shot up in astonishment. "How on earth do
you make that out?"

"For example, when you get your teeth into a project, you
never let go. Like a terrier with a bone. Look at the way you've
persisted with the translation of those diaries. And now your
determination to show that your father could not have been responsible
for that guy's death."

She looked thoughtful. "And there was that dream."

"What dream?"

"The one about the skeleton in the cupboard. I didn't tell you
the first part of the dream, about how I made a connection between the
music of Sibelius and the landscapes of Finland, and then the stories of
the Kalevala, a sort of national legend. And then I found this." She
handed him the exercise book. "I'm really gobsmacked. The dream
seemed real enough, but I just didn't remember that I had actually put

179

all that stuff together. And I would never have guessed that he would actually keep it."

"There you are then," Jude said. "That just backs up the point I was making about you having quite a lot of your father in you."

And now Pippa realised that she quite liked the idea that it had come from him, that doggedness that had earlier informed her determination to make a go of her yoga classes, to care for her father when he had lost the most attractive feature of a keen and enquiring mind, and now to find the real truth behind the mystery of Kalle's death.

3

The first viewers who came to see the house two days later were young middle-aged parents with three children: girl twins of twelve and a much younger male afterthought. The latter was a bit of a pain, poking into corners and trying to open drawers, while his mother gently - too gently - reprimanded. The girls were well behaved and Pippa could see them mentally choosing the room they wanted for themselves.

"This will make a splendid study," the man said when they opened the door on to Father's downstairs work room, and Pippa warmed to him.

His wife had fluffy pale hair and looked the archetypical home-maker. It would be good to have young voices ringing round the house and young feet scampering round the garden. Wouldn't it? The twins did not look the scampering sort though, and the boy would probably be glued to a computer or play station. What would Father make of it?

But Father was not there. The idea was to make a good sale and this family looked interested. But of course they had a house to sell and a bit of mortgage to raise. They would go away and think about it.

The afternoon viewer was a solicitor enquiring on behalf of a client who lived overseas. The client was male; a widower, his wife having died of some tropical bug. By profession he was a water engineer and he was retiring to the UK to be nearer a couple of sisters in the Midlands. These facts, Jude gleaned from the solicitor like dragging blood from a stone. In character, his client sounded as though he might have been related to Joseph Eastman. Was that what made him interesting, Jude wondered? But he could sense that Pippa did not share his feelings. It was not until they went out to inspect the dishevelled back garden that their visitor began to win her round.

"Ah," he said, surveying the untidy but leafy jungle. "I see that you have not joined the concrete jungle brigade."

"Sorry?"

"Perhaps you have not noticed that many of your neighbours have transformed their front gardens into parking lots." He peered over the fence. "And their back gardens into paved patios which require the minimum attention."

"Yes, but ours is a bit of a mess." Pippa noted Jude's use of the possessive pronoun..

"My client has strong feelings on the matter. Having been concerned with the water shortages of Africa, he is appalled by Britain's unthinking attitude towards its own water tables. Concrete does not absorb rain, water tables become higher, floods occur, water in mega millions of gallons is wasted. I believe that is how the argument goes." It was the longest speech he had made. The solicitor turned to go back into the house.

"When is your client returning to the UK?" Pippa asked.

"Mr. Brown is here already, staying with one of his sisters. But he is not very mobile and asked me to make the initial enquiries. He will visit those that I deem suitable."

"But there was no way he is going to tell us whether that includes ours," Jude muttered at Pippa as the solicitor got into his BMW and raised a hand in farewell.

In fact, Hedges and Waters telephoned thirty-six hours later to say that Mr. Brown would like to visit the property at the beginning of the following week. The fluffy pale-haired woman and her husband regretfully would not be making a bid as they had their eye on a different area. Something to do with schooling.

181

Over the week-end, Pippa finished clearing the studio and Jude turned the house into a showcase. Mr. Brown (he can't be called John, Jude said, but he was) - Mr. John Brown was probably in his early seventies with a weathered face, darting blue eyes and wispy hair. He walked with a limp and a stick. Pippa's heart sank. He would never manage the stairs. But, seemingly, he or his solicitor had already thought of that.

"I would turn the upstairs into a separate flat, with its own entrance," he explained. Pippa half expected him to produce ready-made plans from his pocket. "Your downstairs study would be quite large enough for my bedroom, and the rest would be library and working space."

They moved into the garden. "How delightfully untamed," murmured John Brown. And then, as Pippa opened the door to the Studio, he almost did a little dance as he said, "Aaah - and this is where I would write."

"Oh," Pippa said. "My father was a writer."

"Then perhaps his muse may linger to encourage mine," John Brown said.

It was at that moment that Aristotle chose to jump off his cupboard shelf.

"What a splendid animal!" John Brown exclaimed. "I don't suppose he comes with the house?"

It was far too momentous a decision to make on the spot. "I'll think about it," Pippa said.

It was as simple as that. She could hardly believe it.

1

Pippa didn't take John Brown's suggestion regarding Aristotle seriously, for in the end that was up to the two of them. The thought of Aristotle actually belonging to someone else she put in some remoter corner of her mind. He was so much part of her life that it was impossible to imagine him not being there. On the other hand, his presence did add complications to her future with Jude.

As for John Brown, she waited for some snag to arise, but none materialised. It was established that it would take him the spring and part of the summer to conclude his affairs in Malawi, though he would like to complete by the end of May so he could start moving his possessions in and arrange for the conversion necessary to accommodate a self-contained flat. This suited Pippa well. After some research she found another restless Daerlian was spending the summer in Arctic Canada, so another apartment, this time on the High Street, would become available in the middle of May. Happily it was also substantially bigger with a large living room that would accommodate her Monday morning and private classes. She was aiming at transferring the Thursday morning class to one of the day rooms at Freshfields Nursing home.

Beverley called in to see them one morning on her way to Banbury. The twins were with her and promptly disappeared into the garden while Pippa made coffee. They were so alike that she had to guess that it was Paul who was back within a minute to ask, "What's the cat called."

"Aristotle," Pippa said.

"Totty," Jude said simultaneously.

"He's really cool," Paul pronounced.

"Are we talking about the same cat?" Jude enquired.

"Why's he got that funny bump on his head?"

"Ah!" Beverley said. "He's a poorly cool cat," turning to explain to Pippa, "Paul (so she had been right) is going to be a vet and will fall for the mangiest creature," adding quickly, "not , of course, that your Totty is mangy."

Pippa explained about Aristotle's unfortunate night-time encounter when he was young.

"He's really cool," repeated Paul, and hurried off again to examine his imaginary patient.

When they had gone Pippa said, "Why don't you ask Beverley to go with you when you see your Dad."

"Because I'm not taking anyone else unless it's you." He kissed her on the end of the nose.

Over the coming days, he turned his attention to the garden. At this time of the year, now that so much growth had died back, he cleared considerable quantities of ground cover that was just beginning to show signs of revival. He also pruned several dominant bushes hard back revealing several small patches of snowdrops that glinted in the occasional winter sun. He also repainted the garage doors.

"None of this is going to boost your bank balance," Pippa pointed out.

"No," Jude agreed, "but John Brown will appreciate it." All the same, he spent a morning thinking, and then emailed the editor of *Whizz* with several ideas for articles. Four of these were accepted and then the editor said he was looking for a series that would depict Old Europe through the eyes of the New World. Jude spent another few hours thinking and came up with a series which, in essence, would introduce fellow New Worlders to their origins.

"Good idea," Pippa said.

"It came from reading one of your father's books. It struck me that I knew quite a lot of people from what sounded like pretty obscure places, and then I thought that the second or third generation of these migrants probably had lost touch with where they really came from."

"Father would be pleased," Pippa said.

Fortunately the editor of *Whizz* was pleased too. Through a series of emails they set up a number of topics and deadlines which would keep Jude occupied for some weeks to come. When he went

184

out to tell Pippa, she was transferring a colourful selection of polyanthus into troughs to be kept in the conservatory until they could be moved out on to the patio. She put down the trowel and took his hands in her somewhat earthy ones.

"Have you?" she asked, "given thought to what we are going to do when all this father-searching is over. I mean we as in 'thee and me'."

"I think that should be 'thou and I'. And no, I haven't. I thought we'd agreed that we couldn't think beyond Weymouth and Finland."

By the time Pippa was ready to leave, the garden was in good shape. They had also cleared most of the downstairs furniture and were camping out in the living room and bedroom. The house had a hollow ring to it and Pippa was not sorry to be going away. Jude drove her to Birmingham airport but they had a mutual dislike of farewells so he did not linger. Pippa got some duty-frees for Liisu and armed herself with a newspaper for the journey. Ever since she had asked Jude if he had thought about their future, the question had flickered in the back of her mind. She allowed her imagination to flit from Daerley Green to New South Wales and back to Finland. It was impossible to visualise any of them with any degree of permanency. And that was even without introducing the complication of Aristotle.

The flight north took her over an ever more frozen Europe. By the time they were coming in to land at Helsinki airport, the dark forests wore a thick white cloak and the lakes were trapped under ice. Liisu was waiting for her. The warmth of her smile of recognition was especially welcome on this brink of a journey that might reveal so much.

"It's like arriving in a completely different country," Pippa said.

On the drive into the city Liisu said, "We shall have two days here before we go north - I have one or two commitments to fulfill. Kirsti is in remission. Her brother tells me that sometimes she looks so well, he begins to hope that she will recover. But we know that is not the reality."

"Did Kirsti tell you anything about Grandfather Josef?"

"She prefers to tell you. But she has written something, in case you came too late. She has already spoken to Margarit."

185

The Helsinki suburbs were a delight. It was like walking through a charcoal picture until you noticed the luminosity that came from the snow and pale Nordic winter sky, tinting everything in the most delicate pastel tones. Among the snow covered rocks and trees, small children bundled up like colourful footballs, skidded down the slopes on little sledges or laboured up them on their short skis. Pippa thought of the Daerley Green children trudging to school in their waterproofs and decided these Finnish kids had the best of the bargain.

While Liisu was fulfilling her commitments, Pippa went to visit Margarit who lived only a short bus ride away. Despite the language barrier they had always managed quite well. It happened that her husband, Heikki, was at home as he had strained his back, so conversation was not much of a problem, though Pippa resisted any temptation to question them about Kirsti. Instead, she told them about Jude's search for his father, miming the latter's fondness for drink, and then feeling guilty because her hosts clearly found it hilariously funny and she knew only too well there was nothing humorous about it.

It was Heikki who said, "Yes, Kalle had same problem?"

Yes, Liisu's father Matti had mentioned Kalle's fondness for the bottle. Pippa firmly resisted the temptation to pursue the matter further. Liisu was right. It was far better to let Kirsti do things her way.

On the second day, Pippa went to the South Harbour market, remembering how much her own father had liked the place. It was amazing to see it flourishing colourfully under its bright awnings amongst the rather slushy snow beside the white frozen harbour.

That night she and Liisu boarded the night sleeper for Rovaniemi.

2

Liisu's father Matti met them off the train at Rovaniemi. By the time they had had some breakfast in the hotel restaurant overlooking the frozen river, a pastel dawn of pale lemon and rose were streaking the eastern horizon. Pippa was surprised at how good the roads were with their surface of: smooth, hard-packed snow. Beyond the walls of snow that bordered the main road, the forests stretched impenetrably quiet, their stillness broken occasionally by wadges of snow plummeting from a branch. On the drive, she told them of the correspondence she had discovered between her grandfather and Kirsti, without going into too much detail.

"Kalle would have not liked," Matti commented. "My sister Annikki always said he was jealous man. But it is true she also make joke that Kirsti like Josef too much."

"And what about Jude and his father? Did he meet him in the end?" Liisu asked. So Pippa explained how she had gone to Weymouth while Jude was in Australia, but they still had not had a formal meeting though it might happen any day.

"So this is a bad time for you to come to Finland," Liisu said shrewdly. "You have a very complicated life." And no one could argue with that.

In Kittilä, they stopped briefly at the rest home where Kirsti now stayed. Pippa looked briefly in at her, her white hair and nearly white face almost the colour of the pillow against which they rested. It reminded her of those last weeks of Father's life, though his expression had never been so peaceful. That night as she lay in her narrow bed and looked across the room to the other empty one she really missed Jude. Yes, they may have complained about the narrowness of the bed, but they had adapted to it without too much difficulty.

Next morning Matti reported that he had telephoned the rest home and Kirsti was being moved to Rovaniemi for some scans that could not be done here in Kittilä. She would be away three or four days. Pippa stifled her irritation that, had she known, she could have stayed longer in Daerley, perhaps even gone with Jude to Weymouth.

"I have suggestion," Matti said. "While Kirsti is away, we could go to her house and from there to lake where Kalle's body was found. In winter it is not easy because there is no road, only *pulkka* track."

"And what on earth is that?"

"It is a narrow path followed by *pulkka*. This is like a sort of canoe but you travel over snow instead of water."

"So it has an engine?"

187

"Some *pulkkas* do, the new ones. But Kirsti has only old ones and these are pulled by reindeer. She has a man taking care of her reindeer while she is ill."

Pippa could not begin to imagine how a reindeer-pulled canoe would work, let alone how she would control it, but it seemed a good way of finding out. Another surprise was that Matti could telephone Kirsti's reindeer man who had a mobile to make arrangements that they would arrive the following evening. They would spend the night at Kirsti's house, which was accessible by road, then continue with the reindeer to the lake where the tragedy had happened. Pippa did briefly wonder how this expedition would help her to come to any conclusions, especially when the landscape was so unimaginably different from what it must have been. But there was time to fill while Kirsti was away and this was as good a way as any of filling it. Pippa emailed Jude to the effect she would be out of touch for two or three days while she explored the forests in a canoe. She could visualise his characteristic wry expression through the words of his reply: *I refuse to ask how you can canoe through snow-covered forests. Just beware of the rapids.*

Over breakfast next day, Pippa tried again to question Matti about the details of the tragedy all those years ago. He could only repeat that it was indeed a long time ago, that at the time he was busy working on the farm and not paying much attention to anything else. "Though, of course," he added, "I spent much time with your Father Jooseppi when he came here, and said it was bad idea to go and see Kalle. I see he is angry and it is not good idea for two angry people to meet."

"And tell me again what happened when Father came back from seeing Kalle."

"He come back with Kirsti …."

"Oh! You didn't tell me that before."

"I did not tell because it seems not important. Kirsti is in very bad way, red and crying. She said Kalle is gone many days and he must have accident."

"But I thought Kirsti did not love Kalle?"

"No, she love not, but he is her husband; and I do not know what is reason, but she is red and crying. Then brother Pentti comes

188

from Rovaniemi and many people go to look for Kalle, and at last find him."

"Dead."

"Yes, dead. By then Jooseppi has gone back to England. But some days after, Kalle's friend Hans comes from Germany and we go to the place. And there he finds the marks of his boots - or my boots that Jooseppi was wearing, and Kalle has big wound on head. I think police send message to England, but nothing happen."

Pippa thought back to the call she had had from the police soon after Father died. Yes something did happen, but it seemed to have taken nearly forty years. Not really worth mentioning. So, in essence, not much change to the story, except for Kirsti's curious emotional reaction. Perhaps she had been upset because she was afraid Jooseppi would get into trouble. Things didn't seem to be getting any better for Father.

After breakfast, Pippa and Liisu went shopping. Pippa was amused to be introduced to the local pedestrian means of locomotion, a chair on runners. This could be used in the same way as a scooter and could pick up quite a speed on the slippery hard packed snow. By midday the sun had risen well above the tree- and roof-tops and sent immensely long shadows reaching out across the snow. Matti met them at a local café for a snack of open sandwiches before they set off for Kirsti's house.

It was remote indeed. First they travelled south for about twenty miles then took a minor road east for another ten before an even more minor one north again for three or four. How anyone could ever find anything in a landscape that consisted of infinite variations on the theme of pine and snow, Pippa could not begin to imagine, but after a while Matti said "Nearly there," and soon after they saw a lone figure sitting on a tree trunk at the roadside.

"Hei Niila," Matti greeted him.

Niila was a Sami and, unusually wearing traditional Sami dress, unlike most of his race nowadays. Admiring his deep blue smock with the colourful bands of decoration round the hem and sleeves, Pippa wondered why they should want to change this for the universal uniform of jeans and sweatshirts, and concluded that for the most part people did not like to stand out from the crowd. She now saw that Matti had opened the boot of the car and was unloading a pile of what looked like reindeer skins. These turned out to be amazing garments you could pull over your head as an outer covering.

"*Peskija,*" Niila said approvingly.

It was only a couple of hundred yards to Kirsti's house, which was just as well as walking in the thick snow was hard work, especially as the first of the spring thaw was beginning to set in. Niila looked at their footwear and muttered disapprovingly. Indeed Pippa was so busy looking at her feet that she almost fell over the steps of the house before she noticed it: wooden, small, tucked into the trees as though it had grown there a long time ago.

Downstairs there was a large kitchen-cum-living room, which had a tall pot bellied stove at one end of it and an open fire at the other. There were also a couple of beds that could serve as sofas, covered with reindeer skins and fat colourful cushions. It would have been freezing if Niila had not already had both stove and open fire lit, clearly for some time. And, balanced over the fire, a traditional copper coffee pot.

"*Kahvia!*" chorused Liisu and Pippa in appreciation.

Further examination revealed a kind of loft under the eves, with a wooden platform along one wall which could sleep several.

While Liisu pottered about the kitchen area checking where everything was before she prepared their evening meal, Pippa sat on one of the sofa/beds near the open fire. Father had been here, she thought. Had he slept here? How had he looked all those years ago, when she was just a baby and he was at the beginning of his career as an internationally known historian? There were so few pictures of him as a young man to help her to see beyond the austere parent who had dominated her growing up years and from whom she had sought to escape.

"Matti," she said suddenly, needing to know. "What did my father look like all those years ago?"

"He was very good looking, I remember," Liisu said from the kitchen. But it was Matti's opinion Pippa wanted just then.

"Yes, he was," Matti said. "As far as one man can judge another. Thick dark hair."

190

"No beard then?"

"No beard." Matti came to sit beside her. He clapped a hand to his forehead. "At home I have photograph. I cannot understand why I do not think of this before."

"Most people know what their own fathers look like."

"I do not remember what my father look like when I am baby." Matti said.

"You are a very nice man," Pippa said, and Matti looked surprised as she enveloped him in a hug.

Liisu had brought a reindeer casserole from the freezer at home, and the journey had not done much to defrost it, so she now placed it on top of the stove. Then she unfolded the sleeping bags they had brought and spread them in front of the fire.

"I'd like one of the beds down here," she said.

"You girls sleep here downstairs," Matti said. "I will stay with Niila under the roof."

After the meal, no one seemed anxious to linger for long. There was not even a mention of coffee. With so much spinning in her mind, Pippa could not believe she would sleep. But she did, like a log.

3

She awoke several times during the night. There was still a slight glow from the embers of the fire and beyond the thin curtains over the windows, the night was not dark: certainly not with the darkness of an English rural night. There was a lightness drawn from the sky. And something else. Something that pulsated and quivered.

Pippa slipped out of her sleeping bag and went to the window, drawing back the curtain. And gasped. Above her was a sight of such magic she could only stare and stare at the veils of colour - green, rose, yellow, that shifted and parted and met and swirled. At times they seemed to move towards the horizon as though they would disappear, but suddenly they were re-ignited somewhere else and took on a new life. Had Father stood watching them with the same wonder? Though, of course, they would not be visible in the light summer nights. It

191

took her a while to realise that her mouth had fallen open, and to close it. It took even longer to realise she was getting cold. Even then she could only draw away from the window with the greatest reluctance.

"I saw the Northern Lights in the night," was the first thing she said to Liisu.

"Ah, the Aurora, it is like magic. I never tire of it, but probably the first time is the best. Soon it will be too late." After a moment she added, "The Sami say that if you whistle at them they will try and grab you."

"I'm tempted to try," Pippa said.

Soon after Niila came from outside, leaving his shoes by the door. "He says it was minus 25 degrees in the night," Liisu translated. "It will be a cold journey today."

It was. Though it was rather a tight fit, Pippa and Liisu shared the sledge, each of them enveloped in a *peski* over their clothes and more reindeer skins tucked over their knees. They got off to a slow start. The reindeer pulling Matti's *pulkka* expressed its resentment at being handled by a stranger by stubbornly refusing to move at anything faster than a sedate walk. After fruitless cajoling and bullying, Niila exchanged his reindeer for Matti's. The one pulling the girls' sledge was attached to Niila's *pulkka* so had no option but move at the leader's pace. Matti's new reindeer, now resenting its demotion, made every effort to over take the girls' sledge.

"It's breathing into my left ear," complained Liisu. "And its breath stinks." She did not translate Niila's response to her protest.

Despite their coverings, the cold was ferocious. The light wind had risen to a stiff breeze and, however still they kept, the bitter air infiltrated the tiniest crack, seeming to penetrate to their bones. Each out-breath froze to rime on the edges of their hoods. Pippa had a sudden memory of Grandfather Josef's comment in his diary from the Winter War to the effect that the infernos of hell must be a relief after such cold. She wanted to share the memory with Liisu but decided not to risk the frozen arrows that any movement would invite. Instead she concentrated on Niila's chanting rising above the sound of the runners on the snow: a tuneless kind of noise to begin with but which gained a curious, attractive rhythm with time.

192

"It's called a *joiku,*" Liisu explained. "The Sami sing to themselves, usually some long descriptive tale of something that's going on in their lives."

It helped to have something to listen to, but the journey and the cold seemed to go on for ever. Niila had estimated it would take two hours, but detours to avoid fallen trees brought down by the winter gales indicated it would take substantially longer. After the two hours were nearly up, Niila turned and shouted something and their little cortège began to slow down.

"He wants coffee," Liisu said tersely.

Didn't they all? thought Pippa, who decided she had never wanted anything more in her life ever. Except perhaps a cuddle with Jude.

Niila had found the ideal spot, sheltered by rocks on two sides and trees on the other two. On one of the rock faces was a small recess which had obviously been used before for a camp fire, and here in a matter of seconds he made a small fire, placed on it a blackened coffee pot, and produced from his *pulkka* a quartet of carved wooden mugs. While the three reindeer stomped and grunted round them, they drank their coffee which was quite the best Pippa had ever tasted. She thought of Father who would have made the journey on foot, clad in Matti's boots.

"Did you get your boots back from Father, Matti?" she asked.

"Yes, and I borrowed them to Hans Müller."

The coffee had been surprisingly warming and refreshing. Pippa thought she could probably now cope with another couple of hours. In fact it was just under one. Suddenly they crested the brow of a low hill and just below them was the unbroken white expanse that could only be a lake. There was a small hut on the shore and beside this Niila drew to a halt and with some difficult Liisu and Pippa disentangled themselves from their coverings. The wind blew sharply across the ice and they did not linger long before seeking the shelter of the hut. It was quite small inside, almost entirely taken up by a broad sleeping platform and, in one corner, a tall stove with a stack of logs beside it.

"It's what we call a *tupa,* a sort of hut open to any traveller to take shelter when they are travelling in the wilderness," Liisu said.

193

Pippa sat on the edge of it. Had her father slept here? She got up and wandered out of the hut, down the three steps and followed old footprints down to the shore. Nothing stirred. Nothing indicated what tragedy might or might not have happened here over forty years ago. She looked out across the whiteness and then down at her feet in their reindeer skin shoes. Father had not been wearing reindeer skin shoes, but boots that had left their imprint down beneath her, two or three feet below on the lake shore.

Weymouth : early March 2011

1

Jude sat at a table in one of the alcoves of The Mariner, staring into his pint of lager. He profoundly wished that Pippa were sitting beside him. She'd instinctively know what to do. In fact she would certainly have talked him out of making the decision he had taken to go to Weymouth and see his father without a preliminary meeting with Laura. Much as he appreciated what Pippa had done - and of course Laura - he still had this deep-down feeling that this was something between his father and himself, and they needed to sort it. Now that he had just watched his father come into the bar, leaning heavily on a stick, he was less sure. Laura was with him, of course. If she saw him she would naturally wonder why he had not contacted her as suggested. After installing him at a table, happily the far side of room from where Jude sat, she had gone to order their meal from the bar. Afterwards she went back to sit with her husband, her back thankfully towards Jude.

So now what?

Soon after, the barman Jimmie called "Table number seven, your order is ready,".

Jude edged towards the bar, keeping his back to the far side of the room as far as possible.

"You've been here before, haven't you?" Jimmie said.

"Mm," agreed Jude, wishing the man wasn't so darned friendly. He paid, picked up his tray and turned away to discourage any further conversation, but was no nearer any decision on how he was going to make that first stomach-churning approach to his father after thirty-plus years.

He wished he had a newspaper so he could hide behind it, but he managed to find a position where he could no longer be seen by Laura, while his father would not be able to see him anyway. At least the fish and chips were good. When he had finished, he decided against the risks of being spotted involved by ordering another drink or a dessert, and slunk out to the car park via the passageway that led to the toilets. In the campervan, he sat frustrated and furious with himself for his own timidity.

The local campsite was closed at this time of the year, so he slotted himself into a big lay-by used by long-distance lorries. It was hardly a restful night with h.g.vs shunting in and then very early shunting out again, but it gave him time to make a decision. It was a Friday evening, tomorrow was Saturday and presumably his Dad and Laura would be doing their regular visit to the RSPB reserve at Radipole Lake, assuming it was open. He acknowledged it would have made life much simpler if he had made contact with Laura in advance, but he was stuck with his own decision now. And he usually had a way of charming himself out of awkward situations.

The Reserve was open. Sipping a coffee next morning in the Visitors' Centre, Jude saw they had made a good job of clearing the paths, though with his father's lack of mobility it was unlikely he would be walking far. On the other hand, the best hide from which to view was the furthest one, probably about a mile from the entrance if you took the direct route. All the same, it would be infuriating to go there, hang around for ages and then they didn't turn up. Even if he still did not have the faintest idea how he would approach them.

He was about to order himself another coffee, when he saw a VW Polo drive in to the car park. A moment later, he watched Laura get out of it, and after a few more moments observed her remove and unfold a triangular-shaped wheeled gadget from the boot. Soon after, he saw his father ease himself from the passenger seat, take the handles of the gadget and move towards the Visitors' Centre at a quite good pace. He should have realised that they would have invested in a gadget that would make the old man's life easier. Without further hesitation, Jude removed himself from the Centre and headed towards the hides. Glancing back, he saw that the old couple were also heading for the Visitors' Centre so that he should have plenty of time.

2

He set off a brisk pace until he saw a man ahead looking through a telescope. Then he slowed down and paused to make the traditional birder's greeting - "'Morning. Anything interesting?" The man grunted without moving his eye from the telescope. It sounded like "Male".

"Male what?" Jude asked.

There was an annoyed sound. "Not male. Rail."

Jude retreated to consult the bird identification book he had miraculously remembered to bring. Apparently it was part of the same family as coots and moorhens. 'Difficult to observe' the book informed him and more usually identified by its distinctive voice. Hmm. Jude didn't do bird voices. Pippa was better at those. And she'd be furious if he saw one before she did.

What was he thinking of? He wasn't here to get one up on Pippa. He was here on one of the most important missions in his life. Subdued, Jude moved on but at a more modest pace, noting movements in the reeds, remembering their first visit here, at last triumphantly identifying a bearded tit. By the time he reached the main hide, he had calmed down. It was full of rather serious-looking bird watchers and he heard the murmur of 'bittern' being passed down the line. Oh God, they'd be there forever. He would forego his right ever to see or even hear one again if they would go and unclutter the place. Whether the Almighty heard or not, soon after there were excited whispers and pointings and re-directing of binoculars and telescopes, followed by a communal scribbling of notes. And then they were gone.

Despite the bargain with his Maker, Jude was trying to see the bird for himself when he heard the latch of the hide click and said over his shoulder, "Sadly you've just missed a bittern."

"That's all right, mate," returned an unmistakeably Aussie twang. "I heard it. Clear as a foghorn. Beautiful."

Jude turned. "Hello," said Laura. "Haven't we met before. Or is the arm of coincidence getting longer with age?" She installed the old man on one of the benches, scribbled something in her notebook and handed it to Jude. He read *It would have been so much better if you had contacted me first, as we agreed.* He saw that she looked put out.

"We met before," her companion stated without trace of doubt. "One thing about not seeing is you get to hear mighty well. Anyway I wouldn't forget that Aussie drawl. Where did you say you came from? Perth to judge by your accent? My first wife moved to Perth after I left. I just couldn't get on with Australia." He paused. "Well, I was rather crook at the time."

It was uncanny the way his Father looked at him while he spoke. Or appeared to look at him. Jude shook his head to clear his mind which seemed completely to have seized up. All he could think of saying was, "It's really amazing the way you can identify birds before we can even see them."

"Yeah, well, you have to learn to compensate. I got this glaucoma thing soon after I got back to England. But I didn't bother to do anything about it. So I'm paying for that. As soon as someone - my second wife, in fact - marched me off to the specialist, he told me in no uncertain terms what I was doing to myself. They gave me drops but it was too late. So I started to try and train myself: to hear, to feel, to smell. It's amazing what you can do when you try." He stopped abruptly. "Listen to me babbling on like some schoolgirl. It must be the Aussie accent. I kind of feel I know you." He held a hand towards Jude who took it, felt the pressure of his fingers.

After a moment he drew his hand away, stood up. Glancing across at Laura, he saw her anguished expression. He said quickly, "I've just realised what the time is and I have to meet someone in town in half an hour. Do excuse me. It was great to meet you."

"It was good talking," his father said.

Jude pushed his way out of the hide, stumbled back along the path, found a sheltered spot and squatted down. And wept.

He rang Beverley as soon as he reached home and she told him to come over straight away. She opened the door of her cottage, held out her arms and he walked into them. She was much shorter than he was, the top of her head tickling his chin.

"I can't believe you were so stupid," she said, but gently as you would to a small boy who had done something silly.

After a moment she drew him into the cottage and on into its chintzy lounge, pushing him gently so that he let himself sink back on the sofa. Then she poured him a stiff gin. "Now tell me exactly what happened.

So Jude told her, ending with a helpless shrug. "I can't find the words to explain how completely frozen my brain was. I was so scared at blowing the only chance I might have of getting to know my father, that I seemed paralysed."

Beverley nodded. "That sounds unsurprising. Obviously it would have been much better to follow the original suggestion and make contact with Laura first. But you've overlooked a major factor. It's part of your nature to want to do things your way, however stupid it may be. Even as a small boy you were like that."

"Yeah, Pippa says the same."

"Pippa is a wise woman. But all the same, get it out of your head that it was the only chance. Just be better prepared next time." She paused to pour herself out a drink.

"Do you think there still can be a 'next time'?"

Beverley said over her shoulder, "Perhaps better wait for Pippa to get back."

"Mm." Jude said. "I think I better had."

1

Jude reported his failure to Pippa over a crackling line. She was full of empathy. "But it's a pity you're a stubborn so-and-so. It really wasn't the right way to set bout things."

"So Beverley told me in no uncertain terms. I just wished you'd been there."

"As I've wished you'd been here. Especially with such a rotten line. Do charge up your mobile's battery before you call again."

"Yeah. And how about you? Any progress?"

She told him about Kirsti's house and the reindeer sledge ride to the scene of the accident. Or murder. Or whatever. "It was just so unreal, Jude. I tried to imagine Father there on a warm summer's day, wearing Matti's boots, but it was too much for my imagination."

"So what now?"

"The latest news is that Kirsti is coming back to Kittilä soon. I'll keep you posted. What about you? You will try again?"

"Beverley thinks I should wait until you get back,."

"It's not Beverley's decision. I think you ought to go back, only for God's sake get it right this time. Ring Laura first - her number is in my book."

They had only returned from their trip into the wilderness the previous evening. Soon after Jude's call, Pippa found Matti rummaging through desk drawers in the living room and finally producing a small photograph. "Jooseppi!" he announced.

It was a very small photograph. Pippa peered at the central figure of a slim youngish man with thick dark hair and tried as hard as she could to distinguish anything that reminded her of her father. All she could feel was regret that she had no memory of him resembling that personable man. In response to Matti's questioning look, she pulled out her wallet and extracted a photograph of her parents taken not long before her mother's death, and handed it to him. He looked at it for some moments then nodded, as if understanding her mixed feelings.

"I think something happened," he said.

Old age of course. Yes, but what else?

While they awaited Kirsti's return, Liisu took Pippa to visit friends scattered about the countryside. They drank countless cups of coffee. Drove through innumerable expanses of forests, from time to time rose up on to the open fells. They saw the Northern Lights, not always so intensely as that first time, but always magical. And Pippa never tired of them. A couple of times they went skiing at Pallastunturi, Pippa wobbling uncertainly down modest slopes while Liisu slalomed down with grace and speed.

"I'll never get the hang of this," Pippa grumbled, picking herself up for the umpteenth time almost at Liisu's feet.

"You don't need to get the hang of it. Not in Oxfordshire," Liisu pointed out.

Kirsti came back to Kittilä on a Wednesday. The following morning, they had a call from the rest home saying that she would like to see Pippa on the Saturday. After so long, the prospect of meeting the only person who really knew what happened that long ago summer's night in 1970 created a knot of anxiety in Pippa's midriff. She did the only thing she knew that help her mind to find calm and returned to her meditation practice.

Bursting in to the living room at an uncharacteristically early hour, Liisu found Pippa, cross-legged and contained in a silence that was almost tangible.

"Sorry," she whispered. Then. "I may be a good skier, but I couldn't do *that,*" indicating Pippa's lotus position.

Liisu drove Pippa to the rest home on the Saturday afternoon. The staff had warned that Kirsti could not cope with more than a short visit, so Liisu went to wait for her in the visitors' room where a pot of coffee was permanently available. A nurse led Pippa to Kirsti's room, its curtains partly drawn against the low winter sun and the shimmering snow. How many more times, Pippa wondered, was she destined to look down on a pale old face almost the same colour as the pillow against which it rested. Closed lids opened to reveal pale blue eyes.

"Come closer, Jooseppi's daughter, so that I can see you."

Pippa pulled a chair up to the bedside and gently took hold of the pale hand that rested on the coverlet. She hadn't been sure how much English Kirsti spoke and it was good to discover it sounded quite fluent.

"I'm so pleased to meet Grandfather Joseph's good friend," Pippa said.

A smiled flickered across Kirsti's face, taking a score of years from her appearance. "He was my great love," she said. "I can say that now because no one can be hurt. And I always knew that your grandmother was *his* great love." She stopped, her breath fast and shallow.

Pippa stroked her hand. "You must not talk too much or the nurses will send me away. I am only sorry I never knew Josef."

"A lovely man." Again that rejuvenating smile. "You are right. Not talk. But listen. Tell me about Jooseppi."

So Pippa sent her mind back far across Europe and far over the years to her earliest memories of her father. Something told her that Kirsti would not want to hear a prettified version of her relationship with him, so she told it as it was, only softening a little the more abrasive moments of their encounters which had finally sent her to Australia. She could see Kirsti's breathing calming as she listened, and at last the old lady said, "I think he was strong man like his father. Strong men can be difficult. Tell me about your mother."

That was easier. Yet in the telling, Pippa found an affirmation of the close relationship that had existed between her parents. Her mother had understood, accepted, rejoiced in her father's strength and in doing so found fulfilment in her own very different skills. They had never been a closely sharing couple, but two individuals who recognised each other's talents and independence.

A nurse put her head round the door. Pippa saw that Kirsti's eyes were closed, her breathing gentle and regular. "Good," the nurse said. "But I think enough."

2

Liisu looked up from the magazine she was reading in the visitors' room. "Well?"

Pippa poured a coffee. "It was sort preliminary stuff, but I think she approves of me. The boss lady says I can come for a short time tomorrow."

So she fell into a routine of visiting Kirsti nearly every day, sometimes only staying a few moments to hold her hand, because she was too exhausted to speak; sometimes for longer periods. It was during one of those that she began speaking of her brother Pentti. After a moment Pippa realised that Kirsti was not so much talking to her as reminding herself of what had happened.

"When I was very little girl, Pentti saved my life. He is three years older. I fell in river and he jumped in though he could not swim so well. But he managed. After this, he thinks I am his to look after always." Kirsti paused to let her breath quieten. She went on. "When I do something he not like, he reminds me 'you would not be here if I did not save you' - but only in a good way." Pippa wondered if there could be a good way in which one person could claim responsibility for another person's life, but she said nothing.

"Then after Russia took Karelia, Pentti was my only family, and he took this responsibility very seriously." It seemed the only time he did not get his own way was when Kirsti fell in love with Kalle. "Of course he was right, but I could not … did not want to see it. Kalle was strong and handsome and promised me the world, and I believed him. It was only later and slowly that I find he could be something like madman. It was jealousy. In one way he was like Pentti - he thought he possessed me, so that if I look at or speak to another man, he became angry. So angry. At first he only shouted at me …. " She stopped sank deeper back into the pillow struggling for breath.

Pippa said, "You must rest, Kirsti. The nurses will be very angry with me if you overtire yourself."

203

The old lady smiled that lovely smile that stripped away the years. It was easy to see why Kalle had fallen for her and why her brother Pentti wanted to protect her.

"Rest a little," she said. "Give me water please."

They both stayed silent for some time until Pippa noticed that Kirsti's breathing had quietened. Then she said, "Kirsti I feel very badly about making you think about those sad times. It is not good for your recovery."

"Dear Pippa, I will not recover. I stay alive because I want to see Jooseppi's daughter and tell all that happened."

"All right. But we will stop as often as it is necessary. First I want to ask you what your brother Pentti thought of the situation."

"Pentti did not know. He and his wife and first baby had moved to Rovaniemi. Kalle and I stayed much longer in the south. And Annikki, your grandmother, had already gone to Sweden with little Jooseppi. If we had had a child perhaps it would have been better, but it did not happen. There was only Josef and he became my rock. But I had to be very careful that Kalle did not know this so when we were all three together I did not look at Josef or speak to him. But sometimes Kalle was away for some days - for example, in Rovaniemi. Then Josef would visit me and make me feel strong again." She stopped for a moment, before adding hurriedly, "There was nothing bad between us. No sex. Josef was very strong." (*Superhuman , thought Pippa*) "But he spoke so calmly he made me believe everything would be all right. Then suddenly he went away and I never saw him again. It felt like the end of the world, but I could not show how I felt, though when he saw me crying, Kalle knew and was very angry.

"One day Matti, Liisu's father, came to tell us he was going to work on his uncle's farm in Kittilä, and Kalle told him to let him know if he ever wanted more help, as he hated this place. And Matti must have taken him seriously because a few weeks later he wrote to say his uncle was looking for a good worker and Matti had recommended him. And he was a good worker: better with machines and animals than with people, unless they were his drinking friends. Kalle was very happy, and we packed up and went. By then I was happy to leave because without Josef or Annikki there was no reason to stay. Then later, Matti inherited the farm. He was very generous and let Kalle

204

have some land and an old house. Kalle made the old house good, and bought small herd of reindeer…." Kirsti's voice trailed off as her head fell back on the pillow.

Pippa sat quietly watching her until she began to recover. "I shall go now, Kirsti. This is much too tiring for you."

"It is the only thing I can do for Josef and for Jooseppi," she said faintly. "You must not stop me. And there is not so much more."

"I will only stop you for today. I will be back tomorrow."

"One more thing before you go. After Kalle died, I found some papers in his writing. They were written in German and I asked a friend to translate them into Finnish. When I saw they were copies of letters he had written to a German friend, and then a kind of diary, and understood what they were saying, I paid for them to be translated into English because I wanted you to know everything, and nothing shows Kalle's nature better than these writings."

Intrigued, Pippa said, "I'll read them before my next visit."

In fact she did not go back for three days, as she awoke next morning sneezing violently and with a sore throat, no condition in which to visit a frail old lady in her last days. Pippa went for short walks, but otherwise stayed indoors, reading the translation of Kalle's letters and diary over and over again, practising yoga, thinking through all the things Kirsti had told her and remembering her father. But especially reading those writings of Kalle. And especially those diary entries. She tried as hard as she could to imagine what it must be like to be brought up from your first memory to believe that black was white, that a madman was a proud and worthy leader, that in his name and that of the good of your country, anything was permissible, and if a woman did not give you what was your right you were entitled to take it by whatever means. And she failed. She could almost persuade herself that her father had been right to kill him, but one of the things he had indelibly instilled into her was that means do not justify ends.

She was mulling it over yet again as she did some gentle stretching exercises, when Matti came into the living room one afternoon. He backed out hastily, but she called after him to return as she was really bored with her own company. He came back and she saw he was holding a photograph album. As he handed it to her he said, "I had forgotten this. There are many photos from long ago,

205

including one or two more of your father, of Kirsti when she was young. Even Liisu when she was a child."

"Huh!" said Liisu coming in behind him. She grabbed the album and settled on the sofa beside Pippa. "It's just the afternoon for 'do-you-remembers'."

"Well, there won't be many of mine, but I shall enjoy listening to yours."

"They are from very long ago," warned Matti. "But later you will see interesting things."

They were from a *very* long time ago. In the early pages, moustached and bearded male faces and bonneted female ones stared back at them with a composure that gave nothing away. Names and dates were scrawled under each, some in the Cyrillic alphabet indicating there had been a measure of intermarriage in the days when Tsarist Russia held the Finnish reins. Pippa expressed the thought that seemed surprising as presumably as the ruling class, the Russians might have thought of the Finns as inferior.

"Oh, I think they know better than that," Matti said. "We have too many battles for them to have wrong ideas."

"Just look at great-great-grandpapa Matti from 1851," Liisu plonked a forefinger on a ferociously stern face. "Don't you think he has a look of Father?"

Matti came to peer over her shoulder. "It would be strange if he did. He is on your mother's side. Anyway Pippa isn't interested in this old history."

Feigning grumpiness, Liisu flicked her way into the 20th century. Gradually the men became less hairy, the women less matronly. By World War I, they were respectfully and recognisably handsome or beautiful in an old fashioned sort of way.

"Look, *äiti*, Mama!" Liisu had pointed to a portrait of a young woman looking out at the camera from under lashes in a way none of the earlier generations had. Her mouth pouted slightly, like a film star. She was beautiful. "Why didn't I inherit any of her looks."

"Perhaps she wasn't as clever as you," Pippa suggested.

"She was very clever," Matti disagreed. "But she did not have your energy."

206

Liisu pondered a moment about the virtues of energy versus beauty. Pippa finally came up with, "Well a storm is as beautiful as a mountain scene."

They continued through the album. First there was Matti as a young man, and then Matti with another young woman who was not Liisu's mother. "There is my sister Annikki, your grandmother Pippa."

She studied it for a long time, trying to see the worn old face she remembered from her childhood superimposed on the smooth attractive features of this schoolgirl. And not succeeding. Then as they moved on through the years, she began to find a hint of familiarity in the smile and the way she avoided looking at the camera.

"I called her Grannyanni," Pippa reminisced. "Granny was too ordinary and Grannyannikki was too long."

A couple of pages later there were several of Matti and Ana's wedding. They unarguably made a very handsome couple. And on the next page Ana holding baby Liisu, followed by Liisu crawling, Liisu toddling, Liisu laughing, Liisu with a face screwed up in anger, and Liisu trotting off to school. Pippa watched with growing anticipation as the pages turned, waiting for the time when Josef was due to make his appearance. And there he was, leg encased in plaster, standing on crutches, squinting into the sun.

Later there were pictures with a laughing young woman - Annikki, Matti's sister, Pippa's grandmother. And at last one of Annikki holding a baby.

"Uncle Jooseppi," Liisu said.

Pippa looked at the scrap that was her father in the early weeks of his life.

"And look, look," Liisu said excitedly. "There on the same page is Kirsti."

Pippa looked reluctantly away from baby Jooseppi to young, pretty Kirsti with a halo of fluffy fair hair.

"Look, and there is Kalle," Liisu said with less enthusiasm. He was standing beside Kirsti another picture, an arm proprietorally round her shoulders. And, yes, he was handsome, and in a strange way familiar.

There was one more picture of Josef holding the baby. It had been only a very few months after that Annikki had left for Sweden with baby Jooseppi. Josef had never seen his son again. Seeing them all together in these pictures, the reality of it hit Pippa for the first time and she found the tears trickling down her cheeks.

"Now we make you cry," Matti said. "Sorry Pippa."

She shook her head. "It is wonderful to see my father and my grandfather together."

Liisu closed the album. "Perhaps that's enough."

"No, let's see if there are any more of Josef."

There were not, but there was one of Kalle crouching down with a knife, presumably sharpening it. There was something about it that made him seem even more familiar. Pippa went on staring at it for some minutes, then she gave up and handed the album back to Matti.

Later there was a call from the rest home. Kirsti was asking Pippa to be sure to come and see her the next day,

"I think I'm still germy," warned Pippa.

Matti relayed the message to the rest home, but they still wanted her to come.

Pippa and Liisu exchanged glances. It was easy to interpret their mutual agreement that when someone was on the verge of death, the introduction of a cold was probably not a major consideration.

Weymouth : mid-March 2011

The ringing tone stopped and a voice said crisply, "Laura Jamieson."

Before he could change his mind, Jude blurted. "Hello Laura Jamieson. This is Jude … Jimmie here. Is this a convenient moment to speak - that's if you're not too angry ever to speak to me again."

There was a silence that went on for a bit too long for comfort before Laura said, "I have to say I was really angry when I saw you in the hide. I had hoped Pippa had explained how concerned I am at Bob's reaction if you suddenly bounce back into his life."

"I know, I know. She did try to explain. She was right. You were right. I was wrong. But please give me a chance to get it right, and I promise I'll do everything your way."

He heard the suppressed laughter in her voice as she said, "Well, that'll be a first for any Jamieson I've come across so far, including your Aunt Bee," and he began to dare hope he was in with a chance.

He said, "I do appreciate your worries. And I've sometimes wondered whether it would be better if I forgot the whole thing. The fact is that it would be really amazing to have Dad in my life, especially as he seems to be now. Maybe I could even do something for him." Jude felt the tightness in his throat, heard the wobble in his voice, and cleared his throat noisily.

"OK," Laura said. "You've convinced me. Let's think this through. In a strange way, it could be that the hide at Radipole is as good a place as any. We've rather got used to bumping into you there. But how we get over the difficult bit of who you actually are is a different matter."

"Will you let me think about it and perhaps call you when I've got some ideas?"

"Yes, you think about it. But no, don't call me back. If Bob ever got the idea this had been stage-managed, he'd be mad. And let's not leave it too long. Say next week-end?"

He hadn't expected that. "OK, next week-end it is," Jude said beginning to feel he was taking on one hell of a responsibility.

1

Pippa returned to the rest home after breakfast next morning, generally agreed to be Kirsti's 'best time'. A chair was ready for her by the bedside. Someone else was in the room, sitting by the window - Kirsti's brother Pentti. She had made a real effort to look fresh for her visitor, but she still looked as though a puff of breeze would blow her into the next world. Pippa took the thin hand she held out to her.

"Now Jooseppi's daughter, you will hear the end of the story."

She went on, "Last time, I told you how Matti had invited Kalle to go north and work for with him in Kittilä. Later he gave us small piece of land and Kalle bought some reindeer. Kalle had a reputation of being good with animals. I was happy with the arrangement. I thought it would be a new beginning for us both, and easier when I was away from the memories of Josef. I was surprised to find how isolated the house was, but it was well placed for the reindeer feeding grounds. And I do not so much need society. If only Kalle and I could have been good company for each other.

"It was OK for some time. Kalle liked to work outside and he was very good with reindeer. And I was happy to make a new home and to start making *ryijy* again. You know what that is?" Pippa shook her head. "It is a woven rug. You can make own design and colours. In old times people used them on beds. Now they make decoration on wall." Pippa nodded. She remembered seeing several now - there were at least two in Matti's house.

"Then one day I see that he is angry when he comes home. He begins to shout like in the old days. I get up to give him some brandy. That always make him better. Then I smell he already has been drinking. And he hits me in face. It was such a shock, I stood staring at him. Then he was sorry, and wants to make love. I don't want, but I make it so that he is in better mood. After that it happens more and more. Sometimes if I really do not want, Kalle makes it happen anyway."

Pippa remembered the extracts from Kalle's diary and again thought that it sounded suspiciously like rape. She glanced across at Pentti. She knew Kirsti's brother did not speak English, but from the scowl on his face she guessed he understood enough from his sister's tone and gestures to realise what she was saying. "How did you put up with it for so long?"

Kirsti's shoulders rose slightly against the pillow in a small shrug. "Josef asked me that very early. Pippa, it is difficult to explain. I had no money, no skills."

"What about your family?"

"They had stayed in Karelia after the Peace Treaty. I heard nothing from them. Of course, there was my uncle, but he had many children, and he had not been very happy to add me to them."

Pippa nodded. *That damned war.* Kirsti went on, "It was one of the things that brought Kalle and me together. We had both lost family, I in Karelia and he in Germany. Yes, I was foolish. Young and foolish. But Kalle was handsome and strong. I thought he would look after me for always." *Well, Kirsti wasn't the first one to fall for a strong, handsome man.*

A nurse came in with a tray of tea. She looked anxiously at Kirsti, plumped up her cushions, gave her a pill to take. The old lady said something reassuring in Finnish and the nurse nodded and left. Kirsti went on, "And it was not always so bad. There were long periods when things were all right. Kalle was away a lot, especially in summer, following the reindeer to where they found good food. He was always happy at those times, and he did not drink so much. Then in the winter, I went to stay in Rovaniemi with Pentti - my chest was not so good." She smiled. "They were good times." Pentti was smiling too, happy because his precious sister looked happy.

"But didn't you tell him how Kalle treated you?"

The old lady looked at Pippa in amazement. "Of course not. It was not possible. Pentti would have killed him."

And perhaps he did, was Pippa's next thought. She had to pull her mind back from that seductive thought to concentrate on Kirsti's story.

"And so the years passed," she went on. "Kalle started to go to Germany every two years and he always came back very happy. I'm sure he had a woman there. Then one day she came to visit, with her small boy. She was called Greta and the little boy Karl, which is the German for Kalle. But I knew it could not be Kalle's son because I had had tests and knew there was nothing to stop me having babies. But I saw Kalle treating Greta like a wife when he thought I was not noticing."

Kirsti paused, waiting to regain some strength. "Then one day I heard wonderful news. So wonderful that at first I could not believe it. Matti came to visit me and said that Josef's son Jooseppi was coming to Kittilä. Of course I did not tell Kalle. Any mention of Josef made him so angry. I asked Matti ... no, I begged Matti to tell Jooseppi he must not come here - to send me word and I would come to Kittilä to see him. But ....."

Pippa could guess the next bit. You did not tell Father what he could or could not do. After all, he had never met Kalle. All he knew was that Josef had been Kirsti's great love and that he must see her.

Kirsti continued ".... he did not listen. One afternoon there was a knock on door and I opened it and there he stood. I knew straight away it was Jooseppi. He came in and put his arms round me and for a moment it was like Josef had come back from the dead. Then I pushed him away. Kalle was out fishing, but I knew he would be back soon. I told Jooseppi he must go and I would meet him in Kittilä after two days. A few minutes later, Kalle came home."

Pippa found she was holding her breath and let it out slowly. Kirsti said, "He looked round the room and burst into terrible anger, demanding to know who the boots belonged to."

"Boots?" Pippa asked, bewildered.

"Yes, I did not say that as soon as he came in Jooseppi took off his boots as is custom in a Finnish house, and I gave him a pair of Kalle's reindeer slippers."

And suddenly Pippa knew why one of the photographs of Kalle had seemed so familiar. He had been in a crouching position and he had been wearing boots, just like the figure in that dream: the dream of the cold dead figure in the cupboard. With an effort she returned her full concentration to what Kirsti was saying.

"I told Kalle the boots belonged to someone who had brought something from Kittilä. But I am bad liar and there was nothing to show him. He grabbed the boots and started hitting me in a more terrible way than ever before." She started to tremble, clearly reliving the scene and Pentti came over to hold her small hand in his big one. "With strength I did not know I had, I pushed and pushed him. He was rather drunk and he fell back and hit his head on the edge of the fire place. After that I don't remember anything, only that Kalle did not move and I knew he was dead."

There was a long silence while Pentti continued to hold her hand and Pippa's mind struggled to untangle the implications of what she had just heard. And remembered that cryptic comment Father had made in that dream - 'wrong boots'.

Suddenly with a stronger voice Kirsti picked up the story. "Then like a miracle, the door opened and Jooseppi was there. He was too worried about me to go back to Kittilä, and anyway he had only Kalle's slippers.. Then he had seen Kalle return and heard him shouting. He was about to burst in when everything went very quiet. He took the boots Kalle was holding – in fact they were Matti's boots that Jooseppi had borrowed -and put them on, and then we found an old sledge and put the body in it. It took a long time to get to the lake but the nights are light as you know at that time of year. Kalle's boat was there, and I took it some distance and left it on the shore upside down, and walked back through the forest. Jooseppi said we must not bury Kalle because it must look like accident."

She was in control of herself. "But Pentti would not believe I had done this. He thought it was Jooseppi because Kalle had gone to tell the Germans that Josef was Russian and they sent him to a slave camp. And Kalle's friend Hans came from Germany and agreed with Pentti. But Jooseeppi had already gone home to England. For a long time no one asked any questions, because they believed the story about the accident. Then a new Sheriff came to the area from the south, and wanted to make an impression, and started looking into old cases of unexplained deaths. They sent someone to get a statement from Hans in Germany, and they interviewed Pentti who confirmed the trouble between Kalle and Josef. But now Pentti understands I cannot die with such a big lie, so I have written the whole truth and he will give it to the authorities." She smiled. "Perhaps after so long they don't care. But my spirit will be happy."

Pippa was crying now, partly in relief that her Father's name was clear, partly by his honourable behaviour, and partly by Kirsti's bravery in the last days or hours of her life. And clearly they were the last hours. She must leave them together, the sister and brother who had looked out for her all those years and in the end was not there at the moment of greatest need. Pentti made way for her as she got up and leaned over to hold Kirsti's thin frame in her arms.

"Bon voyage," she whispered, and hurried from the room, the tears flowing, but her heart full of pride. She stumbled out to the entrance of the rest home and found a chair in the entrance hall. Wide windows framed a black and white scene that was just beyond winter but not quite spring. It reflected her mood: a limbo somewhere between past and future.

"How about sticking to the present," Jude's voice said in her head.

Liisu found her there half an hour later. She said, "I hope those are tears of joy."

Pippa smiled wanly. "Of relief anyway. But I don't know how I feel. There is a big empty hole where the future used to be full of plans of what to do, where to go next."

"I'll tell you what happens next," her friend said firmly. "We go home and telephone Jude."

Weymouth : mid-March 2011

1

Jude's mobile rang as he was making his way along the Radipole circuit. After listening, he said into it "It's wonderful, wonderful news. God, I wish I were there to give you the biggest hug you've ever had."

Over the ether from a thousand-plus miles away he caught a small sound that seemed to express doubt rather than delight. "Are you OK, sweetheart?"

"I should be over the moon," wobbled Pippa's voice, "but now it's all over, I feel I'm teetering on the brink of a precipice." She gave a gulp, then said more strongly, "But you're on the brink of your own crisis. Sorry, sorry. I'll stop thinking of me and send you every possible positive thought I can dredge up."

"Thanks. And love you," Jude said, aware of his own fragility. "Call me tonight."

As he slipped the mobile back in his pocket, a woman passed him holding the hand of a small boy. "A good idea to start them young," he said cheerfully and the woman smiled.

"I seed a heron," the small boy informed him.

"Saw," the woman corrected automatically.

A few minutes later, Jude sat in the hide, his heart thumping and his stomach churning until he thought he would be sick. Laura had suggested they should meet later in the day when most birders would have gone home. To be on the safe side, he had got there earlier when the hide was still quite full and the excitement pulsating at the unexpected arrival of a pair of great white egrets, much larger than their smaller cousins and without their yellow boots. Then gradually the birders had dispersed until there was only one elderly man. Jude guessed from his speech that he was from within the sound of Bow Bells and had probably never seen a great egret before. He just hoped his enthusiasm would not make him linger too long.

At last the man said, "Better go and show the Missus I ain't scarpered for good."

After the door had clicked closed behind him, the silence seemed to thicken enough to be cut with a knife. Jude had been trying out various appropriate phrases over and over again to match any eventuality, but now he firmly closed his mind to them and looked out at the softening light over the water, as the sun dipped towards the reeds.

He looked at his watch. It would be a good while before Laura and his father turned up and the inactive waiting was really getting to him. He left his identification book on the shelf, open at the page where he had been double-checking the egrets, and left the hide. How did you fill one, two, possibly several hours prior to a life-changing encounter and retain your sanity? He began following the path back towards the entrance, trying to steer his thoughts away from the imminent meeting when he became aware of running feet scrunching closer behind him. He turned as their owner was about to draw level: the woman he had met earlier, panting for breath but managing to gasp, "Small boy disappeared...."

"Name" Jude asked.

"Jimmie." She was close to tears. "My grandson. Oh God."

Jude rattled out "Path divides round the next bend. I'll take the right division, you the left. Do you know your mobile number?" As the woman nodded, Jude thrust his mobile at her and demanded hers. "We call each other as soon as one of us finds him."

He rushed off, leaving her still catching her breath, his mind now totally focussed on pre-empting a potential tragedy. As soon as he reached the division in the path, he slowed down and began to walk quietly, deliberately, scanning either side of the path as he went, paying particular attention to any unexpected movement in the reeds. A nearly four-year-old could be very active, certainly more active than might be desirable among so many swampy reed beds surrounded by so much water. A man balancing a telescope over one shoulder was coming towards him.

Jude asked, "You haven't by chance seen a small boy?"

"A very small boy? Yup. A couple of hundred yards on. Not a good idea to leave him wandering around in this sort of stuff."

Jude quelled his instinct to defend himself against the implied criticism and hurried on, slowing down as he came to a curve in the path and, as it straightened out, glimpsed a very small figure crouching on the right hand side of it. Hair flopping over his forehead, the little boy was totally absorbed in something, stroking the something and singing to it in a tuneless voice.

Jude sent a silent prayer of thanks to whatever gods there might be and sauntered towards the figure. "Hello, Jimmie," he said, "What have you found there? I'm Jude."

"Hello, Choo. This bird is sleepy."

Jude approached. It was a first year blackbird, he could tell from the colouring, and he thought it was very dead. He crouched beside the boy. "I think your nice song sent him to sleep. I shouldn't wake him up."

Jimmie nodded vigorously and resumed his tuneless singing "so that it would go on sleeping." Jude reached into his pocket for the mobile phone he had taken from the boy's grandmother and punched in the number of his own mobile. After a couple of rings a voice said, "Yes? Yes?"

"I'm with Jimmie now," Jude said. "Just follow the right hand path from the fork and you'll find us. There's no hurry. He's just fine."

She gasped her thanks and rang off. While they were waiting, Jude suggested to the little boy that they covered the bird with leaves to keep it warm and Peter trotted to and fro bringing small fistfuls of leaves which Jude spread over the body. In five minutes, the woman was approaching them not even trying to conceal her tears of gratitude.

"You know my Granallis?" Jimmie said, seeming not phased by this unusual circumstance.

The woman crouched down beside the bird, playing for time in which to get herself under control. "My name is Alice," the woman explained. "And Jimmie, you are never, never, to run away like that again. Anyway, what have you found?"

"I've been singing to this bird because Choo said it will help it to sleep."

"My name's Jude," he translated.

They smiled at each other. "I'm so deeply grateful to you, Jude. I don't know what I'd have done if I hadn't found you."

"In fact, you did me a good turn," Jude said. "I was trying to find a way of avoiding thinking about an imminent and possibly life-changing meeting."

"Want to talk about it?" Alice glanced down at her grandson still humming tunelessly to the blackbird and making sure it was properly covered by the leaves.

Jude said, "It's a very long story," and then found that he was telling this pleasant stranger in jerky episodes the convoluted tale of how he came to be in Radipole reserve that day.

She listened intently. At last she said, "Go easy on him, Jude. Admitting you're an alkie is one of the most difficult things in the world - well, for an alkie."

"Don't tell me you...."

She laughed. "No, no. Thank heavens. But my son in law is, which is why my daughter is working and my grandson and I spend quite a lot of time together, and why he is particularly precious. And before you start talking about the long arm of coincidence, there are a lot of them about. Alkies I mean."

Jude put a hand briefly on her shoulder. "And now you have done me a hell of a good turn. And it would be an even better one if we could all go back to the visitors' centre and have an ice cream together."

"Ice creeeem!" shouted Jimmie excitedly, the bird forgotten.

2

An hour later, after they had variously demolished ice cream, a pot of tea and toasted teacakes, Jude waved them off in their car and made his way back to the hide. Though his imminent meeting still made him nervous, he felt noticeably less negative about it. Interesting how one's perspective could change when you somehow removed yourself from the centre of the picture.

The hide was empty and the quality of light visibly altering now that the sun had dipped below the reed beds and streaks of orange and strawberry were beginning to tint gathering clouds. Pippa would have loved it.

He allowed his mind to become caught up in the unfolding phenomena of how much they did enjoy being together. It was all so different from the enjoyment they had shared in Oz: the fun, the busy-ness, indeed the lack of time really to stand and stare. In a way it was rather surprising they had stayed together so long. His thoughts flitted over the occasional affairs when he had been away in New Zealand, or when Pippa had been on one of her trips with the girls. And the oddity of the fact that there had been none after she had left to go back to the UK to look after her father. Was it at that point he had begun to realise how much she meant to him? There had been other changes too: towards his own memories of the sick and cantankerous old man that had been her father. Even goddamit, his reactions towards that weird cat of hers.

And now she knew the truth about what had happened between her father and the man Kalle. He thought of how wan she had sounded, and tried to imagine what it must be like to come to the end of a long quest. Then he reminded himself that he was only now on the brink of reaching the end of his own.

His thoughts were interrupted by an approaching murmur of voices and he was catapulted back into the here-and-now of where he was and why he was here.

"That was a rail," he heard his father's voice say. Jude hadn't heard a thing. And then the door opened and his father edged in with a three-wheel frame - and there was no going back.

"Hello, Jude," Laura's voice said evenly.

Bob Jamieson seemed instinctively to know where Jude sat and turned, glaring at him. "I smell a very large rat. No offence, young man."

"None taken," Jude said. And then he couldn't stop himself. "In fact there is something I want to tell you, sir."

219

Bob grunted. "I thought you might. She talks about you in her sleep, you know. If it weren't for the age gap, I might have been anxious."

Jude couldn't resist, "How can you be so sure about the age gap?"

The old man said, but without bitterness, "You can't be blind for as long as I have and not be able to tell the difference between the sound of an older guy and one young enough to be your son."

The silence seemed to shout at them. Even though he could not see, Bob Jamieson turned his head from one to the other.

"Oh," he said. Then, "Oh!" again. And finally, when the length of silence had become unbearably long, "Someone had better start talking."

Jude opened his mouth. It didn't come out anything like the various ways he had rehearsed but in a gabble of non sequiturs. "I have an English girl friend called Pippa," he said. "I met her in Australia and for various complicated reasons she needed to come back to the UK to find out about her roots. It set me thinking that I would also like to know more about the Dad who had once taken me fishing on the Swan River, and who suddenly did not want to know me and Mother any more."

Bob Jamieson had clasped his hands to stop them shaking. He cleared his throat. "You remember those fishing trips?"

"Yup. They were the best memories. You stuffed me full of ice cream and I watched you fishing and thought I wanted to grow up like that." Jude paused. "Other memories weren't so good. I guess I didn't understand you were so crook."

"Guess I didn't either." Bob held out a hand, and Jude took it. "Jeez that's a big hand. Huh, you've grown and I'm shrinking."

"You're OK," Jude said, because suddenly this rather frail old man with the thinning hair and craggy face *was* OK. "And your Laura's OK."

"She's more'n that. She brought me back to life."

"She did no such thing." Laura's voice was shaky. "She merely joined you on the journey." She became her brisk self. "How

220

about we go home and we can start doing a proper job of filling in the last thirty years. I assume your Pippa is still root-hunting?"

"Mm, in Finland as we speak. We've just been talking." He waved his mobile. "It was odd, really. Everything has turned out as she had hoped, and yet she sounded so … so wan."

Laura nodded. "That can happen to anyone - an overwhelming sense of anti-climax once a crisis is over."

They made their way back to the entrance of the reserve, Bob Jamieson surprisingly spry pushing his frame. Back at the car park, they separated and Jude followed them in the campervan. Inside, the cottage was cosy but uncluttered. Laura went off to put the kettle on.

It was agreed that they would have a session each of holding the floor before giving way to the other, but of course it did not work out like that. The 'don't you remember's…?' and 'Yes, but what about's…?' soon rendered a straight narrative of events impossible. They gave up and just talked, darting backwards and forwards in time, breaking off to recap what had already been said and side-tracking down ways that had no relevance other than the pleasure of sharing what had never been shared before.

The exchange of stories was batted to and fro, with frequent references to Laura for forgotten detail in Bob's case. Jude summarised Pippa's search for the father she had never properly known either, the shock of the news that he might have been responsible for a man's death, her determination to clear his name.

"She sounds quite a woman," Bob said. "Even worthy of a Jamieson."

It was Laura who reminded Jude and informed Bob of Pippa's visit to Weymouth when Bob was laid-up, and how she had gone with Laura to the self-help group where the couple had met. Bob said, "I look forward to meeting your Pippa; but it seems that a great deal of conspiracy has been going on behind my back."

Laura went off to make more tea and some sandwiches. While she was out of the room, Bob suddenly stood up, and instinctively Jude knew what to do. He stood up, too, and they moved towards each other and embraced.

221

"Hi, Dad," Jude said, feeling the thinness of his father's shoulders in his arms.

"Welcome back, son," Bob said, not bothering to conceal the quaver in his voice. "Just wish your mother could know about this."

"Don't you think it's likely that she does?"

There was a grunt. "Not sure I believe in that stuff."

"Hmm. I'm not sure I can continue to not believe it."

Laura returned with a laden tray, paused in the doorway. "That's the best sight I've seen for a long time."

Oxfordshire : early April 2011

1

Kirsti died a few days after her last meeting with Pippa, who stayed on for the funeral. Of course she did not understand much of the service, but it felt right to be there representing Grandfather Josef and her father.

The tiredness that now enveloped her like a fog seemed to drain reality of all life, as though sight and sound and touch were happening in another dimension. Liisu became quite worried and called in a doctor friend who diagnosed depression brought on by exhaustion.

"But I haven't done anything," Pippa protested. "And I'm not taking pills."

She slept a great deal, but it never seemed enough. She had several skimpy little telephone calls with Jude, at first in Weymouth, then in Daerley, but they didn't seem real either. At last Liisu said, "I don't want you to go, but I think you need to be home with your man."

Earlier she would have thought how funny that sounded, but now she merely nodded and went off with Liisu to book a flight.

Jude met her at the airport, took one look at her, and enfolded her in an embrace as though he would never let her go. At home she picked at the casserole he had prepared, then he put her to bed and lay beside her holding her. Love-making was clearly the last thing on her mind, so he went on holding her until he drifted into sleep himself, waking in the early hours to be aware of the gentle breathing that indicated she was sleeping too.

She spent the next day sitting clutching Aristotle and staring out of the window. The next day Jude insisted she went to the doctor. Mac was a no-nonsense Scot, on the verge of retirement, and he dragged out of her the sequence of events of the past weeks. Then he tapped the end of his pencil on his desk and said, "You're suffering from depression, dear girl. With all you've been through, it would be unnatural if you were not."

"I'm not taking any pills," Pippa said automatically.

The pencil went on tapping for a few more moments, then the gruff voice that had advised and supported her through her father's illness said briskly, "Do you want to get better or don't you?"

After a moment, Pippa agreed that she did. Mac grunted, scribbled a prescription and said, "Right. I'll see you in a week's time."

Things seemed to lighten a bit after that. When he found her staring out of the window again, Jude suggested she might do something useful like making contact with her former yoga pupils.

"I'm not starting another class."

"Not suggesting that. Just that you should pick up the threads of normality."

"Whatever that means."

"Did we ever know what it meant?" Jude asked and was rewarded by a flicker of her old smile.

That afternoon she looked in at Freshfields Nursing Home where several of her ex-pupils resided. It was tea time, and they were all there. Some greeted her with guilty admissions that their practice had faded from regular to infrequent to nothing. Three announced that they had continued to meet on a twice weekly basis in one of their rooms. Pippa put them through their paces to make sure they had not picked up any bad habits, and was impressed. She began to think again of the possibility of re-starting the classes while they sorted out their future.

"Sometimes Peter joins us," one of them said.

Peter was the rather more than middle-aged man who had provided them with transport when they had originally come to Pippa's classes.

"You're looking peaky," several of her ex-pupils said.

"It's been a difficult time," Pippa said. "I'll be all right," and found she could actually believe it. She added, "I might come and join you sometimes."

When she got home, she got out some of her yoga books. Then she got our her yoga mat, folded herself into a meditation pose and

224

began one of her favourite breathing exercises, breathing alternately through each nostril, closing one with a thumb, then the other with a ring finger. Jude glancing in through the window saw her and raised a hand in silent salutation to the sky. It was some minutes before Pippa became aware of a car revving in the distance, and paused. She was aware of a hint of calmness that she had not felt for a long time.

Why was it that one stopped doing things that were good for one and then wondered why one was falling apart?

They went out for a pub meal in the evening and that night made gentle love.

"Sorry I'm a mess," she said into Jude's chest.

"You're a beautiful mess. And we'll go and see Dad very soon."

There were still bad times. Mornings were worst when she awoke to peer round the corner of the day. Sometimes she felt trapped in her own head and stayed there, other times the veil gradually lifted and hope returned.

"So?" Mac asked when she went to see him after the first week.

"Had three or four pretty bad days."

"So you had three or four pretty good ones?" He grinned at her annoyingly.

Slowly she was picking up the threads that had made the fabric of her life, and with it the memory of new responsibilities that lay ahead. A phone call from Hedges & Waters, the estate agent, catapulted her into the reality of the moment. John Brown, the purchaser of her house, they informed her, would be returning to the UK unexpectedly the following Wednesday, and would very much appreciate access to the property with his architect.

It was all beginning to sound rather final.

2

It was bad luck that only a few days later Laura rang to say that Bob had collected a bug from somewhere and was in hospital.

225

"I'll wait till you're really better," Jude said.

"No you won't," Pippa said with a return of something of her old spirit. "You'll go and spend some time with the Dad you've only just rediscovered after thirty years. Take it from someone who knows, you'll regret it if anything happens."

Reluctantly Jude agreed and left the following day.

Pippa set about structuring her days: checking on the times of radio or television programmes that would engage her mind; setting periods aside for yoga stretching and breathing exercises; arranging to visit Freshfields most days for tea. Jude rang every day. Bob was stable but they were worried about one of his lungs. There was to be a biopsy. Pippa assured him over and over again that it was better if he stayed there and supported both his father and Laura. Yes, she promised she would let him know if she started falling apart.

And there was John Brown and his architect. They met at the house on the Wednesday morning. He looked younger than she remembered, and his excitement at his imminent move was infectious. The architect was a woman with curly bronze hair and a similar if more professional enthusiasm. Pippa left them discussing where the new outside entrance should go and which wall would be most suitably moved to make room for an extra en suite.

She wandered out into the garden. It didn't sound as if it would much resemble father's house by the time they had finished, and perhaps that was a good thing. The garden was showing signs of a lot of new growth. The bulbs that she and Jude had planted in the autumn had produced a fine show of daffs and tulips. She heard a movement behind her and turned to find John Brown watching her.

They went into her father's old studio. It felt so empty and strange; but she had left the desk there and the cupboard. She noticed the bowl that Father had put down on the floor to catch drips of rain when the wind was in a certain direction.

"We should have fixed that."

"No problem. I think even I can fix that." John Brown paused. "I feel like a twenty-year-old starting a new life," he confided, and she almost told him that is just what he looked like. He added, "And I'll do my best to keep it nice."

"It will be yours to do as you will."

"I know, I know. But I believe places have spirits. I think your father's will be around for a while. And yours." Pippa was glad he felt like that. "By the way where is your lovable monster?"

Pippa looked surprised. "I thought I explained he was in Weymouth."

John Brown's head went back with a roar of laughter. "I didn't mean your young man, I meant the cat!"

Pippa laughed, too. "He's fine. A bit unsettled by all that's going on."

"Well, remember I meant what I said when I asked if he came with the house. Anyway, you've been very kind letting me have advance access. I'm staying at The Trumpet by the way. You wouldn't care to join me for dinner? If you think Lovable Monster Number One would not object."

Pippa met him that evening for a drink in the bar before going into the restaurant. Peter was there with some friends. "Hello, hello," he teased. "Are the mice playing while the cat's away?"

Pippa apologised to John Brown, who shook his head, smiled and said he could not think of a greater compliment.

A few more days passed and the medication really started to kick in.

"I don't like being controlled by chemicals," Pippa complained to Mac on her second visit.

"They are not controlling you, only doing a temporary prop job while you're getting ready to take it over yourself.. And you're looking better."

One of the medication's effects was that she slept as though she had been pole axed. Perhaps that was the reason she did not notice that Aristotle was not his usual self. Perhaps that was also the reason she did not immediately notice it the following week when he went missing. At times, the weariness seemed to permeate the marrow of her bones. She had even told Aristotle about it that afternoon, burying her face in his fur and reporting Mac's conclusions in a passable imitation of his Scottish brogue, which clearly passed Aristotle by.

227

"Early bed," Pippa told him after she had had her daily call to Jude, and they had gone up in tandem. It was at 3 a.m. that she had briefly woken to find that the usual warm lump resting against her legs was absent. "Totty!" she called, assuming he had gone down for a night snack, but was asleep again before she could wonder at the lack of response.

At seven he was still absent and she was out of bed as soon as she awoke. She called him from the back door, then the front door, then back door again. On automatic she dressed, made some coffee, prepared a bowl of cereal, half expecting the familiar *miaoul*. It was inexplicable. Aristotle never went out at night, not since that night when as a young cat he had met something nasty in the dark that had marked him for life. Even in the day time he never strayed far. The flat was only a couple of hundred yards from a conservation area round the remains of a pre-medieval castle: now an interesting network of lumps and bumps crowned by thick vegetation: a wonderful playground for adventurous kids, but not for a nervous cat. Well, at least he now had a collar with his name and her telephone number on it. When the phone rang, she grabbed it eagerly.

"Hi sweetheart!" Jude.

"Oh, it's you."

"And I'm glad to hear your voice, too. Anything up?"

She couldn't inflict something so trivial on him, not when he was worried about his Dad. "Nothing, lover. Just overslept a bit and I'm still surfacing. How's your Dad?"

At least she sounded more her old self. Jude said, "I'm going in this morning. If he continues to make progress, I'll be home in a couple of days. Give my love to Totty."

"Yeah. And mine to Bob."

It was an April-showers sort of morning. Pippa slipped into a waterproof and wellies and went out. After a thorough search of the back garden and peering over surrounding fences, she headed for the castle mound. And stood on its highest point, looking helplessly at the expanse of semi-tamed wilderness. It would take the combined forces of the Thames Valley police to search this lot properly.

228

During the rest of the morning, she trudged round the neighbourhood. *"Dear old Aristotle…"* *"Poor old thing, has he disappeared?"* *"Don't worry - he'll be back. Cats know where they're well off."* The sundry reactions were friendly but unproductive.

Not in the least hungry, Pippa warmed up a saucepan of soup and was about half way through it when the doorbell rang.

Someone must have found Aristotle. She rushed to answer it. On the doorstep stood an unknown girl in her late teens, a very pretty girl with long blonde hair and an anxious expression.

"Have you found him?" It was out before Pippa could stop it.

"Found him?" the girl said. She clearly had not. "Please, are you Philippa Eastman?" The English was slightly and attractively accented.

"I am."

The girl held out a hand. "I am very pleased to meet you. My name is Greta Schmidt, daughter of Karl Schmidt. We have spoken on the telephone."

Indeed they had. "I hope you will be able to help me," the young woman continued.

"I'll try." Pippa took the extended hand, scrabbled into memory. "You had better come in."

She led the girl into the kitchen, put the kettle on for coffee, ditched her half-consumed bowl of soup. "Do sit down. In what way can I help you? I seem to remember it was something to do with your grandfather."

The girl sat down neatly. "Yes, but it is to do with my grandfather and your grandfather. They knew each other, I think."

3

Pippa's mind raced. *Grandfather Josef and someone called Karl. Not, Karl, Kalle.* She reached into a cupboard for cups and saucers. "I never met my grandfather, he died before I was born."

"I did not meet mine because he was killed." Greta smoothed her hands over skirt, folded them neatly on her lap.

If only Jude were here. He was much better at dissembling. Perhaps the best thing was to be as frank as possible. Pippa said, "I think I have heard of your grandfather, but under the name of Kalle. Did he live in Finland?"

"Yes, for a long time. Very far north. But his father was German and he came back to Germany and met my mother, Greta, my grandmother. I have her name." *How simple complicated stories could sound when you stripped them down to bare facts. Clearly this young woman knew nothing of Karl/Kalle's first wife.*

Pippa spooned ground coffee into the glass jug. "When I think about it though," she said. "The Kalle I heard of was married to a Finnish woman and they had no children."

Greta looked momentarily troubled, then her pretty brow cleared. "That I did not know. Then I think my grandmother must be second wife. Their son Karl junior was my father. When my father was still only a few years, he visited the place where my grandfather worked in Finland. And soon after he was killed. My grandfather, I mean."

"That's terrible."

"Yes it is. They say it was an accident, but my father thinks it was not so."

This was getting uncomfortably close. "Why did he think that?"

"I am not sure of the details. My father said there was bad feeling between our grandfathers. He tried to contact your father in case he had some information, but it was not possible."

"My father was a well know historian. He was away a great deal." Pippa began pouring out the coffee, stopped and said sharply "I'm sure you are not suggesting my grandfather killed yours?"

"No, no, of course not. It is only we found a letter from your father to my grandfather and he sound very angry." Greta fished into her handbag and drew out a crumpled sheet of paper.

Could this be one that Kirsti had overlooked or never seen? Pippa took the letter, glanced at it, felt a shock of recognition as she saw her father's writing, and handed it back. "I don't read German." She handed Greta a cup of coffee, nudged the sugar bowl towards her.

"No sugar, thank you. I will read." She fished into her handbag and produced a pair of enormous glasses. "It says *Dear Kalle or Karl, I have recently returned from a place in Germany called Fallingbostel....*"

Pippa interrupted "When was this written?"

Greta glanced at the top of the letter. "In October 1969." Well that explained a lot. "Shall I go on? *I think you know what kind of place that is and how my grandfather will have died there. Until I went there I was not sure ....*" Greta paused to read on and to search for words. *I was not sure that he went there. But there are records and I found his name and his details, the day he died and the date he came here from Finland. You Germans are very efficient in this way. The only thing it does not tell is* why *he was sent there. I think perhaps you can tell me that.*" Greta looked up, puzzled. "Why should my grandfather know such a thing?"

Pippa sipped her coffee. "We have friends in Finland who think that your grandfather hated mine because he was a Russian."

The girl look amazed. "Why should he hate?" So her school hadn't covered that particular bit of history. "I know there were bad people who made terrible things with the Jews, but why should he hate Russians?"

Pippa sighed. As briefly as she could she explained to the girl about the German advance surging through Russia and the equally powerful retreat in which tens, perhaps hundreds of thousands of men and civilians had died.

"War is very bad," Greta said. Well, at least they could agree on that. But Pippa could not bring herself to go further and explain that it was not her father, but Karl's first wife who had killed him. Instead she said, "Perhaps you did not know that your great grandfather was killed in that retreat. That would be Karl's father. Perhaps he felt that could be the way to have revenge."

Greta looked down at her hands, no longer neatly folded on her lap but the fingers twisting in uncertainty. Clearly she was no longer as sure of herself as when she came. The silence went on for quite a long time. At last she said, "Perhaps it is better to … how you say, let the sleeping dogs to lie."

"Perhaps it is," Pippa said. "Would you like some more coffee?"

"Thank you, no. I must go.. My mother is waiting in a hotel in Oxford. She did not want to come. She, too, likes sleeping dogs to lie."

Pippa watched her walk down the path, through the gate, to her parked car. Somehow she did not think they would meet again.

Soon after Greta had gone, there was a gentle tap at the back door. Without much hope Pippa opened it.

"I didn't want to intrude while you had a visitor, but I hear your Aristotle has gone missing," a near-neighbour said. "I just thought you should know that my grandson Kev said he saw him going towards the castle ruins."

It probably came as a bit of a shock to the near-neighbour when Pippa leaned forward and hugged him. "Thanks so much. I wondered whether that's where he'd gone and now you've confirmed it. I'll get over there."

"Would you like Kev to come? And me? It's a big area to search if he's got caught up somewhere?"

"Oh, yes please. That would be so kind. I'll see you over there in a few minutes."

The April-shower morning had developed into a stormy-March evening. They must have searched for two hours or more, though before then Pippa had insisted that Kev should go home and soon after that his grandfather. She soldiered on for another hour, sodden, cold, rain mingling with tears. If Aristotle were not dead, then he had been kidnapped. Though who, enquired the voice of sanity, would want that bit of tatty ginger fur? The tears flowed faster.

Eventually Pippa went home, poured herself a hot toddy, rang Jude and wailed into the phone that Aristotle had gone.

"Gone?" queried Jude. "What do you mean gone? God, not dead, when we've just become mates?"

232

Pippa tried to laugh at this absurdity through her tears, but it turned into a sob. Jude waited until she was coherent, then said "I'm on my way."

"But Bob….?"

" The biopsy was clear. Dad's doing OK. Better than Totty by the sound of it."

She could not have been more grateful. Pippa wandered round the flat, picking things up and putting them down, checking the email, trying to do a crossword, checking the answers on Google then feeling guilty that she had. Finally, commonsense took over and she got a casserole out of the freezer, defrosted it, made a crumble, fished some stewed apples from the freezer.

She had returned to the crossword and was checking answers on Google when she heard the campervan drive in and a few moments later Jude bounding in. It had just struck midnight.

"What on earth are you doing?"

"Checking answers for a crossword."

"Don't you know that's cheating!" Jude pulled her away from the computer, enveloped her in an all-embracing hug.

"There's a casserole in the oven," Pippa said into his tee-shirt.

"Then I suggest we go down and have it, and plan the strategy for the great Totty Search Party."

Aristotle : early April 2011

Something was terribly wrong and instinct drove Aristotle to go to where he needed to be. The instinct had been strong enough to drive him away from his favourite sleeping place to the outside night which he hated. A stranger observing the large ginger cat limping through the empty streets of Daerley would have immediately recognised an animal which was sick but which also knew precisely where it was going

Something terrifyingly noisy approached from ahead and Aristotle squeezed under a hedge. The squeezing hurt but he felt safe as the noise came closer. Lights flashed briefly across his eyes and something huge and dark passed across his line of vision. Then it disappeared and with it the noise became gradually less until it was a faint hum in the distance.

Aristotle waited a few moments before he squeezed himself out from under the hedge. It hurt a great deal. But it was not the pain in his back leg that was the worst. That had been there for a very long time, slowly making it more difficult to go up the stairs or jump on to the bed. It was the pain in his face which had started while his woman and her man were away: a throbbing pain that made his whole head feel as though it was too heavy to carry..

He carried on. Shapes and smells and memories were growing stronger. He had been this way many times without knowing why or when, except that he had been following the same instinct to go where he needed to be. But never before had he had that feeling so strongly.

Now he paused. Earlier he had done this journey at a time when there was a lot of movement and noise. At this particular place it had always been particularly noisy and he stopped to make sure that it was quite safe. But now there was no noise: just an empty space each way as far as he could see. All the same, he would cross this place quickly, just in case. It was not easy to go quickly, and when he had reached the other side of the space, he had to pause again to recover. But things were now more familiar and he felt happier.

Something scuttled across his field of vision. A mouse. At one time, long ago, he would have chased it, played with it, but now he was not interested in any distraction from his purpose. The way became more and more familiar. At one point, automatically, he turned right and followed the line of a fence. The fence stretched further than he remembered and he paused to rest along the way. Then he came out in a more open place and he gave a low *miaoul* of recognition. A few moments later he stopped again. He knew this house and this garden as well as he knew his paws.

He sat in the garden and looked up at the house. And listened. Nothing. No creaks or movement or whisper of breathing. He moved round the side of the house and sniffed at the back door. Nothing.

But he had not come for the house. He limped on down the path to the little garden house which he knew was the safest place in the world.

Then he stopped in dismay. The door was shut. He went closer, sniffed it, prodded with a paw.

It was only nearly-shut.

Probing with his paw, the felt the door move very slightly. He went on probing. It was hard work, and his back legs began to hurt more as he put more pressure on them. But the door was opening … just a little, a little more …. then enough for him to squeeze through.

It felt very empty inside the shed, but without hesitation Aristotle crossed the open space and found what he was looking for: a cupboard, this time with an open door. With one last supreme effort he jumped up on to the shelf where he had been so many times before. There was nothing on which to rest his head now, but he curled up, his chin on his front paws, his bad leg stretched out, and gave a big sigh.

Everything would be all right now.

Oxfordshire : early April 2011

Neither of them ate much. And when they went to bed, neither of them slept much.

"Why on earth would he go off like that?" Pippa said.

"No one could profess to read a cat's mind, least of all Totty's." Jude adjusted the pillow under his head.. "I thought he seemed a bit crook recently."

"Oh? I hadn't noticed."

"Well, you've been crook yourself."

"Tell me about Bob."

So Jude gave her a summary of a series of days of hospital visits and the roller coaster of emotions as his condition deteriorated, improved, deteriorated again. "But now he's really on the way up." When there was no response, Jude noted thankfully that Pippa had drifted into sleep.

They rose soon after six, gulped a cup of coffee and shrugged into their duffle coats. It was agreed that they would walk the circuit of the castle mound in opposite directions so that the terrain would be covered twice. Thankfully the day was still and sunny. Normally the circuit could be walked in an easy stroll of fifteen minutes. They took an hour, then did it once more together. With several side-tracks to investigate movements or sounds, real or imagined, it took another couple of hours.

"He's not here." Jude said. "And by that I mean I don't think he's ever been here. After all the lad only said he'd seen him going in this direction. He could have turned off, side-tracked any time."

Pippa hunted for a handkerchief busily. "He's dead, isn't he?"

Jude handed her a handkerchief. "There's absolutely no certainty of that. He's got stuck somewhere and as long as he has access to water he can manage several more days yet." Pippa snuffled into the handkerchief. Jude added, "I miss the old bugger, too. And I never thought I'd live to say that."

Soon after they got home, there was a gentle tap on the back door. Jude opened it to a small worried looking boy in a hoodie. "I'm

not sure I got it right," Kev said. "Like, it might've been another cat."
He shuffled his feet. "Like, that Totty didn't like me, y'know."

"That's because you threw stones at him," Pippa said, behind
Jude. But he heard the lift in her voice and noted a hint of hope in her
expression.

"He scratched me," Kev said defensively.

"Never mind, Kev." Jude said. "It's really helpful that you've
told us."

"I won't throw no more stones." Kev pulled his hood higher
and mooched off.

"I could almost hug a hoodie," Pippa said.

Aristotle : April, 2011, a day later

On his shelf in the garden house, Aristotle shifted and gave a small moan of discomfort. He was very hungry, but the pain in his cheek dominated any gnawing in his stomach. He looked down from his shelf and knew that he could no longer jump to the floor. He had managed it once or twice but the pain of doing it and of getting back had almost defeated him.

Still, it had been worth the effort. He had crept round the room, exploring as he always had. There were many different shapes but still some familiar smells. And he knew what he was looking for and found it. In the furthest corner was something round with some liquid in it and which triggered memories. He sniffed at it. It seemed all right. He began lapping, slowly at first, and then more quickly as he felt the relief of the liquid going into him.

Afterwards he paused, enjoying the feeling, and looking round. Before the woman there had been a man. He was not like other humans. Other humans made noises to each other, but this man made noises when there was no one else there. Sometimes he made noises to Aristotle, would look inside the cupboard and tickle his head. He did not see the man any more.

But he wished the woman would come back.

The liquid had made him feel a little stronger. He had better get back to his safe place while he still could. He almost couldn't, but at last he did. After some experimenting, he found that if he lay with the good side of his face against the shelf, the bump on the bad side did not throb so much. He found as comfortable position as he could, and set about waiting.

Oxfordshire : early April 2011, later that day

Over the past thirty-six hours, they had been down every street alley, peered over garden fences, asked everyone they knew and many more they did not. Returning from one of their many sorties, Pippa found two messages on the answering machine.

Sorry, Miss Eastman," apologised the young man from Hedges and Waters. *"I did try you several times. Mr. Brown asked if he could have access again to your property to check some measurements. As I couldn't reach you, I thought it would be all right if I took him round. We were only there a few minutes. A few days ago.*

The second message was expressed in an unmistakable Aussie twang. *Pippa, my dear. We have not yet met but my old heart goes out to you. If I weren't stuck in this goddarned bed, I'd be out there with you looking for your Totty.*

"Good on you, Dad." Jude said.

"We must go and see him as soon as this is all over." Pippa waved an arm to indicate the extent of all that needed doing. She scratched her head. "Why do I think that call from the estate agents is significant?"

"Dunno, Love. If there had been any sign of Totty they would have let us know."

"Would they? It could be any old cat." Pippa picked up the phone and punched in a number. After a moment she asked for Stewart, then said, "Sorry to bother you, Stewart. When you took Mr Brown round, you didn't happen to notice a large ginger cat?"

"Your Aristotle? I wouldn't miss him. I have a feeling he doesn't like me very much. Probably blames me for moving him."

When she reported the conversation to Jude, he abruptly slapped himself on the thigh and said excitedly, "That's it."

"What's it?"

"Where Totty will have gone. You know when animals are crook, they are always go back to the place where they felt safest...."

"But his home is *here,"* protested Pippa.

239

"I doubt if it is in Totty's mind. Home, the safe place, will be where he has spent most of his life."

"You really think?" Pippa allowed a glimmer of hope to flicker. "Then let's go."

They were there within five minutes. Pipppa opened the front door. Emptiness, silence.   "Totty, Totty, Totty," yelled Jude.

They searched every room. Emptiness, silence. Less hopefully, they went out into the garden. "Totty, Totty, Totty," yelled Jude.

They searched under every bush and hedge. Emptiness. Silence.

Disconsolately they made their way back to the house. Jude paused and peered in through the window of the Studio, moved on, paused, went back and peered again. Hoarsely, he said. "I can see a tail. A twitching tail."

Pippa unlocked the door, hurtled in, was on her knees, sobbing. Aristotle raised his head with great difficulty, looked at her through slitty eyes, opened his mouth to say *miaoul* but nothing came out.

Jude was exploring the Studio. "He found the water, so he may be all right. Stay with him. I'll reverse the camper into the drive."

Pippa stayed on her knees, gently stroking the animal, noting his flinch when her hand went near the bump on his head, aware of the faintest rumble from somewhere deep within in the limp body. Jude returned with one of the cushions from the camper and they gently eased Aristotle on to it.

"Stewart couldn't have closed the door properly," Pippa said, but there seemed no point in recriminations.

Back at the flat, they put a towel down on the sofa and lifted Aristotle on to it. Pippa got a bowl of milk and put it under his chin and he managed a few laps before giving it up.

"We could use an eye drop," Jude suggested, and went to get one from the bathroom cupboard.

"He's not going to make it, is he?" Pippa said when he came back.

"We'll take him to the vet. Let him decide."

240

They experimented with the eyedrop, and after a while Aristotle got the hang of it and seemed to be taking quite a bit of milk it. Every now and then he would pause and lick the teat of the eyedrop. The low rumble became quite distinct.

"I think he's getting better. Perhaps he's just dehydrated."

"Mmm." Jude checked the phone book, picked up the receiver. After a brief exchange he said, "Yes, four o'clock is fine."

The vet was the other side of the village, behind a garage specialising in bodywork repairs. There were no bodywork repairs in progress, so it was peaceful on this edge of the community overlooking the fields.

The vet was a friend of Aristotle having ministered to him on several occasions, notably after a close encounter with a Jack Russell. The terrier had come out of it with a bloodied nose, Aristotle with a lump out of his leg, which had healed rather more quickly than the Jack Russell's nose. He stood looking down on the cat. At last he said, "Poor old fellow. So it's finally caught up with you, has it?"

He explained that he had forecast at the time of Aristotle's mysterious night encounter as a young cat that the affliction on his right cheek might create problems when he was older. "The Professor vetoed an operation then because it would probably have resulted in the loss of sight in one eye. And he said neither he nor Aristotle cared what he looked like." It was news to Pippa that Father had taken any interest in Aristotle. "They seemed to have an interesting co-dependency, the two of them," the vet went on. "Based on a silent awareness of each other."

They stood in silence, looking down on Aristotle who seemed to be drifting off into sleep.

"So what are you saying?" Pippa asked.

"The best you'd get out of surgery and treatment is a few extra weeks in return for a lot of discomfort. He chucked Aristotle under the chin. "Poor old boy." Without spelling it out, it was clear what his advice was.

"What will you do? How long will it take?"

"An injection. It'll take minutes. Quite painless."

Pippa reached for Jude'shand. "OK," she said. "Now, before I change my mind."

The vet nodded. "It's the right decision. Selfish to keep him going any longer. I'll get it ready while you say your goodbyes." He put a cushion on the examination bench. "Might as well be comfortable.

Pippa rested Aristotle on it gently.

Jude said, "Why don't you hold Totty's paw, and I'll hold yours?"

Pippa snuffled incomprehensibly, put out a hand. Resting a paw in the palm of it, Aristotle stretched it, claws separating, as he did when he washed, probing his tongue between each. But he did not try to wash, just relaxed, his paw limp on her hand..

Pippa snuffled more loudly, gulped, said, "I don't think I can go through with this."

"*Miaoul*," said Aristotle, resting his head back on the cushion.

"He's showing his best side," Jude said encouragingly. "In fact, from this angle, he's really rather handsome." Pippa heard the wobble in his voice, felt his fingers tighten round hers.

The vet came back with the syringe, injected the needle into Aristotle's shoulder, then withdrew.

Jude went on, "Anyway, even if the Aussies weren't paranoid about bringing live objects into the country, Totty would hate it. All those weird noises and smells. Like catapulting some confused geriatric into a class of undisciplined toddlers."

"You're a fool," Pippa said, the tears streaming down her face. "But I love you inspite of everything."

Jude fumbled for a handkerchief, wiped his eyes. "I love you because of everything. Will you marry me?" After a moment, he added, "I think he's gone."

Pippa kept hold of the paw, rested her head back on Jude's shoulder. "I think you're right," she said. "And yes, I will."

Lightning Source UK Ltd.
Milton Keynes UK
UKOW040445080313

207327UK00001B/36/P